"Barbara Michaels' thrillers are always a highly satisfying blend of earthly terrors and supernatural suppositions. This is one of her best yet."
—*Publishers Weekly*

"Mrs. Michaels has a fine downright way with the supernatural. Good firm style and many picturesque twists."
—*San Francisco Chronicle*

"The expertly jigsawed puzzle will keep most readers alert for the missing pieces all the way."
—*Chicago Tribune*

Witch

Barbara Michaels

A FAWCETT CREST BOOK • NEW YORK

WITCH

THIS BOOK CONTAINS THE COMPLETE TEXT OF THE
ORIGINAL HARDCOVER EDITION.

Published by Fawcett Crest Books, a unit of CBS Publications,
the Consumer Publishing Division of CBS Inc.,
by arrangement with Dodd, Mead & Company

ISBN: 0-449-23546-7

Printed in the United States of America

11 10 9 8 7 6 5 4 3 2

For Katie and Cal

One

According to the directions Ellen had received from the
real estate agent, the house was in a clearing in the
woods. Gently perspiring in the hot office, Ellen had
thought wistfully of cool forest glades. April in Virginia is
unpredictable; this particular day might have been bor-
rowed from July, and the small-town office was not air-
conditioned.

An hour later, after bumping down rutted lanes so narrow that tree branches pushed in through the car windows, Ellen was inclined to consider "clearing" a wild ex-
aggeration. She started perspiring again as soon as she
turned off the highway. No breeze could penetrate the
tangled growth of these untamed forests; moisture
weighted the air.

At any rate, this must be the house, though it more resembled a pile of worn logs overgrown by honeysuckle
and other vines. There was a window, shining with an

unexpected suggestion of cleanliness; presumably there was also a door somewhere under the tangle of rambler roses in front. Ellen switched off the ignition and sat staring at the structure. Amusement replaced her initial chagrin over her car's scratched paint and abused shock absorbers.

Clearing or glade, the place was beautiful. Pale-white stars of dogwood shimmered against the green background of pines, and sprays of wild cherry and apple shook feathery branches over the car. Bright-yellow daffodils persisted through clumps of harsh weed, and some of the overgrown bushes threatening the house were lilacs. One was a mass of lavender bloom; the piercing scent triumphed over the smell of her exhaust.

Now that the car's engine was stopped, the place had an uncanny quiet. It was an eerie spot altogether, as mysterious in its way as a gloomy Gothic castle under midnight skies. In these woods time had no meaning. They had not changed in centuries, and there was a feeling of occupation not wholly human. It was a fairy-tale place, but the creatures who came here for twilight revels would not be the sequined, muslin, and cheesecloth sprites of children's stories. Hooved and feathered and furred, they would move upright, with slitted unblinking animal eyes peering out of narrow human faces.

Ellen leaned back and reached in her purse for a cigarette. She enjoyed her fantasies, and she was in no hurry to confront the problematical inhabitant of the house. With a smile, she recalled the warning of Rose Bates, the real estate agent who had sent her here.

"I can't even show you the house," Rose had grumbled. "Ed won't let anybody but him take people there. You'll have to go to his place first. I sure do hate to let you go there all alone. I'd go with you, only that old rascal won't let me in."

Ellen felt a certain sympathy for the unknown Ed. Rose, who had insisted on first names from the start of their acquaintance, was a caricature of her professional type—energetic, cheery, insistent. However, Ellen couldn't complain about Rose's professional zeal. They had driven all over the county in a search for Ellen's dream house. Once or twice Ellen had been rudely hilarious about a square red brick horror that Rose proudly presented as the latest in modern comfort. Rose obviously found her client an irritation and an enigma, and this last offering was one of desperation.

"That house of Miss Highbarger's that Ed just inherited sounds like it might be your cup of tea. It's old enough, goodness knows; parts of it go back to the Revolution. There's about thirty acres goes with it—right on the edge of the Blue Ridge, lots of trees and scenery and all that. Yes, it might do for you. But Ed . . ."

"What's wrong with Ed?" Ellen inquired. "He sounds rather eccentric; he wouldn't—"

"No, no." The other woman blushed. "I wouldn't let you get into anything like *that*. Ed hates women."

"That," said Ellen, "is not necessarily a guarantee."

Rose gave her a shrewd, surprised look. The surprise was not at the sentiment, with which Rose clearly agreed, but at the fact that her client should be familiar with such a cynical truth.

Ellen knew Rose considered her impractical and unworldly. She looked younger than her thirty-eight years; careful diet and professional beauty care, those luxuries of the middle classes, had kept her fair hair shining, had preserved the soft texture of her skin and the slim lines of her figure. It was not only her appearance that the older, country-bred woman unconsciously resented; it was her urban background, her accent, her clothes, her manner.

"It's no guarantee," Rose agreed drily. "There's Joe Muller, out there in Chew's Corners; kicks dogs, shoots cats, beats his wife and abuses his kids. He has fourteen children, and not all by Mrs. Muller. . . . Well, but like I said, you don't need to worry about Ed. He's a mean old rascal, but he's a gentleman. You'll be all right with Ed—if you can find him. He lives off by himself in a kind of shack in the woods. Here, I'll draw you a map."

The map had been adequate. Ellen glanced at it once more. Yes, this had to be the place, and she might as well stop procrastinating. There was still no sign of life from the house. Although she was mildy apprehensive about the eccentric Ed, she hoped he was at home; it would be maddening to have made the trip for nothing. She got out of the car, dropped her cigarette on the ground, and stepped on it; and then jumped back as a voice shook the air.

"Madame! Kindly do not drop pollutants on my property!"

Ellen glanced wildly about the clearing. There was no one in sight. However, a shuddering movement in the rose bushes suggested the possibility of a person behind them. Obediently she bent over and picked up her cigarette butt. Her white gloves were not improved by the gesture.

A more violent shudder of the roses produced, obstetrically, a human form. This was no baby; it was a tall, erect old man with gold-rimmed spectacles and an incredible beard. As Ellen approached she noticed the spectacles were held together with tape and that the beard was curly. It was a gray beard, and it reached the man's belt. His shirt sleeves—and, presumably, the rest of that garment—were of rough blue homespun. The eyes behind the spectacles were a vivid, piercing blue.

"You have come, despatched by that abominable female in Warrenton, in regard to the house of my late aunt?" said a voice from amid the beard.

"I have," said Ellen.

"Then you may come in."

The man stepped back, flinging a curtain of green leaves over his arm as the Scarlet Pimpernel might have flung his cloak. A door was disclosed. Ellen stepped under the roses and entered. The man followed. He did not close the door.

"I am Edward Salling."

"Ellen March."

"Mrs. March? How do you do?"

He bowed with courtly grace. With the same punctilious courtesy, Ellen was offered a chair and a cup of tea. She accepted both, although she was under no illusions as to her host's real feelings. Ed was a gentleman, and would do the proper thing if it killed him, but he wasn't enjoying her company. The haste with which he left the room, to prepare tea, closely resembled flight.

Left alone, Ellen surveyed the room with pleasure. It was surprisingly clean and furnished with austere simplicity. The furniture was all out in the middle of the room, for every inch of wall space, except that occupied by windows and doors and fireplace, was covered with books.

When Ed reappeared with a tray, Ellen was standing in front of one of the bookshelves. She had forgotten her host's wariness; she turned with a broad smile.

"You've got the Henty books! I haven't read them for years; I used to love them."

The cold blue eyes softened a trifle, but Ed was not so easily wooed. He put the tray on the table and gestured, as a nobleman might have done, for her to pour.

"I still read them," he said. "I am able to indulge myself in a rare pleasure: to please myself in all things. You will observe also more intellectual volumes."

The touch of vanity tickled Ellen.

"Yes, indeed," she said. "Do you like Joyce? I'm embarrassed to admit I never could read *Ulysses*. I love his poetry, though."

She continued her assault on Ed's susceptibilities and won a few more icy twinkles before he indicated that it was time to inspect his aunt's house. They would take his truck.

Like Ed's other possessions, the truck was old and impeccably maintained. It lived in a shed behind the house, but did not appear to be frequently used. Ed carefully dusted off the seat before handing Ellen in. As he took his place, she remarked,

"I'd have thought you would have a car with four-wheel drive. It must be hard getting out of here in the winter."

"I don't get out of here in the winter," said Ed.

Ellen felt she ought to have anticipated the reply. She could picture Ed reveling in wood fires, books, and tinned soup, while the drifts piled up outside. Before she had time to feel snubbed, Ed added,

"You seem to know something about motor vehicles, Mrs. March."

It was the first thing he had said that might be classified as a personal remark. Ellen had wondered at his reticence; a seller of property may legitimately question the antecedents of a prospective buyer. Now, to her consternation, she felt a familiar impulse steal over her.

Ellen's "Ancient Mariner seizures" were a well-worn family joke. Her eldest nephew had coined the phrase, claiming that Ellen's glittering eye, as she captured an unwilling listener, was reminiscent of Coleridge's sailor. Her narrative lacked the ghoulish interest of the poem; she talked about herself and her family, in the most innocuous fashion, but she told her victim far more about that subject than he could conceivably want to know. Ellen had become self-conscious about the attacks, but she was helpless to control them when they came on, even though part of her conscious mind remained detached and sarcastic, making silent comments on the imbecility of her conversation. This impish segment of consciousness now chuckled gleefully as Ellen took a deep breath and began.

"Oh, I had to learn something about cars. My three nephews kept dragging home various old wrecks—jeeps, rusty trucks, cars without engines and engines without cars. . . . It was nice for me, they have always done most of the repair work on my cars, and they taught my daughter quite a bit. She's younger than they are, you see, and she has always followed them around like a puppy. I'm going to miss all that service. I'll miss them too, of course. But one has to let them go, doesn't one?"

"So the cliché informs us," said Ed.

"I'm too dependent on them," said Ellen, ignoring this repressive comment. "It isn't the kids who are dependent. They are ready and eager to go. My daughter is going to Europe this summer. Not alone, she's only seventeen, I wouldn't let her set off with a knapsack and her plane fare, like so many of these poor little souls. She's going with a student group. Next fall, if I buy a house this far from Washington, she'll board at the private school she has been attending as a day student. She can come down for weekends, and—"

Her teeth bit painfully into her tongue as the car bounced over a rut in the road. Ed's hands gripped the wheel as if he expected it to come loose. His eyes had a glazed look. The imp in Ellen's mind sympathized, her inane chatter must be positively painful to a recluse who hated women. But Ellen was still in the throes of the seizure and went on remorselessly.

"Two of my nephews are already in college and the third one is going next fall. So I felt this was the right time for me to make a change. The family is breaking up anyhow. And with Jack taking an overseas assignment. . . . He offered me the house—it's in Bethesda, and it's a lovely house, but it wasn't ever *my* house. It was Jack's and Louise's. My sister's. She loved it so much, and I missed her so, I couldn't bear to change anything. She was so young. We never imagined there was anything wrong with her heart. . . . Well, it's been almost ten years, you'd think I could accept it. Jack hasn't, not really. But he's always been wonderful; so cheerful and competent. . . . I was glad I could help him and the boys. Of course it was nice for me too. Penny and I were living in a cramped little apartment in town. I always got along well with the boys, and they really did need someone living at home, you know how boys are. Jack would have had to hire a housekeeper, and it isn't easy to find a good one."

All right, all right, said the inner imp; you don't have to convince Ed Salling of the purity of your motives for moving into your sister's house, with her husband and her sons. You can't even convince yourself, can you? Go on, tell him about Jack. How wonderful he is, how important. You're dying to talk about him.

"The house," Ellen said aloud. She spoke too loudly, combating the silent inner voice, and Ed gave her a puzzled glance as he shifted down, preparatory to turning into the highway. "I've never had a house of my own, not really. First the apartment, and then Louise's house. Now I mean to indulge myself. I inherited some money, you see—from an aunt. . . ."

Not from Louise, said the imp, jeering. Make sure he understands that. Nothing that would have belonged to Louise.

"So you don't need to wonder whether or not I can pay you," Ellen went on, with a feeble laugh. The seizure was wearing off. "I mean, we haven't discussed—"

"I leave that sort of thing to the agent," said Ed disdainfully. "Mrs. March, you don't have to tell me all this."

The mood collapsed, as it always did, into depression and self-contempt.

"I know," Ellen said despondently. "I'm sorry. I get started and I just can't stop. It must be so boring for people."

"I wouldn't say it was boring, exactly."

Ellen glanced at Ed. The beard hid his mouth, but his voice sounded as if he might be smiling.

"If your conversation has any defect, it is not lack of interest," Ed said. "It is lack of coherence. Brevity, too, is conspicuously absent. If I understand you correctly, you have been keeping house for your widowed brother-in-law and his three sons. You have one daughter. Your brother-in-law is with one of those indecent federal agencies that interferes in the affairs of foreign nations. Now that your nephews are of college age and your brother-in-law is going abroad, in order to interfere further, you have decided to buy a quaint old house in the country. Here you will search your soul. . . . I beg your pardon. I am becoming personal, and ironic. I permit myself the latter folly, but not the former. Here, let us say, you will make a life for yourself. An admirable intention. I am strongly in favor of living one's own life. I do not approve of interfering with the lives of others. However, I am about to make an exception. It astonishes me that I should wish to do so. . . . Are you a widow, Mrs. March?"

"Divorced," said Ellen, reeling under the sudden spate of words. "Years ago."

"Then I will give you a piece of advice. If you should decide to settle here, do not mention your divorce."

"You mean, lie?"

"Lying is the most admirable of the social graces. If I do not recommend it in this case, it is only because it is impracticable. You would be found out. I merely suggest reticence."

"You have good reason to suggest that," Ellen said, laughing. "I don't always talk this way. Some situations bring it on; I don't know why."

"I would think you are a naturally candid person. You can afford to be; you don't strike me as the sort of woman who has guilty secrets. However, you must make allowances for the old-fashioned attitudes of small towns. Look about you, Mrs. March. We are coming into Chew's

Corners. A euphonious name, is it not? This will be your marketing center, if you purchase my house."

Ellen looked. She had come from the other direction, so this was her first glimpse of the village. It was only a few blocks long. The houses were elderly and sedate, sitting back from the road and surrounded by fine old trees. There were sidewalks. Along them children rode tricycles and women pushed baby carriages. Ed had slowed, obeying the speed limit posted on the outskirts, and Ellen saw that their stately progress attracted stares from the pedestrians they passed. Ed appeared to be concentrating on his driving, but after a moment he commented,

"They are staring at me, Mrs. March, not at you. I seldom come here. I am, you know, the town eccentric."

Ellen thought of several remarks and decided not to make any of them. They were coming into the business section—and leaving it. It consisted of a gas station, several small frame buildings converted into shops, and one larger establishment—a genuine country store with a covered porch running the full length of the front. On the porch stood a row of wooden chairs, all of which were occupied. The occupants were, without exception, male. As Ed's truck passed they all leaned forward, staring unashamedly.

" 'Grapow's General Merchandise,' " Ellen read from the sign over the porch steps. "What a fascinating place!"

"Mrs. Grapow is one of the town's most successful businessmen (I use the masculine noun advisedly) and also a pillar of the church. I advise you against the church, Mrs. March, and also against Mrs. Grapow. But you will doubtless ignore both pieces of advice."

"Those men," Ellen said. "Were they staring at us? I hope I'm not endangering your reputation, Mr. Salling."

"That would be virtually impossible," said Ed serenely. "Did I not mention that I am the town eccentric? They also call me an atheist. I am a rational Deist, but one cannot expect such clods to understand the distinction. Naturally I have rejected their God. He is an unpleasant old man in a nightshirt, with a habit of persistent interference. What really annoys my neighbors, however, is that I have also rejected their Devil."

"I understand. But it's hard to think of devils—here."

Her gesture indicated the last of the houses on the far side of town—a white-painted frame house with the narrow lines and innate dignity of early Georgian.

"You have not, I think, lived in a small town?"

"No. I was born in Brooklyn, of all places. But I used to visit my grandmother in Indiana when I was small. She had—"

"No more," said Ed, shaking his head. "No more, I implore you. You are a nice woman, Mrs. March—as women go—but I really don't want to know any more than I already know."

"You're nice too," Ellen said with a smile. "I've never been squelched so painlessly."

"I am not trying to destroy your enthusiasm, only to warn you against naivety. Rousseau's vision of the noble savage has been long discredited. Bucolic simplicity has as many vices as urban sophistication."

Ellen felt a slight impatience. She liked this bearded anachronism but she was not prepared to accept his jaundiced view of the universe, or of Chew's Corners. (It was a frightful name, she had to admit.) Absently she wondered what had warped Ed's attitude toward his fellow man. Like so many cynics, he was a disappointed romantic. His bookshelves betrayed that fact.

"Don't worry," she said. "I know all about small towns. I expect the townspeople will be aloof at first, but I'll win them over. I don't have wild parties or a string of lovers, even if I am divorced. If the neighbors don't want to socialize I can entertain myself. I read a lot and paint a little, and garden, and knit, and watch birds. I'm looking forward to birdwatching here, after being in the suburbs so long."

"Oh, yes," Ed agreed morosely. "We have birds."

"There are so many things I've always wanted to do and never had time for. I'm going to learn to play the guitar; reread *War and Peace,* and try to read Proust; study Sanskrit; start an herb garden, and learn to crochet and make quilts and put up preserves and——"

A rusty creaking sound stopped her in midsentence. It took her several seconds to identify the sound as Ed's version of laughter.

"I will say no more," he said.

The truck turned off the highway. A sign read "Private Road." The surface was paved, though very narrow. Trees closed in on the truck. Then the foliage on the left disappeared and high on a hill Ellen saw a house.

"That's not it, is it?" she exclaimed in dismay. The house was a magnificent example of Greek revival, with white pillars along the facade. In size and style it was far too grand for her.

"No, that's the McKay place. Norman McKay is your nearest neighbor. He had the road paved. It only goes to the two houses, but Norman said he got tired of getting stuck every time it rained. He keeps it plowed in winter, too. Owns his own tractor."

"That would be an advantage." A curve in the road shut off Ellen's view of the stately mansion. "What sort of man is Mr. McKay?" she asked.

"Got a degree from Harvard in business administration," said Ed. "He collects antiques, porcelain, and books. I exchange a word with him now and then. He is the only other literate person in the area."

"He sounds like the perfect neighbor."

"No man is perfect."

Ellen was about to reply, with some acerbity, when Ed suddenly jammed on the brakes. He was not going fast;

that fact, and the arm he threw out, kept Ellen from crashing into the windshield. As she righted herself, she caught a glimpse of someone disappearing into the tangled brush along the road. It was evidently this apparition, in the path of the truck, that had caused Ed to stop so suddenly.

The form was that of a boy or young man clad in faded jeans and shirt. His pale-blond hair was worn fashionably long and looked as if it had been trimmed with a pair of rusty hedge shears. All this was normal enough, but there had been something about the figure that disturbed Ellen. The furtive quickness of its movement, perhaps? Or the sly backward turn of the head and the flicker of peering eyes? She was reminded of her earlier fantasies about the woods, and the inhuman things that might slink through in the underbrush.

"I beg your pardon," said Ed, removing his arm.

"Don't apologize. Who was that? Shouldn't he be in school?"

"The halls of Western High School saw no more of Tim after his sixteenth birthday," said Ed. "To their mutual relief. He should be working at something. He prefers to idle about the woods."

"How old is he?"

"Almost eighteen, I believe." Ed gave her a sidelong glance. "I observed your reaction to my statement that Mr. McKay was less than perfect as a neighbor. Tim is one of the imperfections. He is Norman's nephew, and if I am the town eccentric, Tim is the town delinquent."

He stopped the car and jumped out before Ellen had time to pursue the subject. She glanced around. The paved surface ended a few feet ahead. A dusty track, too narrow for anything larger than a bicycle, continued on into the woods. There was no sign of a house, and two tall pine trees, matched giants of their species, were the only unusual features of the landscape. Ed had vanished between these trees. After a moment he returned and got into the truck. He made a sharp right-angle turn toward the two pines and drove between them.

The branches parted and Ellen realized there was a gap between the trees just wide enough to admit a car. Beyond was a brick wall. A wooden gate now swung open. "These trees need trimming," said Ed, in what Ellen could not help regarding as the understatement of the year. "If you purchase the house I will naturally see that they are pruned."

After a moment they emerged into a clearing. Ellen sat staring, even after Ed turned off the engine and came around to open her door.

The house was beautiful, but that wasn't the important thing. It was hers. It reached out invisible arms to pull her in.

According to Rose, the house had been built in the eighteenth century, but Ellen felt sure it must date to a period well before the Revolutionary War—seventeen twenty, perhaps. Originally it had been a standard two-room plan, with chimneys on both ends. Or perhaps— yes, the steep pitched roof had surely been part of the original house. A four-room house, then, with bedrooms above. Some early frontier houses had boasted these amenities. The material was brick; it was now weathered, and covered with green tendrils of Virginia creeper, so that it seemed to blend with the landscape. Later owners had added a frame kitchen wing and a two-room ell be-hind the house. Ellen doubted that a qualified architect had ever been employed; certainly no professional would have endured the screened porch that blurred the simple dignity of the brick facade. But the house showed the in-stinctive feeling for line and structure that is found in many early buildings.

Part of the charm of the house lay in its surroundings. The clearing was slightly over an acre in size. Rounded hills, tree carpeted, enclosed the open space and trees formed a wall all around. There were oaks and maples; and Ellen thought how glorious they would be in the autumn, like great colorsplashed impressionist canvases. Many of the trees were evergreens. In winter they would form a sheltering bulwark for the house. One great oak, towering above the chimneys, must have been almost as old as the house. Its trunk was a brilliant, astounding emerald green. Have to get that creeper off, Ellen thought; it can kill the tree, pretty as it is. Behind the house, massed whiteness, like an out-of-season snow-drift, indicated an old apple orchard.

Ellen turned dazzled eyes toward Ed, but her brain was still adding details. That tree on the left was surely a black walnut. There were climbing roses over the porch and lilacs by the kitchen door. A flagstoned path led through tall grass to the screened porch. What a place to sit on summer evenings, with the roses perfuming the air. . . . The woods were full of white dogwood. A pink one stood by the path.

"I want it," Ellen said. "Can I have it?"

"Not until you have seen the interior."

If Ed had hoped to discourage her by a view of the inside, he failed. Ellen was already in love with the house, and she saw the strength and the grace of design under the neglect of recent years. The kitchen was a horror; there wasn't a single item of equipment later than 1930, and the cupboards had been painted a hideous, peeling dark green. The linoleum was cracked and buckled. Ellen's doting eye visualized the room with pine cabinets and frosty yellow paint. There was a fireplace in the kitchen; the brick wall in which it was located had been the exterior wall of the original house. The room was large, big enough for a trestle table and benches.

Visibly disgusted by her reaction, Ed dragged her from the kitchen. The narrow enclosed stairs didn't bother her,

not even when Ed pointed out that any visitor over five
feet six inches would have to stoop to get under the stair
arch. But in the upper hall Ellen stopped short, seized by
an incredible emotion.

Desire—exultant, fierce, triumphant. Not sexual, not
even physical, but the raw emotion out of which physical
desires are formed. It was as if something had leaped up
out of chaos to receive her with an uncontrollable burst of
joy. It gripped her mind as hard arms might have embraced her body in a welcome, too violent to be without
pain.

It came, and passed, in a flicker of time. Ellen let out
the breath she had just inhaled, and looked around, bewildered.

The upper hall was really only a landing, illumined by
a single small window. The worn pine flooring sloped
perilously toward the stairs. The low ceiling left room for
cupboards on either side of the narrow window. It was a
pleasant little place, but there was nothing about it that
would explain that uncanny surge of rapture.

Ellen glanced surreptitiously at Ed, and her ungovern-
able sense of humor helped dispel the sensation she had
felt. Ed might inspire a number of emotions, but mad
passion wasn't one of them.

She forgot her aberrant moment as Ed threw open the
doors on either side of the landing. The bedrooms were
identical in size, about twelve feet by eighteen. Each had
a fireplace. The sloping eaves and dormer windows atoned
for the decor—early Woolworth, Ellen called it.

"Leak in the roof," said Ed, dourly indicating a stain
that darkened the ugly wallpaper.

"That can be fixed."

"Only two bedrooms."

"There are two rooms downstairs, in the addition. They
could be guest bedrooms, or maybe a single large study
that could be used as a guest room."

"You haven't seen the bathroom," said Ed.

The chamber so designated might have daunted a less determined buyer. The bathtub wasn't old enough to be quaint, it was merely old, and most of the enamel was worn off its bottom. The inner surfaces of all the fixtures were stained rusty brown by the mineral-heavy water of the area.

"It will look lovely with green tiles and a Nile-green bathtub," said Ellen dreamily.

Ed was so vexed he forgot to duck under the stair lintel, and smacked his head. He went on down in a seething silence.

Waiting for him to lock the front door, Ellen examined the screened porch. More expense; new screening would be needed, and sections of the wood framework were in poor condition. But she wanted to keep the porch, although it was an aesthetic excrescence. The insect life of Virginia is varied and carnivorous.

Of course she was seeing the place at its best, horticulturally speaking. Some former owner had been a gardener; there was every variety of flowering plant. Ellen's knowing eye identified the green spears that would be gladioli, the incipient clumps of chrysanthemum, and the feathery emerald embryos of larkspur and foxglove. This was the time of glory for Virginia gardens, but something would be blooming all summer long—rhododendron and mountain laurel, roses of every conceivable variety. Her fingers twitched to be at work. The garden was glorious but neglected; all the shrubs needed pruning, bulbs ought to be dug and separated. . . .

She turned to Ed with eyes so shining that he smiled faintly.

"You are a very poor businesswoman, Mrs. March," he said. "Your expression would raise the price several thousand dollars, if I were myself a good businessman."

"But you aren't," said Ellen. "I'll buy it."

"I suggest you think it over for a few days."

"But I—"

"I will hold the option for you, if that is the term. It probably is not. No matter. We need not go through the formalities of a deposit, or whatever the legal stipulation may be. You have my word."

He stalked off down the path. Ellen followed. She had to run to catch up with him. At the truck, she caught his arm, and when he stopped she turned to take one more look at the house. Her house.

"But I'm trying to tell you, Mr. Salling, I don't have to think it over. I'm absolutely certain. You don't know how many houses I've looked at. Monstrosities, most of them. I'll go straight to Warrenton and—"

"You will do nothing of the kind. I insist that you consider the matter first. Talk it over with your family."

Male chauvinist, thought Ellen.

She said nothing, but Ed appeared to number telepathy among his talents.

"I do not say that because you are a woman. I say it because you are the sort of woman you are."

"I may be impulsive, but I'm not irresponsible," said Ellen haughtily. "If I make mistakes, I pay for them without whining. You may rest assured—"

"What is it?" Ed turned, following her gaze.

"An animal, I guess. . . . It just darted in between the trees."

"There are squirrels and other creatures about."

"I never saw an albino squirrel before," said Ellen.

Ed's eyes widened.

"You saw a white animal?"

"Someone's cat, perhaps," said Ellen; and watched with growing alarm the contortions of the visible portion of Ed's bearded face.

"I had not intended to tell you," he said at last, with a gusty sigh. "It disgusts me even to hint at such a possibility. But in view of your unaccountable and sudden attachment . . . Mrs. March, before you make up your mind, there is something about this house which you must know."

Two

"Your house has a *what*?"

Ellen's brother-in-law put down his butter knife and stared at her.

Ellen poured him a fresh cup of coffee and tried not to think, "Only two more months." She wondered how she could have lived with him so long and not realized the inevitable truth that had struck her only recently. He wasn't even handsome. He was tall, and fatherhood to three energetic boys had kept his figure spare and straight; but his hairline began at approximately the top of his head and the kindest adjective friends could apply to his face was "pleasant." He resembled an ex-football player, but the broken nose had not been won on the playing field; Jack's eyes, now twinkling with amusement behind horn-rimmed spectacles, had always been poor. His eyes were bad and his ears were too big and his hair was too sparse;

and she loved him. She had always loved him, and only in the last months, when she found she must lose him, had she faced the fact. How could she endure a future that did not include his face across the breakfast table every morning?

Well, she would have to endure it. Jack loved her too—as a sister and helpful surrogate mother. Because he was sensitive and kind it would appall him to know of her true feelings. Such a revelation would wreck her hope of keeping his friendship in the future.

Resolutely Ellen returned to the subject she had introduced.

"A ghost," she said. "My house has a ghost. Isn't that marvelous? He isn't even charging extra for it."

A thunder of feet in the hall preceded the appearance of a boy. It was disconcerting to see one human male, however large in size, follow the stampeding sound; one expected a herd of wild horses, if not buffalo. Phil looked like his father, except that he had more hair—much more hair. It was shoulder length in back and nose length in front. Since Phil refused to use hair bands or—heaven save the mark—bobby pins, the front locks were always a hazard to his vision. He had developed a maddening habit of tossing his hair out of his eyes, but when he got interested in a subject he just let it hang.

Phil was in his last weeks of high school. He had explained to his father that there was really no sense in going to school now that his college acceptance was certain. He was going, however.

Phil threw himself into a chair and seized a handful of bread.

"Charging extra for what?" he asked thickly, through his first bite.

"My ghost."

"Your what?" asked a new voice.

Ellen glanced at her daughter, who had just entered.

Penny did not thunder, she floated. She was a dainty creature, with long dark hair flowing loose around a pointed face, but she was dressed like a poverty-stricken farm worker in patched faded jeans and a skimpy T-shirt. The T-shirt fit like a second skin, and Ellen stopped midway between stove and table with a platter of bacon and eggs in her hands.

"Penny! You go right back upstairs and put on a bra. Or an opaque blouse!"

"Bras are out," said Phil, finishing the bread and reaching for a doughnut. "Penny burned hers, didn't you, chick?"

Penny aimed a blow at him, which he ducked without halting his intake of food.

"Nobody wears bras, Mother. They are symbols of sexual repression. Your what, did you say?"

"Did you say you had a ghost?" repeated Phil, spearing a fried egg with a fork and transferring it to his plate.

Ellen caught her brother-in-law's amused eyes.

"You all drive me crazy," she said.

"But you love us," said Phil, reaching for another egg.

"Use the serving fork, Phil, or I'll break your arm," said his father. "And try cutting that egg into fewer than two pieces. Penny, don't talk back to your mother or I'll break *your* arm. And shut up, both of you. How you can be so uncouth, after living with two such well-bred adults, I will never understand."

"I guess you raised us wrong," said Phil thoughtfully.

"No, we raised you right. If you've gone off the track it's because you are inherently evil. Pay for your own psychiatrist. Now, Ellen, tell me about your ghost."

Smiling, Ellen looked around the table. Three faces beamed back at her. I don't know whether I can stand it, she thought.

"Not an ordinary ghost," she said cheerfully. "The ghost of a witch."

"Hey," said Phil approvingly. "Cool."

"Wow," said Jack, to oblige Penny, whose mouth was full. "Go on, ignore the illiterate comments."

"Her husband built the house," Ellen said. Unconsciously her voice took on the old storytelling note she had used in bedtime reading to all the children in turn. "He was a farmer—German, as many of the early settlers of western Virginia were. He came south from the comparatively civilized communities of Pennsylvania into what was then a howling wilderness, the remote edge of the known world. There were hostile Indians, and bears, and wildcats, and forests so thick the sun never reached the ground under the trees.

"It was good farming land, when it was cleared. Grain and cattle did well. All Karl Baumgartner had to do was cut down about a million trees and dig out the stumps and plow the land and plant and harvest. One of you soft modern types wouldn't have lasted a week."

She looked severely at Phil.

"Glad I didn't live then," he remarked.

"There were already a few little houses clustered around the spot where two trails crossed," Ellen went on. "People were helpful in those days; they had to be, there were so few of them. The other settlers helped Karl build a little frame house. But he wanted more. He worked like a demon, even harder than his busy neighbors. In a few years he had a good crop of wheat and a couple of wagons in which to haul it down to the populated Tidewater towns. In ten years he started building a real house.

"His neighbors were surprised and a little vexed when he left the settlement and built his house a mile away, in the middle of the woods. Two or three prosperous settlers had enlarged their homes, but Karl had fancier ideas; his house was built of brick brought all the way from England. His wagons carried bricks back when they went down to the markets. Finally they came back with something else—Karl's bride.

"They say she was a Gypsy. They say she was Spanish, or Egyptian. Something exotic, something different from the sturdy German and Scotch-Irish girls of the region. She was slim and dark, olive-skinned, with great flashing black eyes. . . ."

"You're making that up," said Penny.

Ellen grinned.

"Well, I've never seen a picture of her. . . . It will be nice to have a new audience, one that won't question every statement I make."

"They won't know you as well as we do," said Phil.

"I suppose that part of the story is purely legend," Ellen admitted. "About her Gypsy blood, I mean. She couldn't have been too exotic, because she had a good old English name—Mary."

Penny groaned.

"Mary Baumgartner. That's a terrible name for a witch. She is the witch, isn't she?"

"Try to keep quiet for five minutes," suggested her uncle.

"Mary was the witch," said Ellen. "She was strange and, consequently, unpopular, from the first. She didn't make bread and kill chickens and help with the plowing, like the husky pioneer housewives. Karl hired a girl to do that. And Mary sat in her parlor, which Karl had furnished with the best to be found in Georgetown. She sang strange little songs in a language no one knew."

"Sounds dull," said Penny. "Was that all she did?"

"Obviously not," said Phil, with a laugh. "Karl came home at night, didn't he?"

"He did," Ellen agreed; she was used to the feeble attempts of the young to be daring. "He was mad about her, and insanely jealous. They say she sewed exquisitely, but even that domestic skill failed to impress her neighbors because she didn't make shirts for her husband or mend his socks. She did embroidery."

"Maybe she was Spanish, then," said Penny. "Or French. Educated in a convent, where they learned to do delicate needlework. For altar cloths and things."

"Right," Phil agreed, squinting through his hair. "The songs in a funny language—those poor hicks wouldn't know French or Spanish. And if she was a Roman Catholic she wouldn't dare admit it. The discrimination against Catholics in early Virginia—"

"We know all about that essay on religious tolerance you wrote for American history," his father said repressively. "It's the only respectable piece of research you've done in four years. Go on, Ellen."

"I hadn't thought of it, but I expect they're right," Ellen said. "Mary refused to attend the local church."

"How did she get away with that?" Phil demanded. "People had to go to church at least once a week or they were fined and stuck in the stocks."

He caught his father's eye and subsided.

"This was the frontier, not a settled coastal town," Ellen said. "And by this time Karl was a wealthy man. That didn't prevent the townspeople from whispering, however. Stories began to circulate. People saw Mary walking in the woods at night. They said she worshiped graven images. They said she had bewitched her husband, who was a hard-working, God-fearing man in all things except his infatuation for her. They even said she had a familiar."

"A cat?" said Penny eagerly. "A black cat!"

"No," said Ellen. "Not a black cat; a white one. Karl brought it back from one of his trips to Georgetown. Heaven knows how it got to the wild shores of America, because the description suggested a Persian or Angora, with blue eyes. Mary adored it."

"All sensible people adore cats," said Penny. "Look at the way we spoil Ishtar."

Ellen realized they were all strenuously keeping their eyes from a certain part of the kitchen. She turned. Sitting on the forbidden counter top was an elegant Siamese cat, leisurely devouring the strips of bacon Ellen had left to drain.

"Ishtar!" Ellen yelled, jumping up.

The cat gave her a disdainful look and left the counter, taking the last piece of bacon with her. Ishtar could move with the silence of a cloud, and her leaps were so effortless they gave the impression of levitation. When she was feeling surly, she clumped. Ellen never understood how one dainty eight-pound cat could walk like an elephant, but Ishtar could, and often did.

"Let us return," said Jack, "to the cat of Mary. Do you suppose that really was her name?"

"Maria," Penny suggested.

"Maybe."

"I prefer to think of her that way," Penny said.

"Think, don't talk," said Jack. "Go on, Ellen. The cat of Maria . . ."

Ellen looked down at her plate. Jack knew her too well; he sensed there was something on her mind. But she had no intention of telling any of them about the fugitive flash of white she had seen in the clearing where Mary had once lived. Jack was dubious enough about her decision to move into such a remote area.

"That's all about the cat of Maria," she said lightly. "If she had owned a nice fat pink pig, somebody would have found it uncanny. People talked about her, but nothing serious happened until her husband died suddenly and she was left a wealthy widow.

"They said she had murdered him. The idyll had gone sour; Karl was jealous and accused her of infidelity on several occasions. I think she was innocent of that. Most

of the people in the village shunned her, and the men who
might have disregarded her unholy reputation were in
very practical awe of her husband. So I think Maria was
faithful, in the literal physical sense. But there were quar-
rels—loud, violent arguments, with the lady shouting as
fiercely as the gentleman. The maid overheard them, and
her gossip in the village didn't help Maria's reputation.

"Yet there wasn't much they could do about their sus-
picions. There were no doctors in that remote place and
even if there had been, medical knowledge was primitive.
Karl had no relatives to contest the simple will he left—
'every thing to my wife Mary—' and no handwriting experts to question the signature.

"Instead of selling his farm, or promptly remarrying, as
a decent woman was supposed to do, Mary ran the business herself. She came out of her pretty parlor and rode
the wagons and walked the fields like a man. She was the
toughest master in the whole county and the most ruthless
about collecting rents, and money due her. She could not
be softened, not even by curly-headed kiddies begging
her to give daddy a little more time. She hated children.
She had only one soft spot, and that was for animals.
Over the years she ran what must have been the first un-
official animal shelter in Virginia. Any sick, abandoned,
or hurt animal found a home with her. She doctored them
herself, with herbs and plants she gathered in the woods.
And the wild animals repaid her. Hated as she was, she
was safe from molestation while she harbored wolves and
foxes and a lame wildcat she had nursed back to health."

"Mo-other!" protested Penny.

"That's what the story says," Ellen said blandly. "Of
course Maria's skill with animals only strengthened her
neighbors' belief that she was in league with the Devil. So
did her increasing prosperity. Everything she touched
turned to gold, while her enemies had incredibly bad luck.

Their cows went dry, their children sickened, their houses burned down."

"How could she get farmhands?" Phil asked. "I remember we learned that there weren't many slaves in the western parts of the state at that time, so she had to depend on hired labor. If they all hated her so much—"

"The operative word is 'fear,' " said his father. "You kids are so damned lucky. You've never known poverty; you don't understand how tyranny can intimidate and enslave. She had power because of her wealth, and her reputed supernatural gifts would give her an even stronger weapon. Pioneers lived on the ragged edge. Blighted crops and sterile animals could mean the difference between survival and starvation. If your children are hungry you'll work for Satan himself—and lick his boots if he threatens to fire you."

He glanced at Ellen and smiled faintly.

"Sorry, dear. I didn't mean to turn your ghost story into a lecture."

"I'm beginning not to like Maria," said Penny. "If she was like that—"

"You can't blame her," Jack said. "What else could she do, a woman and an alien? She had to fight or go under."

"You're making her too real," Ellen said.

"Wasn't she real?"

"Oh, yes. At least her name is mentioned in property and tax records of the early eighteenth century. But the rest of it is only local legend."

"Some legend," said Penny appreciatively. "Come on, Mom, let's hear the rest of it. My car pool will be here in a minute."

Ellen tried to recapture her storytelling mood. She had been speaking literally when she accused Jack of making her main character too real. It was easier to be witty about a legend than a living human being, with human weaknesses and worries.

"Well," she said slowly, "there came a time when Maria's animal hospital was almost empty. She had done her work of healing too well; her patients had returned to the woods. One morning Maria failed to appear in the fields, where she was accustomed to supervise the workers. No one complained about her absence. They were happy to be left alone.

"Almost a week went by before some public-spirited busybodies decided they ought to investigate. Maria had no house servants; she had sent them packing when her husband died, and she lived, it was said, in a horrible state of squalor. When the committee approached the house they stopped short, appalled at what they saw.

"The house was surrounded by animals. Wolves, foxes, skunks, rats, even snakes—they sat and lay and sprawled in ranks about the silent house. On the front steps, like a general reviewing troops, sat the white cat.

"The intruders turned to go—to flee, as fast as they could. Behind them, blocking their retreat, was a big black bear.

"So they went to the house, with the animals crowding in behind them. They were witless with terror, but they had enough wits to know death when they saw it. Mary had been dead for almost a week. When the men came out, sick and horrified, the clearing was empty. There was not an animal in sight, not even a cat."

Silence fell. Ellen's audience exchanged glances. After a moment Jack got up from the table, reached for his hat, put it on, and then solemnly took it off.

"That's even better than the one you used to tell about the vampire on Fourteenth Street," said Phil appreciatively.

"How much of it did you make up?" asked Penny.

"Very little, believe it or not. My skeptical friend Ed doesn't believe in ghosts, but he tells a good story. Of course he thinks the people who have reported manifestations are hysterical fools—"

"What sort of manifestations?" Jack interrupted. He was frowning.

"Nothing alarming. Apparently Maria is a rather lazy ghost."

"What does she do? Rattle chains, howl in the night?"

"She doesn't do anything. People have heard noises, that's all. Laughter. Creaking floorboards. The conventional sounds from all the familiar ghost stories. Ed's aunt, who lived there for fifty years, never heard anything."

"Oh, come on." Phil stared hopefully at her through a shaggy brown fringe. "Somebody must have heard something. Or seen something.

"They see her cat," Ellen admitted.

"The ghost of a cat?" Phil was disappointed. "That's nothing to be scared of."

"Not very convincing, either." Jack relaxed, smiling. "You would think local scaremongers could come up with something more imaginative. There are too many stray cats."

"What a rip-off," Phil muttered. "I've always wanted to see a ghost."

"You can console yourself, if you like, by searching for her grave," Ellen said. She knew Jack was watching her closely, and her voice was deliberately light and casual. "She's buried somewhere in the yard. They just dug a hole and dropped her in. She wouldn't qualify for sanctified ground, I guess."

"Hey," said Phil, brightening.

His father kicked him.

"Forget it, you ghoul. There can't be much left of the poor woman after all this time anyhow."

"Aunt Ellen, you are wasted in your present life," said Phil. "You ought to write for the Late Late Horror Movie."

"Come on, Phil," Jack said brusquely. "I know you're doing your best to miss the school bus, but—"

"We haven't heard the end," Phil protested. "How did she die, Aunt Ellen? Not a natural death. That *would* be a rip-off."

The sound of a horn outside announced the arrival of Penny's car pool.

"She was murdered, of course," Penny said, scooping up an armful of books. "Good-bye, everybody. See you later."

She was gone before Ellen could get her wits together. Phil grinned.

"She's got that crazy red shirt," he said tolerantly. "She'll put it on in the car, Aunt Ellen."

"I didn't see any shirt."

"It was wadded up in her bookbag. You know how kids that age are, Aunt Ellen; they have to rebel."

"It's a wonder Penny hasn't murdered you for those half-baked condescending cracks of yours," his father said resignedly. "Get in the car, Phil. You've missed the bus but you aren't going to miss any classes. I'll drop you off on my way to work."

Phil winked at his aunt and wandered out, hands in his pockets.

Ellen got up to clear the table. But the door had barely closed before it opened again. Jack poked his head in.

"How *did* she die?" he asked, in a whisper.

"You're as bad as the kids. She committed suicide, as a matter of fact. Hanged herself. Or is it hung?"

"Damned if I know. Thanks. I couldn't have done a thing today, wondering about it."

Ellen stood at the door watching the car back down the driveway. The house was in one of Washington's older suburban developments; lots of an acre or more in size and ten-year-old trees gave the area a charm the newer subdivisions lacked, despite the greater ostentation of the houses. Jack's blue Buick paused at the end of the drive to let another car pass before it joined the trickle of work-bound commuters.

It would have been easy to stand in the doorway and enjoy a good, sentimental cry; but Ellen had promised herself not to indulge in this any oftener than she could help. With a grimace she turned to face a kitchen in the usual post-breakfast shambles—and a Siamese cat sitting on one of the abandoned chairs, forepaws primly planted on the table as she polished off the rest of Penny's bacon.

"Bad cat," said Ellen unenthusiastically.

Ishtar raised a seal-brown mask and stared at her with innocent blue eyes. After a cool appraisal, the cat decided that Ellen wasn't going to go beyond insults; she returned to the bacon, and Ellen stood leaning against the doorframe, thinking.

She had deliberately chosen to tell the ghost story. There was no hope of concealing it from Jack, and only by being matter-of-fact about the grisly tale could she convince him that it was unimportant to her.

To call Jack overprotective would be unfair to both of them. He gave her exactly the degree of support she needed at any given moment, and if that support was sometimes greater than she ought to have, that was her fault for asking—not his for giving. One of the reasons why the house in the mountains appealed to her was because it was a complete break with her former life and habits—a change she owed to herself, and to the people who had been propping her up, in one way or another, for ten years. She depended on the children, on Jack's boys as well as on Penny, more than they realized. Because she owed them so much she had to let them go, and she could only free them by being capable of standing alone, asking no more of them than the freely given love which is a hard-won gift, not an obligation. If she owed the kids that, she owed Jack even more.

She really did love her new house. It reached out to her

as no inanimate thing had ever done. But she wished Ed hadn't told her that gruesome story!

She said, "Damn," and the cat, now on the table, questing among the plates, cocked a wary ear in her direction before deciding that the expletive had not been directed at her. Ellen was vaguely aware of Ishtar's misbehavior; she was more preoccupied with the things she had left out of her ghost story.

She had not mentioned seeing a cat—a white cat. Jack was absolutely right, it was a feeble sort of ghost to invent. She had been more disturbed by the idea that Maria's frail ivory bones lay somewhere under the green grass of her front yard. Jack had seen that she was disturbed, but he knew she was too sensible to be seriously upset. The bones were only part of the cast-off cocoon, the outgrown shell of the nautilus. . . . "Build thee more stately mansions, oh my soul!"

On the whole, Ellen thought she had carried the whole thing off rather well.

So why hadn't she told Jack how Maria had died?

According to Ed, whose talents as a raconteur were certainly wasted in his present location, the investigating committee had found the woman's body hanging from a hook. But the comments of her family that morning had crystalized Ellen's uneasy feelings about the death. If Maria had been a member of the Catholic faith, suicide was a deadly sin. Why should she kill herself? The legend held no hint of illness, of consciousness of sin, that would drive a woman to such a deed. Suicide conflicted with Maria's theoretical religion and with her personality, as demonstrated by her ruthless behavior. She had known the woodland pharmacopoeia; if she had found signs of a fatal illness, would she not have resorted to one of the natural drugs available to her, rather than seek such a painful death?

Ellen gave herself a vigorous shake that vibrated the silver-gilt curls on her head.

"That is enough of that," she said aloud, and advanced purposefully toward the table. The words might have had a double meaning, but Ishtar went by actions, not speech; she vanished and Ellen started gathering up egg-stained plates.

ii

On Saturday they all drove down to see the house. Jack was silent for most of the drive; he had asked her not to sign a contract until she had had another, critical look at the house. He meant until *he* had had a look at the house, but was too tactful to say so. Phil and Penny were in manic moods, laughing and singing and making outrageous jokes; they thoroughly approved of Ellen's back-to-nature movement.

To Ellen's relief, the house worked its magic on all of them, even on Jack. Impatient with the deliberate movements of their elders, the younger pair rushed off to explore the house. Their shouts of approval, broken by a howl from Phil when he hit his head on the stair arch, floated back to Ellen as she stood with Jack in the living room.

"It's a charmer," he admitted, rubbing his chin and smiling. "I don't blame you, Ellen; I'd like a place like this myself someday."

"Oh, Jack, I'm so glad."

"Wait a minute, now, I haven't said I approve. Charm is one thing, termites are another. Let's go slowly and see how many flaws we can find."

The tour took almost an hour. Ellen's anxiety returned as she watched Jack poke and probe and mumble. He made no audible comments, nor could she tell from his expression what he was thinking. It was not until they stood once more on the walk before the house that Jack cleared his throat and prepared to pronounce. The young people were off in the woods somewhere; Ellen could hear them shouting to one another.

"I hate to admit it," Jack said, "but the place is in amazingly good condition. Oh, there's a lot of minor work that needs doing, especially inside. It will cost you a mint to remodel the kitchen and bathroom. You'll want another bathroom downstairs, and the plumbing needs a thorough overhaul. Ditto the wiring. The well pump looks as if it's about to go, and the septic tank probably hasn't been touched in thirty years. But the basic fabric is sound. Those walls will stand for another century."

"What about the price?"

"Lower than I'd expected. There are going to be more and more people wanting to get away from it all, as the cities expand. You won't take a loss if you resell."

"Then you advise me to go ahead."

"No." He smiled at her, and her treacherous heart quivered. "I'd be much happier if you bought a nice new townhouse in Potomac or Chevy Chase."

"I'd hate a house like that."

"I know you would. And I feel the attractions of this house. Its imperfections don't offend, they make you itch to get in there and fix them up. I'm being selfish. I want you to take something you would detest just to relieve my anxieties. Which is a helluva thing to ask anyone, much less someone for whom I feel as I do about you."

"You know your opinion means a great deal to me."

"That's why I shouldn't have had the crust to give it to you. Forget my feelings. Only be sure, Ellen, that you will be happy here. You won't be afraid, alone and isolated?"

"I'm probably safer here than I would be in your dear suburbs."

"Physically, yes. It's your state of mind I'm concerned about."

"I knew I shouldn't have told you that story! Do you really think I'm that neurotic?"

Jack looked astonished, and then amused. He threw back his head and laughed heartily.

"My dear girl, believe me—your ghost is the one thing I'm not worried about!"

back his head and laughed heartily. "..."
"My dear, g do. believe me — your ghost is the one thing I'm not worried about."

Three

The next two months passed with unbelievable speed. At the beginning Ellen wondered how she was ever going to complete the complex chores that lay ahead—preparing three people for departure to scattered parts of the world, selling the Bethesda house, and getting her new house in order. In his unobtrusive way, Jack did a good deal of the work. He took care of all his own preparations; and if Ellen sewed on a few buttons that didn't need sewing, he never knew about it, and she felt entitled to that final indulgence. Jack sold the house, managing to be on hand when it was necessary, despite his killing schedule at work. He even made Phil and Penny help with the constant cleaning Ellen insisted upon. Later, when she had time to think, Ellen wondered whether Jack hadn't sold the house for less than he might have obtained, just to put an end to her exhausting orgies of house cleaning.

The speed with which her new house was readied for

occupancy astounded Ellen and left her city friends vocal with envy. Either the old-fashioned virtues of hard work and reliability still lingered in small towns, or else Ed Salling had greater influence with local workmen than he would admit. Plumbers, electricians and carpenters came and went; each time Ellen drove down to inspect the house she found another job done.

The two older boys, Arthur and Sam, came back from college in the middle of the upheaval. After inspecting the house in the mountains they called a family conference and informed Ellen that it was ridiculous for her to spend all that money on work they could perfectly well do themselves. Her objections were firmly overruled; the three boys, equipped with sleeping bags and a case of canned spaghetti and meatballs, moved into the house and painted every piece of wood that showed. Penny seethed with frustration. Her school didn't dismiss until the end of June, so it was only on weekends that she was allowed to wallow in paint and plaster.

The last week was a whirlwind of activity. When Ellen looked back on it afterward she couldn't recall a single action clearly; it was a blur of moving figures carrying ladders and furniture and suitcases, pounding nails and hanging pictures, hemming new drapes and laying rugs. When her family left, all the heavy work was done, but there were enough minor chores to keep her busy for a week. And that, she knew, had been deliberately planned.

She stood in the doorway the final morning, waving as the station wagon drove off. The day before they had all put Penny on the plane for New York, where she would meet the chaperoned tour she was joining for a month in Europe. Jack was leaving next day; the boys would spend some time with friends in Washington before scattering on their summer activities—Arthur to a job as counselor at a boys' camp, Sam to spend three months working in a northern city before returning to finish his doctorate, and

Phil to a Canadian hiking tour with cousins of Jack's. The last she saw of them was the red flare of the car's taillights as it passed between the pines at the end of the drive.

The red lights blurred around the edges, and it wasn't only because of the rain, which fell with appropriate dreariness. Ellen brushed the tears from her eyes, sniffed twice, and turned briskly back into the house.

She put a record on the hi-fi and settled down with the boxes of books that occupied a large part of the living room. The fireplace was flanked by built-in bookcases, freshly painted by the boys. A fire flickered on the hearth; Jack had lit it, as his last gesture. The therapy of music, literature, and a fire worked wonders with Ellen's spirits, but the unpacking didn't progress quickly; the books had to be dusted and arranged, and Ellen kept finding old favorites she hadn't read for a long time. When the doorbell rang she was deep in the third chapter of *The Immense Journey,* and she had to flex her stiff knees before she could stagger to the door. The doorbell sounded again before she reached her goal, and she reminded herself to look for an antique knocker. The bell was an unnecessarily modern intrusion.

She had not been exaggerating when she told Jack she was not afraid to be alone. She opened the door without hesitation; but at the sight of the group on the porch she recoiled.

The man wasn't alarming. Quite the contrary. Tall and broad-shouldered, he wore an aged mackintosh dripping with rain. His hair, flattened by wet, was prematurely silver, to judge by the youthfulness of his smiling face. Ed Salling had pointed him out to Ellen on a former occasion, so she even knew who he was. But the dogs flanking him on either side would have made most people run for cover. They were huge Dobermans, black as midnight.

"Mrs. March? I'm Norman McKay, your nearest neighbor. I live up on the hill."

"Oh, yes." Ellen extended her hand. "Mr. Salling mentioned you. Won't you come in?"

"I'd like to, if I won't be interrupting. I didn't drop in earlier because I knew how busy you were, but I saw your family leave a while ago and thought it might reassure you to know you have friends at hand."

"That is kind," Ellen said warmly. "You're not interrupting anything that won't be going on for the next month. I was just about to take a coffee break anyhow."

She stepped back from the door. Instead of following her, Norman stooped and took the dogs by their collars.

"I hope the dogs didn't frighten you?"

"Oh, no," Ellen lied valiantly.

"I wanted to introduce you formally so you wouldn't be alarmed if you met them on one of your walks. They won't attack unless ordered to do so, but the very sight of them can be frightening if you come on them unexpectedly. Bruce—Champion—meet Mrs. March."

Ellen extended a hand to each dog in turn. Ordinarily she was not afraid of dogs, but she appreciated Norman's firm grip on the collars of this pair. That it was unnecessary she could well believe, for the animals appeared to be very well trained. All the same, it was a considerate gesture, indicating unusual thoughtfulness.

The dogs sniffed her hand politely and then lay down, simultaneously, like well-drilled acrobats—or machines, Ellen thought involuntarily.

"That's amazing," she exclaimed. "I didn't even see you give a hand signal."

"I did, though." Norman grinned boyishly. "Behind my back. I can't resist showing off. Do you mind if they wait on the porch?"

"Of course not."

Ellen led the way into the living room, an apology for its cluttered state on her lips, but before she could speak Norman exclaimed.

"Books! Books that have been read! What a beautiful sight."

"Messy is the word I would have used." Ellen laughed.

"You have no idea how wonderful it will be to have a neighbor who reads. I feel like an alcoholic who has just called on a new arrival and found the living room full of bottles. An immediate empathy!"

"Then I won't worry about how you will amuse yourself while I get the coffee."

"No, indeed."

When Ellen came back with a tray her guest was sitting cross-legged on the floor amid the scattered volumes of a set of Dickens. He leaped to his feet when she came in and took the tray from her. *I wonder how old he is,* she thought. *He moves like a boy. . . .*

Norman's enthusiasm for her favorite authors strengthened Ellen's first favorable impression. By the time he rose to go they were on first-name terms.

"I hadn't meant to stay so long," he said sincerely. "Are you sure I can't help you put these away before I go?"

"Thank you, no. But I appreciate your coming. It's nice to know someone is nearby."

"Call any hour of the day or night. But you've nothing to worry about," he added reassuringly. "We haven't had a serious crime for two hundred years."

It was, Ellen thought, a rather odd interval to mention. Did he mean that there had been a serious crime in the village two centuries earlier? But Mary Baumgartner had lived almost two hundred and fifty years ago. . . .

Before she could make up her mind whether or not to pursue the subject, there was an outburst of barking from the porch.

"Someone coming," Norman said, frowning. "Are you expecting company?"

"No. Perhaps they scent Ishtar. They wouldn't attack a cat, would they?"

"You have a cat?" Norman said, in a peculiar voice.

Cat lovers insist that felines exhibit evidence of extrasensory perception; certainly Ishtar had a habit of appearing, apparently out of thin air, when anyone mentioned her name. She came stalking through the archway into the living room, tail erect and switching. Instead of stopping at the sight of a stranger, as she usually did, she advanced steadily upon Norman, blue eyes fixed unblinkingly on his face. Ellen was surprised to see Norman retreat. His face had lost some of its color.

"I'm sorry," she exclaimed, making a grab for the cat. "I know some people are allergic. . . ."

Ishtar writhed, yowling, and with a grim expression Ellen carried her to the cellar. When she returned to the living room, followed by a chorus of hoarse Siamese complaint, she saw that her guest was wiping perspiration from his face.

"Ridiculous, isn't it?" he said wryly. "No, for God's sake, Ellen, don't apologize, that just makes me feel a bigger fool. I can't help it, though. The doctor says it's the worst case of ailurophobia he's ever encountered."

"Oh, dear," Ellen said in distress. "I hope that doesn't mean you can't visit me again."

"No, it's not like an ordinary allergy. As I understand it, allergic distress can be caused by animal hair in the air or on the furniture. It doesn't bother me to know there's a cat in the house, so long as I don't see it, or—or touch it." A long, agonized shiver ran through him, and he smiled apologetically. "See! The very idea gives me gooseflesh. I'm sorry to have repaid your charming hospitality with this absurd performance. Next time you must come see me—and not because I'm chicken. I'd like to show off my library and the few bits of bric-a-brac I've picked up. What about dinner tomorrow? I'll call for you."

"I'd love to," Ellen said, following him to the door. "But you needn't—"

"Of course I needn't. I want to. You won't have to suffer bachelor cooking, I have an excellent couple living in. Martha is a narrow-minded old Puritan, but she cooks like an angel."

As he opened the door, another chorus of barks burst out, and Ellen ducked involuntarily. Norman laughed.

"Now that is real tact," he said. "Pretending to be afraid of my poor little dogs to make me feel better about my reaction to your vicious cat. Ellen, thank you. This was a joy. I'll see you tomorrow. About seven? Good."

As soon as he opened the screen door the dogs darted out and ran across the lawn. They were silent now, but their silence was more menacing than the deep barks had been. They seemed to be in pursuit of something. Ellen shivered sympathetically, thinking of a rabbit or squirrel fleeing before that pair of white-fanged behemoths.

There was no car in sight, and as Norman followed the dogs into the woods Ellen realized that there must be a footpath connecting the two houses. I'll have to find it, she thought, watching the tall, erect figure vanish among the trees. This was definitely an acquaintance worth pursuing, as Jane Austen might have put it. She had not expected to find such a paragon right on her doorstep—a man who was attractive, wealthy, cultured, and intelligent. He even had a sense of humor. Her female friends in Washington would gloat over Norman; some of them had been thrusting eligible males at her for years, and speculating dangerously about her immunity.

Well, why not, she thought defiantly. A few years of solitude would be restful—but thirty or forty years? The rest of her life? Jack would never marry her. He would probably be captured by some glamorous European, and then she couldn't even count on seeing him as a friend. For him she would always be good old Aunt Ellen.

However, Norman had one deficiency as a potential husband. Apparently it would have to be him or Ishtar.

Ellen smiled. From the cellar came sounds that suggested that somewhere in the nether regions a Siamese cat was being skinned alive.

Ellen marched to the cellar door and opened it. A streak of fawn and brown fur hurtled out. It thudded against the front door and scratched and sniffed for a few moments. Then, realizing that her quarry was gone, Ishtar suddenly sat down and began to clean her stomach with an air of great concentration.

"Ha," said Ellen. "He got away. Made you look like a fool, didn't he?"

Ishtar did not look up. She rolled over onto her back, lifted one leg, and began working on a different section.

Ellen watched this feeble attempt at indifference with a smile. Gradually the smile faded. She had heard of ailurophobia but had always imagined it was the equivalent of the squeamish distaste she felt for large squashy insects. She didn't like them; but she never turned faint, or fled from a beetle. Poor Norman. It was a painful and embarrassing affliction. She fully believed his assertion that he couldn't control his feelings. No man would put on such an exhibition by choice, especially in front of a woman. And Ishtar . . .

Ellen glared at the cat, who pretended not to notice. Ishtar probably realized the man's weakness and was prepared to take advantage of it. Cats always made up to the people who hated them the most. Depending on how you chose to look at it, it was a touching manifestation of trust, or a malicious pleasure in human discomfort.

"Terrible animal," she said fondly, and bent to pick up a demurely purring Ishtar. "Does she want some liver, now, bad cat? Don't worry, darling, I wouldn't marry anybody who didn't like you. . . . Of course I'm sure Jack would take you if—"

Ishtar sank her teeth into Ellen's hand. She didn't draw blood, but the fangs left perceptible dents. Hastily Ellen put her down.

"I should know better than to talk in front of you," she said, watching the affronted animal stalk away. Every inch of Ishtar's elegant form radiated contempt. Ellen raised her voice.

"I was just speculating, you know. I can't imagine that the problem will ever come up."

Ishtar didn't even turn her head. Ellen laughed, but her laughter had a faintly hollow note.

That evening, sitting before the fire, Ellen surveyed her kingdom with possessive pleasure. She felt as smug as Ishtar, who had forgiven her tactlessness and was now lying on the hearth rug with her paws tucked under. Ellen had dreaded that first evening alone. She could hardly believe in her own mood; she found herself probing tentatively into areas of possible discontent as one pokes at a sore tooth. No doubt the visit of an attractive new neighbor contributed to her feeling of satisfaction, but it was more than that; it was the house. The large low-ceilinged living room was snugly enclosed against the rain. Firelight shone on the paneling and glinted redly off Ellen's collection of antique glass, which occupied some of the shelves beside the fireplace.

The house was not entirely silent. Every house has its own distinctive orchestration of sounds—wood creaking, the purr of various appliances, noises from without. Ellen's subconscious had learned the sounds of this house and accepted them. She rocked luxuriously and mentally reviewed her new domain.

There were still chores to be done—pleasant chores, such as shopping for a doorknocker and curtain material, grubbier tasks like cleaning the cellar. It was a genuine old-fashioned cellar, not a basement; it smelled of dank earth and was virtually windowless. The boys had intended to clear out the accumulated debris, but after inspecting it they reported that the collection was too fascinating to discard without further investigation. Old newspapers and magazines, broken machinery, boxes full of moldy books and discarded finery—as Phil said, you couldn't tell what you might find down there!

Ellen smiled as she remembered his eager face. Phil hoped for skeletons; his tastes still ran to Lovecraft and Bradbury's grislier tales.

Ellen wasn't worried about finding relics of Mary Baumgartner, although the lower regions of the cellar did rather resemble an archaeological *tell*, with layers of superimposed discards from former inhabitants. As a confirmed antique hound, she was looking forward to rummaging. The cellar wasn't much worse than some of the shops she had visited. According to Phil, there was even a "mysterious" boarded-up door in a lower subcellar room below ground level. Only lack of time, and his father's outraged prohibition, had prevented Phil from attacking this fascinating structure with an ax. She must ask Ed Salling about the door sometime. . . .

When the fire died, Ellen went upstairs in the same mood of peaceful content. Her low-eaved bedroom was cozy and welcoming. Someone had laid a fire here, too. Ellen knew who the someone was, and she smiled as she knelt to light it. The room wasn't cold, but it would be so luxurious to lie in bed listening to the rain outside and watching the glow of firelight.

She decided to read a while until the flames died down. The room couldn't have been more peaceful. Her reading lamp shed a bright circle of light on the book without disturbing the soft gloom of the far corners, and the purring of Ishtar, curled up on the foot of the bed, blended with the sound of the rain. Involved in the adventures of Becky Sharp, Ellen read on.

Then it happened. She dropped the book with a harsh gasp, her hands flying to her throat. Ishtar groaned irritably and turned over, but did not wake. Gradually the thud of Ellen's heart quieted but she still sat twisted about, staring into the dim corner by the door.

Of course there was nothing there . . . nothing that could have cast a shadow like the one that had suddenly appeared, at the very edge of her vision. The shadow had vanished as she turned. But—heavens, how real it had seemed! Ellen put a hand to her forehead and found she was perspiring.

She glanced at the sleeping cat and a sheepish smile curved her lips. Ishtar was lying on her back with all four feet sticking up into the air; she looked as ridiculous as a Siamese cat is capable of looking. Well, Ellen thought, that proves it couldn't have been a ghost. Cats were notoriously susceptible to the supernatural.

Ghost, indeed, she told herself, picking up her book. Your eyes are going bad, lady. Maybe you need a checkup. But Becky's abortive romance with Jos failed to hold her attention. She kept glancing surreptitiously to the left, where the shadow had stood.

When she turned out the lights, there were shadows to spare. They moved and twisted as the flames created them. Ellen lay awake watching them for some time. But none were even remotely like the sharp-edged shape she had seen. It had resembled the figure of a woman, with long, full skirts and flowing hair.

Four

The following evening Ellen dressed for her dinner engagement with a meticulous attention to detail. Weighing the comparative merits of three different pairs of earrings, she realized how long it had been since she had had the time or the inclination to fuss over her appearance. When the children were small, there was never time; getting them fed and settled for the evening before the sitter arrived left no time for primping. Later, Penny had tried to get her to experiment with makeup and wigs, but by then Ellen had lost interest. She hadn't dated for years, and her only outings had been to concerts and embassy parties with Jack.

With a flash of insight she thought: You were afraid, that's why you didn't bother—afraid of attracting attention from men you didn't care about, afraid people might think you were trying to be more attractive to Jack.

Ellen shook her head at the sober image in her mirror.

Jack was gone, but Norman was very much in evidence; it was time she started thinking about how she would look to him. On the whole the reflected image pleased her. It was a bit sedate, but not bad for a woman who was slipping downhill toward forty. Her pink linen dress had its own jacket; a pink-and-mauve chiffon scarf softened the tailored lines. Ellen leaned forward, peering at her face. It was not without wrinkles; the only way to keep those blemishes from appearing was to cultivate a complete impassivity of countenance. Experimentally she grimaced at herself and decided that most of the lines had come from laughter rather than from frowning. She couldn't give up laughing just to keep her face unlined. If Norman preferred the smooth vacuity of youth, as so many middle-aged men unaccountably seemed to do, then she was out of luck.

Her eyes were drawn irresistibly to the row of photographs on her dressing table. Penny's smiling face—young but certainly not vacuous, Phil's wide-lipped grin; Arthur and Sam trying not to look sulky because they had been forced into suits and ties; . . . and Jack. His hair was brushed uncompromisingly back from his forehead and his eyes looked straight into hers.

She was still looking at him when the doorbell rang. Gathering up purse and gloves, she stood for a moment by the window looking out over the wooded hills that had already become dear and familiar. She had not done much yardwork. The ground was still damp. Soon, she promised herself, she would get to work weeding and clipping. She had been indoors for two days and needed exercise—mental and physical. It wouldn't do to sit and moon over Jack's photo like a dreamy teen-ager.

The doorbell rang again and Ellen hurried downstairs.

"I see you are ready," Norman said. "Admirable woman!"

As he stood smiling at her, with the sun gilding his hair, Ellen couldn't help being struck by the contrast be-

tween his youthful good looks and Jack's beloved but
homely face. Again she wondered about Norman's age.
He had to be in his thirties. . . .

"Yes, I'm ready," she said. "But won't you come in for
a minute?"

"If I do, I'll linger, and Martha is a fussbudget about
time."

He spoke casually but Ellen saw his eyes; she didn't
need to glance back to see what had prompted his reaction. Ishtar was thudding down the stairs. Ellen went out
the door so hurriedly she almost stepped on Norman's
toes.

Norman's car was a revelation of his personality that
Ellen had not expected. She wasn't much interested in
cars except as a means of transportation, but a few types
of automobile are immediately recognizable, even to a
novice. Once seen, the massive elegance of a new Rolls
Royce is not easily forgotten. Norman's Rolls was black
and immaculately tended. Ellen winced as he squeezed
the car through the branches of the twin pines. Ed had
trimmed the trees, as he had promised to do, but the
space that was wide enough for her Corvette cramped the
Rolls. Norman made no comment, but Ellen saw his
mouth tighten. Well, she thought, if you cherished a Rolls
Royce, you had a right to be fussy about it.

The car helped prepare her for Norman's house, which
she had seen only from the road. It was impressive
enough from that angle, but at close range it made her
feel like a Cockney charwoman visiting Buckingham Pal-
ace. The house was very large, pushing out wings and
ells at unexpected angles. Like the car, it was lovingly
tended. The grass had the velvety softness she associated
with centuries-old English lawns. A circular drive, bor-
dered by flowers and shrubs, passed the pillared portico
and the broad steps that led to the front door. No gravel
for Norman, Ellen thought, trying not to calculate how

much that driveway must have cost. A flying bit of stone might mar the gleaming finish of the Rolls.

Norman stopped the car in front of the steps. A man came into sight from behind the house. He was a tall, lanky fellow of indeterminate age. Norman introduced him as Will Hendrick, his handyman. Hendrick responded to Ellen's greeting with a stiff nod. He got into the car and drove it away.

"He's not talkative, but he's reliable," said Norman. "The car is his great love; he washes it every day. If he had his way, I wouldn't drive it at all. Come in, Ellen. Welcome."

Norman needed little prodding to take his guest on a tour of the house. He obviously loved it and was proud of every object in it. Like Ellen's house, it had a central core that went back to Colonial times, but little external evidence of this age remained visible; the house had been extensively remodeled. Secretly Ellen preferred her own brick walls and rough beamed ceilings, but she had to admit that Norman's house was a magnificent example of what money and taste could produce. Its decor was eclectic, in the best sense of that much-abused word; every object, every piece of furniture was a work of art in its own right. When they finally settled down in the spacious living room, with its wide French doors opening into wooded hills and a spectacular sunset, Ellen was almost afraid to sit down. She had never owned a dress made of material as expensive as the imported French velvet covering the chair.

"It is magnificent," she said, seeing that Norman was waiting for praise. "I've never seen a more beautiful house. Did you do all this yourself?"

"Some of it." A slight shadow crossed Norman's face. "My sister-in-law redecorated the house when she married my brother. . . . I'm a terrible host, Ellen; what would you like to drink?"

Ellen accepted sherry; it seemed the proper drink for the gracious room. She had taken only one sip when a woman entered carrying a tray.

"This is Martha," Norman said. "The best cook in Virginia."

After placing the tray on a nearby table, Martha straightened and looked Ellen squarely in the eye. She was the image of the jolly cook of fiction—round and fat and pink-faced, with soft gray hair drawn back into a bun at the back of her neck. Ellen took an immediate and unreasonable dislike to the woman. Perhaps it was the coldness of the gray eyes, which seemed to measure and judge her.

The judgment was negative. No warming spark touched the woman's face. She acknowledged Ellen's existence with a few cool words and turned to go, after mentioning that dinner would be served in half an hour.

"Fine," said Norman. "Where . . . that is . . . is Tim here?"

"He is not," said Martha shortly.

"Oh. . . . Well, when he comes in, send him here, will you, Martha? I want Mrs. March to meet him."

"Hmph," said Martha.

When she had gone, Ellen looked ruefully at her host.

"I'm afraid I didn't make a hit with Martha."

Norman roused himself from some private thought that had left his face lined and older.

"No, no, don't get that impression. Martha doesn't approve of my drinking. She and Will belong to a strict tee-totaling sect. She won't serve liquor in any form, not even wine at dinner. Naturally I wouldn't ask her to violate her principles, even though I don't share them; but I'll be darned if I'm going to give up my harmless glass of sherry! We've compromised. I drink and she ignores it. Actually I think I'd miss her silent condemnation. I'm so accustomed to it."

"You're tougher than I am. Condemnation bothers me, even when it's silent."

"Really? You mean you'd give up your sherry?"

"No," said Ellen. "I'd fire Martha."

Norman laughed.

"Not after you had tasted her cooking. Disapproval is a small price to pay for ambrosia three times a day."

After sampling the hors d'oeuvres, Ellen had to admit he had a point. She ate far more of them than she should have done. Norman continued to chat pleasantly, but Ellen wondered whether he was quite so indifferent to Martha as he pretended. Something was bothering him; he kept glancing at the clock, and occasionally he would fall silent in the middle of a sentence. His nervousness was contagious. Ellen found herself watching the clock too. As the hands approached the hour Martha had set for dining, Norman said suddenly,

"There's something I must tell you. About my nephew—"

He stopped speaking, his eyes focused on the doorway. Ellen felt a prickle of nerves as she turned to see what had made him stop so suddenly.

The boy who stood in the doorway had to be Norman's nephew, Tim. He was also the boy she had seen once before, when Ed had stopped the car in order to avoid hitting him. He resembled many of the adolescents she had known in Washington. The shaggy, shoulder-length blond hair and the faded patched jeans resembled the styles her nephews preferred. The bare feet were in vogue, too, but Tim's feet were black with mud; a trail of dirty prints marred the shining hall floor behind the boy.

He must have done that on purpose, Ellen thought, with a flash of irritation. If he had been ten or eleven— but this boy was old enough to know better. Old enough and big enough; he was as tall as his uncle, and although his arms and chest had not filled out completely, they were impressively muscled.

Then she looked at Tim's face, and she knew why she felt uneasy. She had seen that expression before.

During the last few years Ellen had done volunteer work with delinquent children in Washington. The children had been of all types: black and white, rich and poor, from ghetto squalor and from the most expensive suburban developments. All of them had psychological problems that varied in intensity as well as in kind. Ellen had learned early in the game that it was impossible to find a single underlying cause for the various forms of delinquency. But she had become very familiar with "the look," as she called it—the blank, shuttered faces that rejected contact with the outside world. These children were the hardest to deal with; they suspected adult sympathy as much as they feared adult censure.

"Oh, there you are," said Norman. "Come in, Tim, and meet our new neighbor."

Tim did not respond at once—another symptom Ellen found familiar. After an interval that extended to the point of discomfort, he walked slowly across the floor, leaving a fading trail of muddy prints. He came to a stop directly in front of Ellen. He stood too close, so that he loomed over her. She had to tip her head back in order to meet his eyes.

"Hello, Tim," she said.

Tim said nothing. He continued to watch her with the same unblinking stare. My God, he's big, Ellen thought involuntarily.

"Sit down, Tim," Norman said nervously. "And—and have a Coke, or something. Dinner will be ready in a minute. I'll bet you're hungry. Been out in the woods all day? You know how active they are at that age," he added, addressing Ellen with a false heartiness she found quite painful.

Tim didn't move. Ellen sensed Norman's embarrassment, but there was nothing she could do about it. Later, she wondered how long they would have stayed in their various positions if Martha hadn't come in.

"Dinner's ready," she began, and then exclaimed, "Tim! Look at that filth in the hall! You get right out of here and wash those feet. Wash your filthy hands, too. You aren't fit to eat at a decent table. Now you just move and move fast, young man, or—"

"All right, Martha," Norman said quickly. "Hurry up, Tim. Please?"

It would have been inaccurate to say that Tim obeyed. He left; but his walk, and his expression, got the point across—he was going because he felt like going, not because he had been told to go. Norman rose and offered Ellen his arm. He looked so unhappy she couldn't help sympathizing, although she suspected he was not handling Tim very well.

"Adolescents are all monsters, aren't they?" she said lightly. "I've been through it with four of them, and there were times when I thought I'd lose my mind."

Her bluntness struck the right note. Norman brightened.

"They are all frightful, aren't they? I guess I get upset too easily. I haven't had your experience."

"They like to upset you. Bland indifference to the most outrageous behavior is the only safe response."

Norman seated her at the right of the high chair marking the head of the table and went to the sideboard, where he dealt expertly with a bottle of wine. The table was beautifully set, with fine old china and heirloom silver. Ellen had to admit it boggled her imagination to visualize Tim's muddy feet under that table.

"It's comforting to talk to you," Norman said, as he poured the wine. "I don't know what to do with Tim. I never was any good with children. I was horrified when I realized Bev and Joe had appointed me Tim's guardian. But I could hardly refuse, could I? There are no other relatives."

"Surely you underestimate yourself. They must have thought you capable or they wouldn't have appointed you."

"They had no choice," said Norman. There was a note of bitterness in his voice. "Oh, I suppose Joe trusted me. I had been handling his business affairs, so I was a logical person to appoint as executor. But Bev never thought much of me. She used to laugh at me. . . . The thing was, she didn't expect to die."

"Nobody does," Ellen said gently.

"I guess not. But Bev—she was so alive. More alive than anybody I've ever known. Everything was exciting to her—a new dress, an ornament for the living room, the first robin in spring. I couldn't believe . . ."

During this speech Martha entered with the soup and began to serve it. She served Tim's place as well, although he had not yet appeared. Ellen was surprised when Norman went on talking, despite the cook's presence.

"I couldn't believe she was dead. The police said it was the other driver's fault, but she always did drive too fast. . . . They were both killed instantly, which was a merciful thing. Joe's death was a shock, too, of course, but Bev. . . . She was so alive."

"She was a sinner," said Martha suddenly. "She broke her parents' heart and she ruined that boy."

"Now, Martha," said Norman deprecatingly.

The cook left the room with a sniff and a backward look. Norman glanced at Ellen, who was finding it difficult to conceal her shock and disgust.

"I'm sorry, Ellen. Martha isn't an ordinary servant; she's been with me for ten years, and she helped raise Tim. Her ideas of discipline are as old-fashioned as her attitude toward alcohol, but she has a point. Bev was lax with Tim; she'd keep him out of school to go berrying, things like that."

"I hope Martha doesn't discuss his mother with Tim," said Ellen, tight-lipped.

"So do I," said Norman. He added pathetically, "I told you I was a wretched sort of guardian. If you can give me any advice, Ellen . . ."

Ellen was softened by the appeal, although she still itched to tell Martha a thing or two. With a faint smile she said,

"You don't know me very well, Norman, or you wouldn't say that. I'm only too free with advice. God knows I'm no expert, but I did work with disturbed children for some years, and I'm a pushover for young people. I can't believe a boy like Tim is beyond help."

"He's not a bad boy," Norman said. He looked at her anxiously, and Ellen's tender heart contracted. She had heard that pitiful statement so often.

"He's a handsome boy," she said gently. "He resembles you strongly."

"Shame on you, hitting at my vanity like that. Tim looks a lot like his father; and when we were small, people used to think Joe and I were twins. But it takes a keen eye to see the resemblance, with that perpetual scowl of Tim's."

Ellen's offer of a sympathetic ear had been genuine, and she was honestly curious; but she didn't want to discuss Tim now, when he was apt to appear at any moment.

"This is wonderful consommé," she said. "You didn't exaggerate Martha's talents."

The soup was an unsuccessful attempt at divertissement, for Tim's bowl remained untouched. When Martha came in to change the plates, she took Tim's full bowl without glancing at her employer. When she brought in a superb roast, with its accompanying vegetables, she looked at the empty chair and shook her head.

"You ought to cut off his food for a few days. A little starving might teach him to appreciate good food."

"Now, Martha—"

"You're too soft," the woman grumbled. She gave Ellen a provocative glance, and Ellen knew she had been eavesdropping. She met Martha's hostile eyes with a look so coolly contemptuous that Martha turned away without further comment. As she left the room, Tim entered it. The timing was too perfect. Tim lurking at one door, and the cook at another—heavens, Ellen thought, what a house this is!

Tim had washed his hands. Literally. The line left by soap and water stopped an inch above his wrists. Ellen wondered about his feet. They were now covered by worn old sneakers, but Ellen suspected the mud was still there.

Tim began to eat in silence. Norman's attempts to draw him into the conversation won only grunts.

Ellen would have enjoyed the meal if it had not been for Norman's discomfort. After the first moment of surprise she had not been disturbed by Tim. She had seen too many like him and had learned that Norman's self-conscious good cheer was the worst possible tactic. She ignored Tim with perfect equanimity and chatted about abstract subjects; in fact, as the meal progressed she almost forgot about him. It was something of a shock, therefore, when the silent figure opposite her suddenly addressed her.

"You've got a cat, haven't you?"

"Yes, I do," Ellen said amiably. "A Siamese. Do you like cats?"

"No," said Tim. "No, I don't like cats. Do I, Norman?" He didn't wait for an answer. "Neither one of us likes cats. But I don't dislike them as much as Norman does. Do I, Norman?"

Norman's face was pale. Watching him in helpless sympathy, Ellen knew he was afraid—but not of the object of his phobia. He was afraid of the same thing that sent a shudder down her backbone—the blaze of hate in his young nephew's eyes.

"Ailurophobia is a painful thing to have," she said. "I've never heard that it was hereditary, though. I wonder if anyone has researched the subject?"

Tim's eyes dropped to his plate. He began wolfing down a masterpiece of the pastry maker's art—strawberry tart with a crust like air. Norman relaxed with an audible sigh. Ellen felt a little like an animal trainer trying to calm a leopard by talking soothingly to it. So far it seemed to be working. She went on in the same level voice.

"They say children acquire prejudices against animals, food, and the like from their parents. I've always doubted that. My kids love the vegetables I loathe, and vice versa. But of course ailurophobia is more than a prejudice; it's a physical illness. Perhaps a chemical imbalance—"

"No," said Tim, without looking up. "It's hereditary, all right. We've had it for a long time. Haven't we, Norman? It goes back to our ancestor that was killed by the witch's cat. She hexed him, and he murdered her. Didn't he, Norman? Then the cat clawed—"

"Tim!" Norman's pallor disappeared under a flush of anger. "Let's not have that crazy story, at least not while we're eating."

"I'm through." Tim pushed back his chair and stood up. Then he did something that shook Ellen more than anything he had yet done. Bowing in an ugly parody of courtesy, he said in a high-pitched voice,

"Please, ma'am, may I be excused? Pretty please?"

Ellen was spared the necessity of finding an adequate response. Tim swung abruptly on his heel and strode out of the room.

Norman began to apologize, but Ellen scarcely heard him. She was trying to figure out why the bizarre little performance had been so disturbing. Malice—yes, that was a source of distress, particularly since she hadn't given Tim any cause to dislike her. Another disconcerting element was her awareness of Tim's masculinity as he moved, for once, without a slouch or a shuffle. He might be retarded emotionally, but physically he was almost a man, and he could move with a young man's animal grace. Ellen had a habit of speaking without premeditation when she was strongly moved, and now she said,

"What a devil he must be with the girls!"

"Don't say that!"

Norman's voice was harsh. Ellen stared at him.

"I'm sorry, Norman. That was stupid of me. He hasn't —I mean, there haven't been any—"

"Not yet. Nothing serious . . . yet. Oh, my God, what am I going to do?"

Norman covered his face with his hands.

"Now," Ellen said gently but firmly, "that won't help. I'm sure you are worrying unnecessarily, Norman. Tim is going through a difficult stage—"

"He's almost eighteen." Norman took his hands from his face. He was flushed, but there were no traces of tears. Ellen was glad of that; she wasn't used to dealing with masculine weeping. She suppressed a sudden unfair memory of the way Jack had been accustomed to deal with the malefactions of his young.

"How long do these stages last?" Norman went on. "This one has been going on for seven years."

"But what has he actually—" Ellen stopped as Martha came in with the coffee. If Norman wanted to discuss Tim in front of Martha she couldn't stop him, but she had no intention of joining in the critical chorus. She felt sure the woman had overheard the entire episode. Her face was pursed with the nasty satisfaction of a Puritan who has just discovered a sinner sinning, as expected.

Norman answered the unfinished question as Martha gathered up the dessert plates.

"He's done a lot of things. Malicious mischief, vandalism, cruelty to animals—"

Ellen let out a low exclamation and Martha eyed her severely. The woman balanced the heavy tray as if it had been empty. She had arms like a stevedore's.

"Better watch that cat of yours," said Martha.

"Now, Martha—" Norman began.

"You gotta tell her. You're too soft with that boy, always have been. Tell her about the squirrel he cut the tail off, and the baby rabbits——"

"Martha!"

"All right, all right," Martha muttered. "But you tell her. Doesn't matter what he does to varmints like squirrels, but some people set store by animals. Those fancy cats cost money. Some folks carry on about them as if they was human."

She marched out with the tray. Norman patted Ellen's hand.

"I'm sorry, my dear. Why, you're as pale as a ghost!"

"My phobia," said Ellen, trying to smile. "I can't stand stories about cruelty to children or animals. I'm a sentimental fool."

"There's nothing foolish about that attitude. But Martha is right, it wouldn't be fair not to warn you about Tim's habits with animals. When he was small I thought pets would be good for him. But he—well, the only animals I can keep are the dogs. They are too big and too dangerous for Tim to hurt, although he torments them as much as he safely can. They detest him, and I'm always afraid they'll do him an injury."

"It was Tim yesterday, wasn't it—at my house, when the dogs barked and then rushed off into the woods?"

"I'm afraid so. But don't worry about any danger from Tim. He's a solitary creature; spends a lot of time roaming about the woods. But he's never attacked anyone. At least—not an adult."

"You don't mean he attacks children!"

"I mean he fights," said Norman, with a sudden grin. "He used to, at any rate. When he was ten or eleven I got an average of two calls a week from outraged parents whose kids Tim had beaten up. I'm afraid I discounted that. You know how boys are."

"That kind of aggressiveness is often a sign of trouble, though," Ellen said. "The sudden death of his parents——"

"That's right," Norman said eagerly. "It was a normal reaction, wasn't it? He was ten when Joe and Bev were killed. I expected the boy to be disturbed."

"It's normal in a sense," Ellen said cautiously. "But often children need help to adjust to a loss as severe as that."

"He had help. He saw three different psychiatrists over the next five years. It didn't do any good. He doesn't fight now, but only because the other boys leave him strictly alone. They learned not to provoke him."

"Is he seeing a psychiatrist now?"

"Not at the moment. The last man I consulted said he couldn't do anything without some cooperation from Tim. He wasn't getting it."

"Whom did you see?"

The names Norman recited made Ellen's eyebrows lift.

"You went to the best, all right. How on earth did you get Abrahamson to take you on? He's usually booked up ten years ahead."

"I was ready to do anything by that time," Norman said. "You do agree that I've tried?"

"My dear man, you certainly have. There are no better names in the field."

"I can't help being fond of the boy," Norman said forlornly. "Even though he hates me. . . . Oh, yes, he does. I have to recognize that, though it hurts me. Ellen, I've been incredibly inconsiderate, depressing you with all this. Let's talk about something else. I wouldn't have gone into it if Tim hadn't behaved so badly. I'm such a stupid optimist; every time he meets someone new I hope he'll respond, be pleasant. . . . And I hope the newcomer won't start out with a prejudice against him. That happens, you know."

"I know exactly what you mean. If you expect a boy to behave badly you increase his propensity to do so. But I'm not prejudiced, Norman. I wish I could help Tim."

"Even when you know about his cruelty to animals?"

"He couldn't get near Ishtar, she's too cautious."

"But if he did?"

"What did you just say about prejudice, and expecting the worst? Norman, believe me, I've worked with children who had worse problems than Tim."

"Thank you, Ellen. And now we really will talk about something else."

He still looked depressed, and as they walked toward the living room Ellen was moved to make a gesture she was normally wary of making. Slipping her arm through his, she said lightly,

"Don't you know I'm psychic? My crystal ball tells me you've no need to worry. Tim will turn into a model citizen."

"Are you really psychic?" Norman asked with interest.

"Of course not. I don't really believe—"

"In that sort of thing? I sincerely hope you don't, Ellen. You're in the wrong house, if you're at all susceptible."

"Oh, Norman, not you, too! Ed Salling almost refused to sell me the house. Do I strike everyone as a feeble-minded female?"

"I didn't mean that. . . ."

"Then tell me about my witch and your ancestor. Or was Tim making that up?"

Norman cocked his head and looked at her speculatively. The pose made him appear almost as young as his nephew. After a moment he smiled.

"You're all right. It isn't morbid curiosity, is it?"

"Just curiosity, plain and simple. I told you I was a busybody."

"Can't blame you for being intrigued. Ghost stories are always fun, aren't they? It's true that my ancestor, Peter McKay, was one of the first settlers in this area. He was a tough character and a Bible-toting fundamentalist. Did Ed tell you anything about our local church?"

"He warned me against it, but he warned me about a lot of other things, too."

"He would. But the church is something of a curiosity. It's an unusual sect—unique, so far as I know. No, don't get any wild ideas about Devil worship or Black Masses. It's nothing like that, just an extreme form of pessimistic Calvinism. Infant damnation, predestination, prurient Puritanism—the works. Peter McKay became a convert and an elder. It is quite possible that he came into conflict with Mary Baumgartner, if the stories about her are true. But that's as far as I can logically support the legend Tim mentioned. Mary's death was officially suicide, and her cat is probably apocryphal. Cats are the conventional familiars, aren't they?"

Ellen sipped the brandy he had served as he talked.

"Black cats are conventional, but a white, blue-eyed Angora, at that period, is distinctly unusual. However, that's a side issue. How did your ancestor die?"

"Who knows? He died in 1756, which was the period of the French and Indian Wars, so maybe his demise was violent. But there are no reliable records."

"And the ailurophobia? Is it really hereditary?"

Norman showed signs of impatience.

"Again, who knows? My father hated cats, but a lot of people do. Men of the old school wouldn't admit to such a weakness if they had it."

His mouth had a wry twist, and Ellen decided she had better not pursue the subject.

The rest of the evening passed pleasantly, considering its inauspicious beginning. Norman played some of his favorite records, and they were still talking about music when he drove her home. The conversation had wandered so far from the subject of ghosts and hallucinations that Ellen's conscious mind was free of any such associations. It was therefore a considerable shock when she saw the shadow again.

She was undressing, and humming the theme of the

Mozart piano concerto Norman had played. There was no preliminary flicker of light or movement; suddenly it was there, distinct and sharp-edged.

When Ellen recovered her wits several seconds later, she was crouching against the wall, with the nightgown she had been about to put on clutched to her chest. From the foot of the bed Ishtar stared curiously at her. The cat's expression conveyed well-bred surprise.

This time it took Ellen's thudding heart longer to resume a normal beat. Ridiculously, she turned her back upon the room before slipping the gown over her head. When she turned, the low-roofed, shadowy chamber met her with the welcoming grace it had always showed. Ishtar was purring. The breeze from the open window was as warm as a caress.

"I've got to have my eyes checked," Ellen said aloud.

When she turned out the light, the darkness held no threat. One does not see shadows in the dark.

Five

By the end of the week Ellen had almost forgotten about her optical illusion. It could hardly have been anything else, for it lacked all the attributes of a supernatural apparition. Ellen was familiar with the literature of the subject. She enjoyed a ghost story as much as anyone else, and since several of her friends had been interested in the occult, she had visited fortune-tellers and even participated in a séance or two. Her family had kidded her about her prophetic talents, which usually took the form of warnings to procrastinating youth: "If you don't put that bike away, someone is going to steal it!" As Jack had pointed out, it was this kind of reasonable anticipation that built a fortune-teller's reputation.

Ellen's attitude toward prophecy, palmists, and spiritualism had always been one of open skepticism. She did not consider herself suggestible; surely, she argued, any tendency toward mysticism would have blossomed rampantly in Mary Baumgartner's house. Instead the house seemed cozier every day. And when Ellen thought of the former tenant, as she sometimes did, it was with pity and curiosity, not with fear.

Since the weather continued to be fine, she got a lot of outside work done. Once, as she dug poison ivy from under the massive oak in the front yard, she found herself staring at a slight depression between two of the great roots. She stopped digging for a moment, the trowel motionless in her gloved hands. Poison ivy is hard to dig up. The established roots are long and thick. If she dug deeply enough . . .

The idea held no terrors. The story was vague, the yard was large—and it had been a long time. If she did, by a wild coincidence, come upon some scrap of mortality, it would really not disturb her. For a while she dug a little more slowly, that was all. By the time she had the root up, she had forgotten the whole thing.

She thought of Mary again later in the week, when she explored the cellar. It was a hot morning, and the idea of working in the cooler part of the house had appealed to her, but after a few hours she was ready to quit. The cellar was too damp for comfort. At least, Ellen thought, pushing back her hair, I won't have to worry about the fire hazards of old papers and rubbish. The papers weren't old enough to be valuable, but she hated to throw them out; the kids would find headlines of the forties and fifties interesting. She emptied two trunks of rotting clothes, however. Judging from the refurbished gowns she had seen for sale in expensive Georgetown shops, old clothes were "in," but these were too far gone. Ellen's nose lifted fastidiously as she bundled cloche hats and mildewed calico aprons into a plastic garbage bag.

Phil had been right about the mysterious door. There were a good many doors in the cellar; it had been subdivided and enlarged over the centuries. But there was no doubt about the door Phil meant.

It stood in a corner of the lowest part of the cellar, a reeking little black room at the bottom of a flight of steep stone stairs. The stairs were what reminded Ellen of the witch; they looked old enough to have been built by Mary's husband. She swept her flashlight around the room. The electricity had not been brought into this section, and with reason; the place was unsuited for storage or for any other function. The rough stone walls were green with moss. The material of the door was hard to see, for that structure had been completely boarded up, not once, but several times, as the wood had rotted in the damp air.

Ishtar had refused to accompany her mistress into the subcellar. She stalked back and forth at the top of the stairs emitting lugubrious Siamese complaints. A susceptible person might have viewed this behavior as significant, but Ellen knew better; Ishtar hated nasty wet places and she was never reticent about expressing her opinion. Ignoring the cat's howls, Ellen stood still, waiting to see if any supernatural residue would trouble her sixth sense.

That sense remained quiescent, but others objected, particularly her sense of smell. The place stank. With a shrug Ellen turned to retrace her steps, and was welcomed by a scolding cat. She worked in the yard for the rest of the day.

She had occasion the following day to consult Ed Salling about a minor flaw in the plumbing repairs, and asked him about the door. Ed looked disgusted.

"Why, it is the witch's tunnel," he said sarcastically. "That is the way by which Mary Baumgartner reached the woods where she held her assignations with the Devil. Does that reassure you, Mrs. March?"

"I just wanted to make sure nobody could get into the house," Ellen said meekly.

"If there was a tunnel, which I doubt, it has probably collapsed."

"If there was a tunnel," Ellen said, "it was probably an escape route. If I had Mary's reputation, I'd want one."

Ed looked interested, but refused to demean himself by pursuing such an irrational subject, so Ellen left. The plumber appeared that very afternoon and repaired the leak. Ed might be irritating, but he was certainly conscientious.

If anything bothered Ellen during her week of work and rest, it was not her witch, but the neighborhood delinquent. The first time she set off for a walk in the woods she was a trifle uneasy; it would be demoralizing to have Tim's large and hostile form pop out at her unexpectedly. She was even more concerned about Ishtar, but to her relief the cat stuck close to home. An unfortunate encounter with a skunk, at the beginning of the week, taught Ishtar that the woods might harbor foes even a Siamese cat couldn't overcome. After her meeting with the skunk Ishtar spent three days in the woodshed, howling like a chained eighteenth-century maniac. Thereafter she confined herself to the yard and found much there to interest her. A mighty hunter, despite her mere eight pounds, she kept presenting Ellen with gifts of moles and field mice.

Ellen did not meet Tim in the woods, and it was not long before her nervousness wore off and her walks became a great source of pleasure. The forest was formidable; Ellen never went into it without boots and heavy gloves, no matter how hot the day. There were the normal hazards of brambles and poison ivy, not to mention the probability of snakes. The underbrush was as hard to penetrate as a tangle of barbed wire. Ellen knew the biting strength of the deceptively thin strands of honeysuckle, and took to carrying a knife. She also carried a compass when she went far afield. The hilly slopes were broken by streams and ravines, and it was very easy to lose one's sense of direction.

Yet the rewards made the effort worthwhile. Sitting on a fallen log in a tiny clearing dappled with sunshine, she

saw families of black-headed quail march past, all in a
line like old-fashioned schoolchildren out for a walk. She
counted birds she had never seen—hairy woodpeckers
and wood thrushes, barn swallows and ruffled grouse. She
found small trails which human feet had never made; and
once, following one of these animal highways, she met a
fox trotting home with dinner for its cubs. The wind betrayed the hunter; the fox did not sense her presence until
it saw her, rounding a turn in the path. A shaft of sunlight
striking through the trees turned the animal into a bril-
liant-copper red statue as it froze, eyeing Ellen with steady
appraisal before it finally turned and disappeared into
the bushes.

Ellen, shaken, let out a long breath. Some of her
friends belonged to suburban hunts; the sport was tradi-
tional in Virginia. She had never approved of the sport,
which depended for its thrills on the terror and pain of a
hunted animal; now, watching the shaken foliage where
the fox had passed, she herself was shaken by an unaccountable fury of grief and anger. It was as if she had
entered the hunted animal's mind, had experienced the la-
boring lungs and aching limbs. . . . And felt, simultaneously, a wholly human awareness of injustice. Foxes
hunted only for food. When they killed, they killed
quickly.

As she started back toward the house, Ellen decided
she would post signs forbidding hunting of any sort on
her property. It would be a fitting gesture, carrying on a
tradition begun by Mary Baumgartner, two centuries before. Ellen smiled faintly. The impact of that strange moment of identity was fading. Now she was getting sentimental, thinking of Mary as hunted and beleaguered,
sympathetic to the wild creatures of the woods because,
like her, they were the victims of human cruelty.

Next day Ellen drove into Smithville to buy "No Hunting" signs and visit a library—an amenity Chew's Corners
did not boast. It took her the rest of the day and part of

the following morning to post the signs; the farther boundaries of her property were high in the hills and attainable only on foot.

She returned from the final expedition in time to see the mail truck pull away, and hurried eagerly to the mailbox. Her family were excellent correspondents; she had already received notes from the boys and from Penny, and this morning she found a real prize—a thin envelope with Jack's familiar scrawl.

His writing was typical of him, she thought, savoring the very feel of the envelope. It was a rapid scrawl—he did everything quickly—but it was surprisingly legible. She made herself a cup of coffee before she opened the letter, and sat on her shady porch to read it.

"Want to hear something funny?" it began, with characteristic abruptness. "I'm homesick. It's not fair. The kids who are thrown out of the nest are the ones who are supposed to suffer. Near as I can tell, not one of them felt a qualm. I'm the one that sits here staring at family pictures and wishing I'd never left home. . . .

"To add insult to injury, I can't assume you are missing us. I'll bet you're having the time of your life. I picture you in your Ideal House, smugly sipping tea with Ishtar on your lap, or wrestling with weeds while your hair comes loose and curls around your ears, using language a lady isn't supposed to know—language you learned from my rotten sons—and thanking God daily you rid yourself of your contentious brood at last. I don't know whether I ever told you, Ellen, how much I appreciate what you've done for us. I've tried; probably I never succeeded because the words don't mean enough. But if ever a woman was entitled to some peace and quiet, you are. You earned it."

Ellen's eyes were too blurred to read further. She put her hand on the back of the cat, who was sleeping in her lap. Jack knew her so well; his picture was only too accurate. A tear fell on the cat's furry face and Ishtar swiped irritably at it before she curled up and slept again.

Ellen almost wished Jack had not written. She had thought she was progressing in her effort to forget him, but the letter brought him back so vividly that she could picture him in her mind. The shape of his hands, the funny hazel-green of his eyes, the very, very high forehead about which Jack was slightly sensitive. . . . At least he didn't comb pathetic strands of hair across his bald spot, as some men did; he was too honest to kid himself about that any more than he did about more important things.

Such as his feelings for her. He couldn't have expressed himself so warmly, so openly if those feelings had been other than those of a brother toward a beloved sister.

Ishtar was sitting on Ellen's handkerchief. Ellen wiped her eyes on the back of her hand and went on reading.

The rest of the letter was impersonal, full of funny but discreet comments about Jack's activities. His sense of humor extended to his own profession, and that, Ellen knew, was a rare attribute. Many people can laugh at everything except themselves. Ellen laughed aloud over his description of a diplomatic reception, and the people who had attended it.

The letter went into a particular little box on Ellen's dressing table, but that was as far as she would let herself go. "No blue ribbons," she announced, staring at her reflection in the mirror. In fact, it was high time she got out of the house and saw people. She was getting too introspective and too imaginative.

Coming to a sudden decision, she took off her faded hiking jeans and reached for a dress—something light and cool, it was going to be a hot day. She would drive into town and stop at the store for the chocolate chips and coconut and condensed milk needed for a very rich cookie recipe. Then, when she got back, she would bake the very rich cookies and eat them. All that hiking justified a few additional calories. Then she would sit down and write Jack a nice cheery letter about the quaint homely charm of Chew's Corners.

Her spirits rose as she turned onto the road and headed for town. She had seen very little of Chew's Corners and was looking forward to patronizing Mrs. Grapow's general store. Originally she had stocked her larder lavishly from the supermarket in the busy town twenty miles away, but from now on she would make use of local products and merchants. There must be an orchard in the area, and fields where she could pick her own strawberries.

Chew's Corners was built around a crossroads. Both roads were small county highways, so there was not much traffic. The town was only a few blocks square, but Ellen had caught glimpses of several interesting old houses.

She parked the car on a side street, and saw a curtain move in a front window.

Smiling, she got out of the car. She did not lock it; that would be a churlish gesture toward her new town, especially with one of the inhabitants watching her. She walked down the street, away from the highway.

It was late in the morning and the sun struck warmly on Ellen's bare arms. It didn't take more than half an hour to cover the entire town, and it had less of interest than she had thought. Some of the houses were old; she spotted a handsome sunburst fanlight and a wonderful old gazebo in full Greek Revival style, complete with pilasters, architrave, and cornice. But the overall effect was subtly depressing. The evidences of decay were not obtrusive, yet the town was dying. Many houses were boarded up. One had been a handsome old Georgian mansion. Little boys had broken all its windows and the house stared sadly out across an expanse of weedy lawn.

Ellen hoped for better things from the church, but she was disappointed. It was severe in style, a simple box of

white-painted wood with a stubby, graceless steeple. The
windows were of clear glass; inside, Ellen caught a
glimpse of straight wooden pews and plain white walls.
With a shudder of aesthetic distaste she turned from the
cold austerity of the church to the cemetery beside it.

By contrast, the worn gray stones and green grass
looked warm and friendly. Gradually, however, Ellen realized that under the kindly facade of nature the cemetery
was as austere as the church. She had hoped to find addi-
tions to her casual collection of bizarre tombstone art and
quaint epitaphs; and, though she scarcely admitted it to
herself, she was rather hoping to find a stone with Mary's
name. Proper burial in consecrated ground is supposed to
quiet any potential ghost. However, there were no old
stones to be seen. Certain neglected weedy areas might
have been the sites of centuries-old graves, but she fancied the town might not like nosy strangers digging
around the remains of their ancestors.

The recent headstones were plain blocks giving a name
and two pertinent dates. There was an occasional biblical
quotation; as she read these, Ellen wondered about the
faith that chose epitaphs so lacking in hope. "All flesh is
as the grass" and "There shall be weeping and gnashing
of teeth" were two of the mildest. Nowhere could she find
any mention of the resurrection.

Ellen turned with relief to the world of the living. She
approached the general store with great curiosity and
some trepidation. A woman dressed in a cotton house-
dress had nodded to her and a child had given her a smile
before hiding behind a bush in its front yard. The town
did not seem unfriendly. But the idea of facing the row of
loungers on the porch of the store daunted her. She
mounted the wooden steps and saw that she must pass six
men before she reached the door.

They were all elderly men; with inner amusement Ellen
deduced that the porch was the local substitute for golf
course and country club—the Senior Citizens' Association

of Chew's Corners. The faces that turned toward her were angular and leathery brown, and curiously alike.

She was not greeted with a round of applause, but the reception was affable; a few of the men said "Morning," and the others nodded. Ellen beamed back at them, relieved to find them so amiable.

The store was shady and dark after the bright sunshine without. As Ellen's eyes adjusted, a wave of nostalgia swept over her, bringing memories of small-town stores half a lifetime away.

There was a candy counter, with trays inside and big glass bottles of colored sweets on top. Names like "jaw-breakers" and "licorice whips" came into Ellen's mind. At the back of the store a brown, highly varnished wooden grille bore a sign reading "U.S. Post Office." The shelves to the right carried bolts of fabric, shirts and overalls, and boxes discreetly labeled "Ladies' Undergarments."

Other shelves held groceries in bottles and cans and packages. There was one small freezer. The cracker barrel has vanished into the American past, but this store had plenty of barrels; they contained seeds and feed of various kinds. The room was large and it was cunningly arranged to hold the absolute maximum; a bundle of brooms, looking like a weird modern flower arrangement, hung from a beam. There was even a magazine rack to the left of the door.

Then Ellen's eyes finally reached the woman who stood behind the counter.

Later, when she was groping desperately for explanations for so many things, Ellen found no difficulty in explaining her initial antipathy towards Mrs. Grapow. The woman was enormous—the biggest female creature Ellen had seen outside a barnyard or zoo. She was not fat, nor was there anything bovine in the expression of the broad face whose eyes were watching Ellen with open curiosity. She was simply a very large woman, tall and big boned, with the massiveness that overtakes such women later in life unless they diet strenuously. Mrs. Grapow's long-sleeved dark print dress and gray hair compressed into a bun made it clear that she would view dieting as tampering with the will of the Lord. "If He had wanted me to be thin, He would have made me thin."

Ellen put on a smile and approached the counter.

"I'm Ellen March," she said. "I've just moved into the old—"

"The witch's house," said Mrs. Grapow. Her voice was another shock; instead of the booming bass Ellen had expected, it was high-pitched and whiny. "Yes. I heard Ed sold the house to a city woman."

"The witch's house! Do you still call it that?"

"There's some places where people don't forget things," said Mrs. Grapow. "What was you looking for today, Miz March?"

After a moment Ellen realized she was being addressed in dialect, not in the latest mode advocated by women's liberation.

"Oh. Chocolate chips, condensed milk and—do you have any coconut?"

Mrs. Grapow turned. With one sweep of her arm she collected the items named and put them on the counter.

"Anything else?"

"I'll just look around," said Ellen, fascinated and amused. "I must need lots of things."

Mrs. Grapow's expression indicated that she thought poorly of a housewife who had to "look around," instead of shopping with a carefully prepared list; but she said nothing. As Ellen turned from the counter, another woman entered the store. She was a faded blonde of approximately Ellen's age, although her lack of makeup and her shapeless cotton print dress made her look older. She nodded to the storekeeper and gave Ellen a sidelong smile before sorting through some hosiery on a rack by the counter.

Ellen turned to the paperbacks and magazines. She could never resist a book in any form, although she had a good supply of old favorites she meant to reread. The selection was certainly not broad. For the most part it consisted of cookbooks and light romances. There was a conspicuous absence of covers with bare-chested adventurers of either sex. Apparently the men in town did not read and the women preferred sedate fiction. For some reason Ellen found the selection depressing.

Before long two more women entered. The second was panting audibly, and it dawned on Ellen that she might be the cause of the midday shopping spree. Turning, she saw Mrs. Grapow eyeing the shoppers with a smile—if an expression so grim could merit that word.

"All right, ladies," she said. "This here is Miz March. Might as well meet your neighbors, Miz March. Miz Muller, Miz Roth, Miz Janssen."

The three women converged on Ellen.

Mrs. Roth was the blonde who had first come in. Ellen deduced her marital status by her wedding ring; Mrs. Grapow's speech patterns did not distinguish between wife and spinster. Mrs. Muller also wore a ring. She was a nervous-looking woman who kept twisting her hands like Lady Macbeth. Hair, face, and dress were of the same pallid gray. Miss Janssen was apparently unmarried. A fat, jolly-looking woman with gold pince-nez, she was the most loquacious of the three. Using a direct frontal assault that took Ellen by surprise, she soon extracted Ellen's vital biographical facts, including her age and marital status and the number, sex, and ages of her offspring.

Ellen was more amused than offended by the unsubtle tactics of the questioners. Poor souls, she thought tolerantly, they haven't much to talk about. She fancied, however, that meaningful glances were exchanged when she admitted to being divorced. She had not forgotten Ed's advice, but she had no opportunity to evade the question even if she had wanted to. There are only two ways of responding to a question such as "Is your husband dead?" It would have been churlish to reply, "None of your business," although for a moment Ellen was tempted to say just that.

However, this was just preliminary skirmishing. Miss Janssen leaned forward, adjusted her pince-nez, and introduced the main topic.

"We worry about you, all alone out there, Mrs. March. I wouldn't sleep a wink in that awful house! Aren't you nervous?"

"Not at all. I sleep like a log."

"Oh," said Miss Janssen flatly.

Mrs. Roth thrust her face close to Ellen's.

"Have you heard things? Seen things?"

There were only three of them; three ordinary women —and Mrs. Grapow, who was certainly not ordinary. . . . Suddenly Ellen felt encircled—closed in. Mrs. Muller was breathing heavily through her open mouth. Mrs. Roth's eyes were wide with anticipation, and Miss Janssen looked like a bloated bird of prey, waiting to pounce.

Ellen's imp awoke and stretched its wings.

"Well . . ."

With a concerted gasp, the three women edged closer.

By the time Ellen reached the car with her bag of groceries, she had recovered herself and was beginning to feel ashamed. How she had led those poor women on! Not that she had actually said anything . . .

No, said her inconsistent imp; you didn't say it, not explicitly, but those women are now convinced that your house is haunted and that you are in communication with the ghost of Mary Baumgartner. You ought to be ashamed! They were only trying to be friendly. Even Mrs. Grapow . . .

No. There the imp was going too far. There was absolutely nothing friendly about Mrs. Grapow. She was too proud to ask impertinent questions, but she had listened eagerly enough to the answers elicited by the others.

None of them were really very nice women. Their avid curiosity was morbid and not exactly tactful.

When Ellen drove up her driveway, there was a small white cat sitting on the gatepost.

Ellen stopped suddenly; she didn't want to startle the animal. In this she failed; the cat left the post in a white blur and disappeared.

"I wonder what the good ladies would make of that," Ellen muttered.

Her weird tale had not included cats or shadows. It had been a fictitious masterpiece of suggestion involving groans and sobbing cries and a rocking chair that moved by itself. She was glad she hadn't mentioned the cat to her ghoulish audience. It would be just like them to send out an equally gullible husband with a silver bullet to exterminate some poor stray or feral barn cat.

On Saturday Ellen had to shop again. After her first encounter with the ladies of Chew's Corners, she was no longer so keen on making use of local merchants, but she had invited guests for Sunday dinner, and by the time she had finished a series of minor chores there was not time to drive twenty miles to the supermarket.

She was pleasantly surprised when she pulled up in front of the store. On Saturday mornings the broad porch became the teen-age hangout instead of the Senior Citizens' Club. Like that of many dying villages, the population of Chew's Corners was predominantly elderly, and there were only a dozen or so adolescents in the whole town. They were all present, brightening the morning with their colorful clothes and their young, cheerful voices— sitting on the steps, perched precariously on the railing, buying Cokes from the big red machine. Ellen found them irresistible. Hastily she made her purchases, and on the way out she stopped to buy a Coke which she really didn't want. It was not long before she was seated in one of the chairs, with the whole group crowding around.

They were shyer or less bumptious than their urban

counterparts; their speech bristled with "yes, ma'am" and "no, ma'am." Jeans and shorts predominated, but there were no see-through blouses or skimpy T-shirts, and the shorts averaged a couple of inches longer than the abbreviated garments Penny habitually wore.

A few individuals stood out from the group even on that first day. A tall boy named Steve, with blond sideburns practically meeting under his chin, was apparently the town Casanova. He posed by the porch railing, pretending to be indifferent to the giggles and glances of the girls. His eyes tended to dwell on one girl named Joyce. She was not the prettiest of the girls, but her vivacity and bouncy red-gold curls made her the most attractive.

Some of the young people were memorable for the opposite reason. They were conspicuously unattractive. Bob Muller was obviously self-conscious about his acne; his attempt to conceal the blemishes by letting his beard grow was a failure, for the beard, though coarse and black, was too sparse to hide anything, including Bob's negligible chin and obtrusive upper lip. His sister, Prudence, belonged to a type Ellen had learned to regard with suspicion. Her giggles were too frequent and too high-pitched. She was pathetically plain, except for big blue eyes that had an unfocused look, and she wore a frilly blouse and full skirt that made her heavy hips look even wider.

Joyce was the spokesman for the group. Sitting crosslegged on the floor, she talked till Ellen's head began to spin.

"The high school is over in Smithville," she explained, in answer to Ellen's question. "Yes, ma'am, there's a bus. Gosh, is that a ride in the winter! The good old state doesn't get around to plowing these roads half the time."

"You're lucky you don't have to walk miles across the snowy fields," said Ellen.

"Like Abe Lincoln?" Joyce grinned. She looked, unpredictably, so much like Penny that Ellen felt a pang.

"No, ma'am; we'd just stay home and be ignorant—wouldn't we, Steve?"

Apparently this was part of an established esoteric joke. The whole crowd burst into laughter, and Steve, whose beauty made wit unnecessary, grinned and tossed his yellow mane.

"In the summer we all work," Joyce continued. "Some of us at the orchard—what, ma'am? Oh, yes, ma'am, that's Borden's orchard up at Cosmo. Right now we've got cherries and strawberries. . . ."

The conversation became strictly practical and ended with Ellen making an appointment to come out one day to pick and buy fruit. She had offers of assistance enough to strip the orchard.

"What are you going to do with all that fruit?" demanded Prue, squinting unattractively. (She needs glasses and won't wear them, Ellen thought.) "I don't suppose you know anything about canning."

"That's dumb, Prue," said Joyce, before Ellen could defend herself. "I bet Mrs. March knows how to do most everything."

"Well, I don't know much about canning," Ellen admitted cheerfully." Maybe one of you could teach me."

"My mom would be glad to help," said Joyce.

"She's real good at canning pickled peaches," said Prue, with a sly smile.

This seeming compliment produced another, softer murmur of laughter. Joyce flushed angrily.

"Just 'cause one jar burst—"

"One! It was like the Fourth. Or a war."

Joyce rose in a smooth coiled motion. Seeing that mayhem was imminent, Ellen was about to intervene when suddenly the whole group froze.

For a few seconds they looked like a still from an action film. Then Joyce sank back onto the floor and Steve combed his hair, and the other activities recommenced, but in silence and slow motion. It did not take Ellen long to identify the cause. Slouching down the road came Tim.

If she hadn't known his background, Ellen would have taken him for the offspring of illiterate tenant farmers. His shirt was a disgrace, his jeans verged on indecency. His sun-bleached blond hair flopped over his forehead as he walked, eyes straight ahead, hands in his pockets. He came toward the store and climbed the stairs; and Ellen saw that the kids shrank back, as people once shrank from the presence of a leper. Joyce moved closer to Steve, who reached for her hand. Prue stared avidly; Bob's close-set black eyes narrowed.

The silence continued while Tim was inside the store. He soon came out eating a candy bar, descended the stairs, and crossed the street. He had not acknowledged Ellen's existence by so much as a look, so she didn't speak. The tension in the air distressed her. Norman had mentioned that the kids kept out of Tim's way, but he had not prepared her for this intense, positive hostility.

Tim was passing in front of a vacant lot across the road when it happened. Ellen knew perfectly well which member of the group was responsible; what she didn't understand was where he had gotten the rock. It was the size of a man's fist, and was accurately thrown. It caught Tim on the side of the head. He dropped to his knees and then fell forward, face down in the dusty weeds.

Ellen was halfway down the stairs before he hit the ground. She knelt beside him, and Tim stirred and sat up. A streak of blood ran down his cheek. His face was ashen under his tan.

"Hold on," Ellen said, catching him by the shoulders. "That was a nasty one, you may have a concussion. Lean on me."

"Lean . . ." His dazed eyes cleared as they focused on her face. "Lean on you?"

"I'm softer than the pavement."

His head drooped and for a moment she thought he was going to let it fall onto her shoulder. Then he raised it again, and the expression on his face turned her cold. She spoke as she would have spoken to one of her former cases.

"Don't start anything, Tim! You're in no condition to fight. He'd knock you flat."

"Yeah," said Tim, considering the point. "That's right. . . . Later."

"No, not later." She shook him gently, her hands tight on his hard shoulders. They were as rigid as rock—with anger or pain, she could not tell which. "Leave him alone. That was a coward's trick; but if you hit back, you'll only get yourself in trouble."

He regarded her steadily. There was no expression at all on his face; such disciplined immobility was frightening in a boy of his age. Finally he said,

"I'm all right. Leave me alone, will you?"

"You're not all right. I'll drive you home."

"Like hell you will." He pushed away the handkerchief with which she had started to wipe his face. "For God's sake, stop that! It makes me look so great having Mommy taking care of the little boy. Want to kiss it and make it well?"

He stood up. Ellen accepted the rebuff without resentment; she was prepared to grab him again if he fell, which she thought quite likely, but he kept his feet. He swayed slightly as he walked away, but he did not look at her.

Ellen returned to the store. Standing at the bottom of the steps, she let her eyes wander slowly over the group. None of them were able to meet her eyes, but she did not see the face she was looking for.

"Where is Bob?"

"Inside," Joyce muttered.

"That's consistent," Ellen said clearly. "Yellow all the way through."

She went into the store. Behind the counter Mrs. Grapow stood like an immense idol, her arms folded. No one else was there.

"Where did Bob go?" Ellen demanded.

"Out through the back." Mrs. Grapow indicated the door leading to the storeroom. Studying Ellen's flushed face, she added, with apparent irrelevance, "You met his mother. She's a saintly woman, married to a foul-mouth sinner. She never misses a church service. A good woman has a price above rubies."

"She may be a saint, but she's raised a rotten son. Do you know what he did?"

"That young demon had it coming," said Mrs. Grapow flatly. "Lucky if he doesn't get worse."

Ellen was so angry she couldn't think of any comment devastating enough to penetrate the storekeeper's complacency. Then words came into her mind from a source she would not have consciously sought, and she said them aloud.

" 'He that is without sin among you, let him first cast a stone. . . .' "

Mrs. Grapow's reaction was profoundly satisfying. Her face flushed a deep ugly wine color and her eyes narrowed until they were slits in her broad face. Ellen waited, to give her a chance to retort, but apparently Mrs. Grapow's knowledge of Scripture was limited to the Old Testament.

Ellen spun on her heel and marched to the door. There she paused, and spoke in a voice that was audible outside as well as within.

"I don't know, or care, what Tim has done. Nothing justifies a cowardly attack like that one. If he does something wrong, call the police; that's what they're for. I'll call them myself, if there is any further violence—no matter who commits it."

As she stormed across the porch, Joyce reached for her.

"Please, ma'am, don't think we wanted that. We don't like Tim, but we aren't all sneaks."

Ellen stopped.

"Why do you all dislike Tim so?"

"He killed my dog," said Joyce.

"And beat up my kid brother," added Steve.

"Set fire to the barn."

"Chased Mom's chickens till they died."

"Wait a minute," said Ellen, as the string of accusations lengthened. "Did he really do all those things?"

"Sure. He's a devil," said Joyce.

"When he was small, perhaps. But now . . ."

"My dog disappeared this last winter. When I found him, somebody had . . . had hurt him before they killed him."

"But don't you see," Ellen said gently. "If Tim does these things, it's because he's sick. He needs help—not rocks on the head."

"The rock was a bad thing," said Joyce soberly. "But you can't help him, ma'am. He's got the devil in him, like the preacher says. When he was little there were times when he'd act nice. We were nice, too. . . . Well, some of us were. And then he'd turn right around and do something awful, to the people that were the nicest."

"That's another symptom of his sickness," Ellen said earnestly. "Don't you see. . . ."

She stopped. They didn't see. How could they? Few adults are capable of compassion toward those who injure them.

"Okay," she said, with a faint smile. "We'll have to see what can be done. In the meantime—no more rocks, all right?"

"No, ma'am!" The chorus sounded sincere.

"And you'll come out to the orchard next week?" Joyce asked.

"If it doesn't rain. I hate berry picking in the mud."

"It won't rain," Joyce said, with a glance at the cloudless blue sky. "The almanac says no rain for a week."

"I'm not so sure," Ellen said soberly. "There's a storm building up. It could be a bad one. I can feel it in the air; can't you?"

Six

Luckily there was little traffic on Highway 624. Ellen drove home in a fog, too preoccupied with her own thoughts to pay attention to the road. She regretted her final comment; the kids had no talent for symbolism, they would probably go home and tell their parents the crazy new lady at the witch's house was setting herself up as a weather prophet. Absently she contemplated the sky and realized that her prediction might well come true. It was an unusually muggy day, and there was a slight haze in the air.

Selfishly, she cursed the incident that had spoiled what was otherwise a pleasant encounter. They were nice kids, most of them, and she was hungry for young companionship. Strange that the two least appealing members of the group were brother and sister. . . .

But of course it wasn't strange when she stopped to think about it. Mrs. Muller had struck Ellen as more piti-

able than contemptible. No doubt her "sinful" husband
was responsible for her beaten look, although Ellen had
doubts about Mrs. Grapow's definition of the word. A
half-forgotten memory rustled in her mind and she
frowned, trying to remember. Hadn't the real estate agent
mentioned a man named Muller who was a wife beater,
drunkard, and all-around rat? She was almost sure that
was the name. Maybe Mrs. Grapow was right, for once.
Though surely nothing was more likely to incite a bully
than that gray, doughy helplessness of Mrs. Muller's. Why
didn't she leave her worthless husband, or hit *him* over
the head with a rock?

Which brought her mind back to the real cause of her
distress. All the way home she kept remembering Tim's
look and the tone of his voice when he said, "Lean on
you?" It was as if the very idea of support, of help, were
totally foreign to him. Which was ridiculous, of course.
His uncle was ready and willing to help, if Tim would let
him.

Ellen sighed. There was no use fighting it. Something
had to be done about Tim. She sighed because she knew
her symptoms. She had been through this sort of thing
before, and it was never easy. The results were so unpredictable. An occasional heartwarming success was coun-
tered by a series of disappointments. There was Bernie.
Bernie had been one of her first cases, the polestar that
kept her working with disturbed kids through failure after
failure. Big, lanky, frizzy-headed Bernie, "the worst kid in
the neighborhood," was now a successful law student,
deeply involved with Legal Aid. And there was Hank,
now married, with a baby, and assistant manager of the
local gas station; Pat, whose new husband knew all about
her unfortunate slip at the age of fifteen; Marian, who
was on her way to moderate success as a model after
using her extraordinary beauty to make money in a less
socially acceptable profession.

And on the other side of the ledger were other names and faces, all burned indelibly into her heart by the pain of failure. Which would Tim be? He would be in her ledger; she was hooked, and she knew it.

Ellen stopped the car outside her house with a decisive jab at the brake. She would call Norman and invite him to her dinner party next day. It was short notice, but she owed him an invitation, and if she didn't offer it soon he would think she had been offended by Tim's behavior.

Little does he know, Ellen thought with a wry smile. He's in for it now, as Jack used to say when I got interested in some youngster and nagged the parents till they did what I wanted them to. Jack always said . . .

Turning her mind firmly to the menu for the next day, she carried her groceries into the house.

Norman accepted her telephone invitation with such pleasure that Ellen felt ashamed of her delay. She had not meant to plunge into a lecture about Tim just then, but she felt it necessary to mention the rock-throwing incident.

Norman's reaction was one of weary acceptance.

"No, he won't tell me about it; he never tells me anything. It was nice of you to go to the rescue, Ellen."

"What else could I have done? I was really scared, Norman. He could have been killed."

"There would have been general rejoicing in town," Norman said grimly.

"The rejoicing wouldn't have lasted long. Not after I'd told the police what happened."

"Police?" Norman repeated sarcastically. "We-uns don't call the cops about our little troubles, Ellen. This community is the most anachronistic, hidebound. . . . But I shouldn't complain. Tim would have a record as long as my arm if my fellow citizens weren't amenable to settling out of court."

"I see why you feel that way, and in a way I agree with

you. But you can't keep the police away if someone is seriously hurt. You minimized the severity of the problem —for my benefit, I know. But after what happened today—"

"Well, accept my thanks for your help. I daren't hope you got any thanks from Tim."

"Quite the contrary."

"Oh, my." Norman's voice was so depressed that Ellen had to laugh.

"My dear man, I'm too bullheaded to be put off by bad manners. You can't expect a boy to accept feminine fussing gratefully. My nephews would have cussed me out for babying them in public. They're very conscious of their masculinity at that age."

"You are a good woman, Ellen."

"I'm a nosy busybody," said Ellen cheerfully. "And I've got several ideas about Tim. But we won't discuss them now. See you tomorrow?"

"Wonderful. Oh . . . I hate to mention it, but the cat . . .?"

"Will spend the day in the nice fresh out-of-doors."

"I thought you had decided it was wisest to keep her in. I'll never forgive myself if she should come to harm because of my nutty phobia."

"If it worries you, Ishtar will languish in the woodshed. Now you are fussing, Norman. Stop it."

Ellen spent the rest of the afternoon cooking, which she enjoyed. As a busy mother of four, she had seldom had time for the slow, complicated recipes that are the most challenging. Now she could grate lemons and melt chocolate and mince onions to her heart's content. She had even bought a small kitchen scale so she could try some of her hoarded European recipes without having to translate their weight measurements into the American equivalents.

By late afternoon she had baked a Sacher torte of dangerous richness and was chopping the vegetables for the daube that was to be the main course. Peeling and cutting up fresh tomatoes took a long time. The recipe also called for chopped carrots and bacon, black olives, and top sirloin marinated in wine overnight and larded with salt pork. When Ellen finally had put it together, she sealed the earthenware casserole with a strip of dough and heaved a sigh of self-congratulation. Six hours in a slow oven, and that concoction would put Martha in her place.

She had planned a late-afternoon walk, but, absorbed in her work, she had not noticed the withdrawal of the sunlight. Now, glancing out the window, she realized that she was a better prophet than she had realized. The sky was overcast with rain clouds.

So she spent the rest of the day cleaning the kitchen, which was in need of attention. Even that chore was fun; the kitchen was now a charming room with natural-pine cabinets and pale-yellow counter tops. Copper and chrome gleamed when Ellen was finished. She read for the rest of the evening, and when she retired she saw no shadows but the ones cast by her reading lamp.

The rain held off, but the next day was dark and threatening. As she frosted her cake and made salad and rolls, Ellen kept glancing anxiously out the window. The threat of bad weather did not deter her guests; they arrived on time, with scathing comments about the condition of her driveway and the inadequacy of her directions.

When Norman's car drove up, Ellen realized she had forgotten about Ishtar. Snatching the cat from the lap of a guest who was wearing a dark suit—Ishtar preferred those fabrics on which cats hair stood out most effectively —she had only time for a hasty explanation to her guests before rushing Ishtar off to the woodshed.

The party was a success, and Norman was a social sensation. Even the men seemed to like him and the two women kept giving Ellen meaningful looks. Dot Gold was more direct, when she came into the kitchen to help Ellen serve the meal.

"He's a nice guy and a good neighbor," Ellen said, cutting short a flood of questions. "And that's all, Dot. I wish you'd stop trying to marry me off. I'm perfectly happy the way I am."

"I'll stop; you seem to be doing all right by yourself. He's much nicer than the ones I've shoved at you over the years. And rich. . .!"

Ellen changed the subject.

As they lingered over second cups of coffee, Dot's husband Peter drew their attention to the weather. It had worsened; the clouds over the mountains hung like gray sacks bulging with rain.

"Like the udders of big gray cows," said Dot poetically. "How beautiful!"

"Beautiful, hell. I've got to drive through that stuff," her husband replied unappreciatively. "I hate to break up the party, Ellen, but I think we can outrun this if we get started right away. The sky to the east doesn't look bad."

"I should have warned you," Norman said with a smile. "Our local weather prophet has predicted a bad storm."

He indicated Ellen, who stared openmouthed. She had forgotten about her comment.

Dot laughed.

"Is Ellen up to her old tricks? She's always predicting rain, Norman. In this climate that's an easy way to build a reputation."

"But I wasn't . . ." Ellen began, and then broke off. She could hardly explain the real meaning of her statement in front of her guests. "What a town," she added. "Do you mean they are gossiping about that already?"

"They don't have much to talk about in these places," Peter said with city-bred tolerance.

"Little do you know," Ellen muttered.

Reluctantly she accompanied her guests to the door. She had to admit that if she had been in their place, she would have fled. As the station wagon pulled away, the first drops of rain began to fall. Norman said,

"Better close the window, Ellen. Before I leave I'll look around the yard to make sure you haven't left anything outside. Thanks for a fantastic meal. I'm planning an underground campaign to get rid of Martha so I can offer you the job."

"But won't you stay for—"

"I'd better get the car home. Will would never forgive me if it got wet. Don't come out, dear; I'll have a quick look around and then take off."

Ellen hurried in. The curtains at the front windows were flailing as the wind rose. As she ran from room to room, closing windows, she thought gratefully of Norman's help, and of what he had said. That "dear"—unthinking, of course. Endearments were common currency these days. People used them as casually as first names.

She heard the car drive off, though she did not see it; the view from the upstairs window was blocked by foliage, now weaving wildly in the wind. As she wrestled with a bedroom window, she suddenly remembered the cat. Ishtar hated storms; she would be terrified out there in the woodshed.

Snatching up a scarf, Ellen ran down the stairs and out through the kitchen.

The shed was concealed from the house by an arbor, now thick with roses. Its door was never locked, but it was kept shut by means of a wooden bolt that turned on a central swivel. Ellen pushed the bolt up and opened the door. She was mildly surprised not to hear any sounds from within, but she was not alarmed until she called the cat's name and got no response. A search of the shed soon convinced her that Ishtar was not sleeping in a retired corner. Then her stomach started to feel funny. It was hard to believe that the bolt could have turned accidentally. It was stiff, and required strong fingers to move it. Neither could she believe that Ishtar had left the shed and refastened the door. Someone had let her out.

Ignoring the rain that turned her coiffure into a mass of wet curls, she ran around the yard calling. There was no reply. Ishtar would respond if she were close by, but she would not venture out through the rain if she had found a dry hole somewhere in the woods.

The alternative was one Ellen hated to contemplate. Tim had asked about the cat. Once before, to her knowledge, he had prowled around the house, and he would have been unobserved if it had not been for the dogs.

Ellen ran back into the house and went to the telephone. It was six o'clock; the sky was dark with storm clouds. The line buzzed ominously when she dialed, and Ellen could hardly hear the answering voice. She started to shout, as if sheer volume could cross the distance.

The incoherence of her alarm added to the difficulty of communication, but finally she made Norman understand. She could hear the concern in his voice, despite the bad connection. He sounded quite shaken.

"I closed the shed door," he said. "It was open and banging when I went out there, so I latched it. God, Ellen, I'm sorry; I should have looked around, but you know how I am about cats. . . ."

"It's not your fault. I was in a hurry when I took her out there. Maybe I didn't bolt the door securely. The wind could have blown it open."

"I hope that's the explanation." There was a pause. "I'll go out and look for her, Ellen."

"No, no, not in this weather. She'll come home eventually. . . . Norman, where is Tim?"

"I don't know."

He reiterated his apologies. Ellen cut him short. She went from door to door, hoping to find a drenched and angry animal crouched outside one of them; but the evening darkened and there was no sign of Ishtar. Unable to sit still, Ellen got a raincoat and a flashlight and went around the yard, shining the light up into trees and calling. The rain was falling so heavily she could hardly breathe. If the cat was out in this . . .

There was nothing more Ellen could do. She went back to the house and forced herself to tackle the dishes. The kitchen was a mess; seeing Peter's anxiety, she had refused help with the washing up. It was a relief to have something to do, but her mind continued to fret at the problem. It was bad enough to think of Ishtar being lost in such a storm, but the alternative was worse.

The weather didn't help. Not only did it make a search impossible, but it pounded and howled like some creature trying to break in. Ellen was pacing the floor when she heard a sound, over the roar of the rain, that made her skin prickle. Had Norman sent the dogs out to search for the cat? He couldn't be so stupid!

Pressing her face to the window, she tried to see out. It was useless; rain and starless night produced a blackness such as she had never seen. The baying of the dogs had stopped, but that didn't mean they had turned homeward. Normally they were a silent pair. Then the howling broke out again, closer, and Ellen whirled as she heard another sound. The screen door of her front porch had slammed.

She ran to the door. The porch light was on; she had left it lit in a forlorn hope of attracting the cat. She did not open the door. Instead she looked out through the glass pane set in the upper panel.

Against the blackness of the storm-swept night, the enclosed porch was like a stage set. The sole actor was upstage and center. He was crouched by the screen, his back to Ellen. His posture was that of a man who is suffering from a painful wound, or from cramps. The soaked condition of clothing and hair made him look stripped for action, and brought out the fine lines of bone and muscle. Despite his hunched posture he did not look at all pathetic; a leopard might have held that pose just before it sprang.

Ellen's hand went to the doorknob, but she did not open the door. She had gone to Tim's rescue once before and he had not appreciated her efforts; it would be stupid of her to let him into the house when she was alone and probably cut off, even by telephone. If he sought shelter from the rain, he could sit on the porch.

Then her fingers closed like clamps over the knob, as the dogs' renewed howls burst out. She didn't have to see them to know where they were, or to sense what they were after. Even as the realization came to her, the darkness beyond the porch condensed and hurled itself against the outer door. The screen bulged and tore. Ellen had a brief, nightmarish glimpse of blazing eyes and long white fangs.

Tim sprang up and away, toward the house door. It was to Ellen's credit that she was already turning the knob before she saw what Tim held tightly in both arms. The screen door wouldn't hold, not against a hundred pounds of canine fury, and she couldn't stand there and watch the boy torn to pieces before her eyes. Tim's arms were clasped across his chest; his shirt was torn and his brown skin streamed with blood. For a moment she thought the dogs had already been at him. Then two sharp brown ears rose up above the torn bloody sleeve of his right arm; and Ellen flung the door open as the dog's heavy body hit the screen and ripped it from top to bottom.

One leap took the boy through the door. He tripped, or fell, face down on the floor, and Ellen slammed the door shut. It quivered as she shot the bolts. The dog let out a last howl of frustrated fury. She heard its claws shred her brand-new paint.

Shakily, Ellen turned. Tim was prone, his head pillowed on his bent arm. Beside him, like an Egyptian goddess surveying the sacrifice, sat Ishtar. She was as wet as if she had been fished out of a bathtub. With a snort of disgust she began to lick herself.

The dog was still scratching at the door, but Ellen knew it couldn't get in. The thick oak panel would hold. As she stared, too shocked to move, Ishtar stretched out a long neck and began licking Tim's wet hair. The long locks got tangled up with her tongue; she spat and returned to her personal toilette.

Tim's back was heaving up and down like a bellows. Clearly he had been running for his very life. The blood on his breast and arms was probably Ishtar's contribution. She would not be in any mood to distinguish between rescuer and enemy, with the hounds on her trail. But the dogs had left their mark too. The left leg of the boy's jeans was ripped to the knee and there was a mangled wound on his calf.

The rhythm of Tim's breathing changed, and Ellen forced her rubbery legs to move. She turned him over, with difficulty; he was heavy, and his limbs had the adolescent quality of seeming longer than they really were. His eyes were closed, and he looked very young and pathetic.

Pity was not Ellen's only emotion, however. Her thoughts might have found utterance in such words as "Thank God Penny can't see him now!"

With its conscious defenses down, the young face was as innocent as a baby's. It was also dangerously handsome. When she had complimented Norman on his nephew's looks, she had understated the truth, this was the first time she had seen Tim's face without a sullen scowl or a snarl of hate.

Gently Ellen brushed back the tangled hair. The hard young cheek might have belonged to one of her nephews. She had often stolen in as they slept for a furtive caress they would never have permitted while awake.

Tim's eyes opened wide, and Ellen spoke quickly, before
he could gather his wits.

"This is getting to be a habit," she said with mock severity. "Can't you think of less painful ways of attracting
my attention?"

For a moment Tim's eyes mirrored the amusement in
hers.

"Not so painful," he muttered, trying to sit up.

"Tim." Hands on his chest, she held him down. "You
are going to hate this, but I have to say it. Thank you. I'm
a silly old lady, and I love my cat."

"No problem."

Tim's eyes closed. He was still pale, and the day-old
bruise on his temple stood out like a dark stain.

Ellen looked with dismay at her blood-streaked hands,
and glared at Ishtar, who had finished her ablutions and
was watching the tableau with detached interest.

"You're a fine one," Ellen said severely. "Scratching
the poor guy to pieces when he's trying to save your silly
neck. Sharper than a serpent's tooth to have—"

"Thankless cat?" said Tim, with a faint sputter of
laughter. He had opened his eyes, startled at her first exclamation, and was listening with visible amusement. "Do
you always talk to animals?"

"Usually there isn't anybody else to talk to." Ellen realized that this statement smacked of self-pity. She added
briskly, "Cats are ideal conversationalists. They don't talk
back."

"I bet this one does."

Tim reached up a long arm. To Ellen's surprise Ishtar
not only permitted the caress, she rolled over on her side
and began licking Tim's head. It was an uphill job, her
expression implied, but wet things had to be dried, and
people were always saddling her with the dirty work.

"She does." Ellen stood up, holding her hand away
from her skirt. "Stay right where you are. Ishtar has a

paw on your head and she'll probably bite you if you move. I'm going to put some antiseptic on those scratches and see if I can reach a doctor."

"Doctor!" In defiance of order, Tim tried to sit up. Ishtar's claws came out and he sank back with a yelp.

"For your leg. Honestly, Tim, I'm afraid to touch it. You might be lame if it isn't properly fixed."

"Forget it."

"But—"

"I said forget it. The telephone lines are probably down, they always go when there's a slight breeze. Anyhow, he'll be along in a minute."

Ellen knew Tim was not referring to the doctor.

She had kept Norman out of the conversation; if any relationship could be established between herself and Tim, it would have to exclude Norman, at least in the beginning. She was not surprised at the bitterness in Tim's voice, but his precise meaning eluded her. He didn't elaborate. The closed-in look was back; his face was impassive, and his mouth was set like a vise.

The dogs had been silent for some time. Now one of them barked. A voice spoke in sharp admonition, and footsteps thudded across the porch.

"Right on schedule," Tim murmured.

Ellen went to the door.

Heavy in glistening oilskins and hat, Norman's body filled the doorway. Beyond him Ellen saw the dogs. They were lying by the torn screen, their eyes fixed on Norman.

"Don't worry," Norman said quickly. "They wouldn't move now if the roof fell in. Ellen, are you hurt? Your hands are all. . . . My God! Tim!" He pushed past her and dropped down at the boy's side. "Son, did they get you? How bad is it?"

Tim waited till the anxious hands touched him. Then he stood up, with a deliberation that made the movement a calculated insult. He staggered as he put his weight on the injured leg. Norman's arms went around him, and only Ellen saw the look in Tim's eyes.

"Get your hands off me," he said tightly.

"That leg . . . you can't stand . . ."

Tim let out a string of epithets. The words didn't shock Ellen; she had heard them before. What shocked her was the concentrated venom with which they were spoken.

Then Ishtar took a hand. She had retreated when the door opened, with the combination of speed and dignity possible only to a cat. Now that the dogs were shut out, she advanced on the object that had fascinated her before; and, as before, Norman fell back. He released his hold on Tim, who caught at a chair for support. The grin on the boy's face as he looked from the cat to his uncle was one of the ugliest expressions Ellen had ever seen. With a word she seldom used, Ellen dived for the cat. A smooth brown eel, Ishtar eluded her; and Tim began to laugh like the demon he had often been compared with.

Ellen finally captured the determined cat, who had backed Norman into a corner. Tim ended the evening's performance by collapsing. Ellen was too far away to help him and Norman was too deep in the grip of his phobia; the boy's limp body hit the floor with a force that rattled the glasses in the corner cupboard.

Thrusting the cat into the cellar, Ellen hurried back. Norman had not moved. For a moment the two adults faced each other. Then Ellen sat down abruptly in the nearest chair and Norman passed a hand over his wet face.

"How much are you asking for the house?" he inquired.

It took Ellen a while to understand. Then she laughed feebly.

"I'm not going to sell my nice house."

"After tonight I would think you'd run from the sight

of us," Norman groaned. "What a performance! Crazy boy, neurotic uncle . . ."

"Tim saved my cat, Norman. He brought Ishtar home. I'll never believe now that he isn't worth fighting for."

"I wish I could believe it. We still don't know how the cat got out. Let me pour you some brandy, Ellen. You're as white as a sheet."

"Tim needs a doctor more than I need brandy." Ellen knelt down by Tim. "He's suffering from shock, and that bite is a mess. He may need surgery. Stop fussing about me, Norman, and call a doctor."

"The lines are down. Anyhow, the nearest doctor is twenty miles away. I'll take him in the car, it'll be quicker."

"You can't carry him by yourself. He's as big as you are."

"I'll get Will."

He hurried out.

Ellen got the afghan from the couch in the living room and wrapped it around the boy. Tim was still unconscious. Again Ellen breathed a devout prayer of thanksgiving that her daughter was safe in Europe. It had been an unpleasant evening in more ways than one. And Tim . . .

He looked like the fallen hero in an old Errol Flynn film. Outflung arm, muscular chest streaked with blood, romantically torn clothes—and that fine-boned, beautiful face. Ellen sighed. She took his face between her hands. He was so cold.

She was still holding him when Norman returned with the handyman. Tim's lean length was no problem for Will; he lifted the boy in a single heave and carried him out, head hanging.

"I won't stay to thank you," Norman said. "He does look bad. I hope—"

"He'll be all right. The young have amazing powers of recuperation."

"You should know. Well . . . *á bientôt* . . ."

The dogs rose as he passed between them. Norman looked back.

"I'll have the screen repaired tomorrow," he said, and vanished into the storm with the dogs following.

Long after the car had left, Ellen stood in the open doorway. The slit in the screen door gaped. It was a shocking reminder of what might have happened, had she not reacted quickly—and if Tim had not been such a good runner.

Seven

Will came by the next morning to repair the screen door. The storm had passed in the night, but it had left considerable damage in its wake. Ellen's drive was a muddy bog and the yard was strewn with fallen branches.

Ellen went out on the porch when she saw the station wagon, the car Norman used for rough work and bad weather. The telephone line was still down, and she was full of questions. Will answered her in monosyllables: Yes, Tim was all right. No, he was not in the hospital. Yes, the roads had been very bad.

Ellen finally gave up and left him alone. He was an unprepossessing fellow; either he was a little slow mentally or he was afraid of women. She inclined toward the latter theory. The man hadn't looked directly at her once.

She spent the rest of the day wading around her flooded yard picking up debris. By evening the telephone lines were repaired; Ellen was informed of this fact by a call from her Washington friends inquiring after her welfare. They gave a horrendous description of their drive home. They had not outrun the storm after all.

Ellen had just hung up when the phone rang again. This time it was Norman.

"I thought you might be anxious," he explained. "Yes, Tim is fine; a dozen stitches, but no serious damage. He was lucky. If I've warned him once I've warned him a hundred times. . . ."

"Norman, I know you've seen several psychiatrists, but you must try again. There's a man in Washington who is wonderfully successful with boys of Tim's age. His name is Worth, and I could . . ."

Norman sighed.

"I guess I'll have to tell you. Someone took a shot at Bob Muller last night."

"Oh, no."

"Oh, yes. He wasn't hit. Scared the devil out of him, of course. His father was raging around town this morning swearing he was going to kill Tim. It cost me fifty dollars to cool his paternal anxiety."

"Does Tim have a gun?"

"What kind of fool do you take me for, Ellen? There isn't a weapon of any kind in the house. They found the rifle, in the bushes—it was a .22 belonging to Josh Carter. He's a bachelor, and his house is never locked."

"That doesn't prove Tim did it. Why, he got here at—"

She stopped. Norman wouldn't have mentioned the incident if Tim's alibi had been any good. In her mind a picture formed and would not be dislodged—Tim's expression as he sat on the dusty grass with blood on his face, saying, "Later."

"But my cat," she said. "He saved—"

"Ellen, Ellen. I hate to curb your optimism; it's so beautiful. But I must warn you. Tim isn't always—sick. There are hours, even days, when he opens up, when I think I'm reaching him. At least I used to think so, before I realized this thing is cyclical. In his good spells, he's perfectly normal. But the bad times come on without warning, and they are getting closer and closer together. Don't trust him with the cat."

Ellen remembered Joyce's description of Tim's behavior. She had implied the same thing.

"I don't care," she said stubbornly. "If that is the case, it is all the more imperative that he should have treatment."

"I'm beginning to think you are the best thing that's happened to me in twenty years," Norman said, after a moment. "Thanks, Ellen. Of course you're right. I'll talk to Tim. Maybe you would talk to him as well?"

"I'd be glad to."

"Wonderful. You could come over for cocktails one day and sort of casually bring up the subject—"

"Of how badly Tim needs a psychiatrist? I'll do my best, but that isn't easy to bring up casually."

"You'll do it. You're our fairy godmother. And do we need one. . . . Which reminds me, have you been to town today?"

"No. I was afraid of the roads."

"They're okay now. I wondered whether you were aware of your new status. Mrs. Grapow is going around telling everyone you're a weather prophet. Or is it prophetess?"

"Oh, for goodness' sake!" Exasperated, Ellen explained what she had meant.

Norman laughed.

"That figures. Just take it easy around Mrs. Grapow, Ellen. You might not think it, but she wields a lot of power in this town. She holds mortgages on half the farms around here."

"You're kidding. That beefy, stupid-looking—"

"Stupid is as stupid does. As Ed puts it, she has 'worn

out' three husbands, and she inherited from each of them."

"Well, she doesn't hold a mortgage on this house. . . . I hope the storm didn't do much damage in town?"

They talked about the weather for a while and then Norman hung up. Ellen read in the living room and went to bed early. She had gotten into the habit of staying downstairs until she was ready to sleep, and undressing in the dark.

For the rest of the week she was busy. The rain brought out weeds she never knew were there, and the honeysuckle seemed to grow while she looked at it. One day she met a friend for lunch in a town forty miles away, which boasted a famous country inn; they spent the rest of the day antiquing, and Ellen returned home at twilight exhausted and grubby and the proud owner of an old dry sink. Stripping and refinishing this relic took the rest of the week, so it was Saturday before Ellen had occasion to go to town. She was willing to admit that she had been waiting until the young people were off work; except for Norman's, theirs were the only faces in town she wanted to see.

They were out in full force when she drew up in front of the general store. Bob Muller was among them. Ellen had decided to ignore him; the shooting incident did not alter her essential moral position, but it did weaken her argument from a pragmatic point of view.

The others greeted her with the ease of old friends, and she let Joyce escort her to a chair and buy her a Coke. As she sat down, Mrs. Grapow appeared in the doorway. She greeted Ellen with a nod and stood with her massive arms folded across her chest.

"Didn't see you in church Sunday," she said.

Aha, thought Ellen; that explains part of her antagonism. She thinks I'm a horrible heathen of some sort.

"I wasn't sure I'd be welcome," she said.

"Why wouldn't you be?" Joyce asked.

"After all, I am a stranger."

"You've gotta work out your own salvation with fear and trembling," said Mrs. Grapow.

This cheerful statement was received with silence. Steve stopped humming and Joyce's smile faded.

"I had guests last Sunday," Ellen said blandly. "I was too busy to come."

"Vanity of vanities," said Mrs. Grapow. "Everything is vanity."

Ellen tried not to smile. It really was impossible to take Mrs. Grapow seriously; her quotations were either inaccurate or not apropos. Ellen's imp was in full control, and she didn't even struggle against it.

"There was the marriage at Cana, wasn't there," she murmured, gazing soulfully at Mrs. Grapow. "And the lillies of the field. 'They toil not, neither do they spin.' Not that I didn't toil last Sunday, cooking and cleaning. . . . However, I might come to church tomorrow."

Mrs. Grapow's face turned red. Maybe she isn't so stupid, Ellen thought; she knows I'm kidding her. Or maybe she's angry because someone has the effrontery to talk back to her. Doesn't anyone ever disagree with this virago?

"Maybe you wouldn't like our church," Mrs. Grapow said, abandoning Scripture in favor of a more direct attack, "We're Protestants."

"Why, so am I," said Ellen heartily. "Isn't that a coincidence? What sort of Protestants are you?"

Mrs. Grapow drew herself up.

"The Earthly Church of the Wrath of God."

Ellen laughed.

It was to be some time before she fully comprehended the fatality of the laugh, but she regretted it as soon as it came out. From anyone but Mrs. Grapow the phrase might have been a joke. But Mrs. Grapow had no sense of humor. And to laugh at someone else's faith was, Ellen felt, the height of bad manners.

She bent down and brushed at her calf.

"I forgot to warn you I'm terribly ticklish right there," she said to Joyce, who was squatting beside her. Poor Joyce stared, openmouthed, and Ellen turned back to Mrs. Grapow.

"Really," she said, her face now quite sober. "I don't believe I'm familiar with that church. Is it related to the—to the—"

But for the life of her she could not think of any conventional Protestant sect that could be compared to Mrs. Grapow's without insult to the former.

"Isn't related to anything," said Mrs. Grapow hoarsely. "It's been here since the town was founded. It's the only way to God. The only way that ain't a snare and a illusion."

"I certainly must come tomorrow," Ellen said sincerely.

Mrs. Grapow muttered something and went inside. Ellen had the feeling that she was lurking and listening.

The young people relaxed visibly when the presence had been withdrawn. Steve started to whistle, and one of the other boys did a dance step. The music distracted Joyce, who was still looking bewildered.

"Anybody going to the dance next week?" she asked loudly, glancing at Steve.

"Sure," Bob Muller answered promptly. "You're going with me, Joyce."

"Who says?" Joyce turned a disdainful shoulder. "I guess I just won't go."

"You don't have to have a date," one of the other girls said, with a sly glance at Joyce. "We'll all go together, okay? Dad will let me have the car."

"I'm not going if I don't have a date," said Joyce.

"You've got—" Bob began.

"A date with a human being," said Joyce rudely.

She stood up and walked over to the Coke machine.

On the way she passed Steve, who stared straight through her and went on whistling.

It wasn't hard for Ellen to figure out what was going on, even without the nudges and grins of the others. Steve and Joyce had had a quarrel. Ellen was amused but sympathetic. She had nursed too many cases of what is erroneously called puppy love to underestimate the severity of the disease.

Joyce had trouble with the Coke machine. She fumbled, dropped her coins, and made critical comments. She was only a few feet from Steve, but she might have been in the next county for all the attention he gave her performance. He looked at Ellen.

"That was some storm you put on the other night."

"Glad you liked it," Ellen said gravely.

Joyce laughed, and most of the others smiled. A few of the faces remained sober, however.

"Do you give lessons?" Joyce asked, returning with her hard-won Coke. "Maybe you could teach me to do it. I'd like to rain on some people."

"Oh, you have to start young," Ellen said. "I learned the technique at my mother's knee, as a lisping toddler."

This time Joyce was the only one who laughed.

"I bet you can tell fortunes, too."

"I haven't got my crystal ball with me."

"How about reading my hand? Here, I'll cross your palm with silver."

She dropped a quarter into Ellen's lap and extended a slim, calloused hand.

"Not much silver in that anymore," Ellen complained.

"Oh, come on. Please."

Ellen smiled into the laughing, upturned face. Joyce had a constellation of freckles across her snub nose; her green eyes danced and her curls shone like polished copper. She was as cute and harmless as a kitten; but as

Ellen took the outstretched hand, she felt as if the sun had gone under a cloud.

Joyce knew she was joking, but there was a sudden tension, a sharpening of interest, among the others that might have warned Ellen. She disapproved of playing games with the occult; it was potentially dangerous for delicately balanced minds. But as she hesitated, she sensed a movement beyond the darkened doorway, where Mrs. Grapow lurked like a wolf in its lair.

Ellen bent over the girl's hand.

"I see," she intoned. "Yes—I see you have been picking fruit. Is it blackberries? No, wait—it's coming. . . . It—yes, it was—red raspberries!"

A burst of laughter broke the tension.

"Oh, come on," Joyce pleaded.

"A long life and a merry one," Ellen said, pretending to trace the lines in the berry-stained hand. "Two husbands—no, three—and children—four, five, six, seven—"

"Stop right there," Joyce laughed. "That's too far away. Can't you see anything closer?"

She was still smiling, but there was a look in the green eyes Ellen couldn't resist.

"I see you dressed up," she said, peering at the hand. "How pretty you look . . . roses in your hair—white roses. . . . You're going to a party. There's a boy with you. I can't see his face, but he's tall and fair-haired. He's wearing jeans. . . ."

That was a safe bet, anyhow, and so were the roses; if Joyce hadn't thought of wearing them, she would now. From the corner of her eye Ellen saw Steve leaning forward, as if he were trying to see the vision she had described. Joyce was blushing.

"Thank you," she said.

The bolder souls pushed forward.

"Me next!"

"No, me!"

Recklessly Ellen predicted trips abroad and handsome dark strangers and letters with good news. Some of her statements aroused mirth; a howl of laughter burst out when she told Alan Bates he was going to be a great surgeon. He was an intellectual-looking boy with thick glasses, but apparently his mates thought poorly of his brains.

Then a hand was thrust through the others, so close to Ellen's face she recoiled.

"Now me, it's my turn, tell me something. Something good."

Again, a shiver of warning ran through Ellen. She hardly recognized Prue's voice; it was harsh and urgent, and the girl's eyes shone feverishly. Ellen took the pudgy hand in hers.

"Honey, it's just a joke," she said gently. "You know I can't really—"

"Tell me! Please!"

"I see you in a white dress," Ellen said reluctantly. "And a veil. You're getting married."

"What does he look like?"

Someone snickered. The sound only increased Ellen's sympathy; the fact that Prue's problems amused the other kids made them even harder for the girl to bear.

"Well, he's tall," she said. "And broad-shouldered. . . . And his hair . . ."

"Blond," said Prudence, like a prayer. "Blond?"

"Yes, that's right."

She could no more have withheld this promise than she could have waved a forbidden ice cream cone in front of a younger child. Prudence sighed. Her eyes were misty.

"I've got to go," Ellen said, rising. The game had lost its savor; even the fun of teasing Mrs. Grapow paled in the face of Prue's small tragedy. She had a desperate crush on Steve, and she didn't stand a chance against Joyce's charm. Ellen was pretty sure who Steve's date for the dance would be.

She backed the car out of the parking space and then hesitated, her foot poised above the gas pedal. Through the car window she saw the group framed by the squared-off shape of the porch roof and railings. The sunlight shone in their hair—tawny and brown and black, Joyce's flame-bright curls and Steve's yellow mane. They were engaged in an animated discussion—probably about her predictions. Nostalgia gripped her, not only for her own younger days but for the other youth she had enjoyed vicariously. My God, she thought sincerely—I do miss my kids!

One last glance in the rear-view mirror showed a crow among the bright flock on the porch. The sight of Mrs. Grapow turned Ellen's mellow memories sour. What was she saying to the kids? If it was a quotation, Ellen felt sure of its general tenor.

ii

Ellen had not been trying to propitiate the storekeeper when she said she meant to go to church next day. Wild horses couldn't have kept her away; she spent half the morning trying to invent a theology for a faith with a name like the one Mrs. Grapow had given.

At any rate, Ellen thought she could safely assume that the Earthly Church of the Wrath of God was puritanical in taste. She dressed accordingly, in a severely tailored gray shirtwaist dress with long sleeves, but as she got into the car she was already regretting her attempt at conformity. It was going to be a scorcher. There was not a cloud in the sky; the leaves hung motionless in the still air. By the time Ellen got to town, the dress was sticking to her and her nylons felt like wool slacks. It was a safe bet that the church would not be air-conditioned. People who are preoccupied with God's wrath think physical discomfort is good for the soul.

This little white church looked sleepy and pretty in the sunlight, with the emerald green of grass and trees softening its rigid lines. Ellen was chagrined to realize that she was late. Apparently the service began before the conventional eleven o'clock. She hurried up the path, feeling perspiration trickling down her ribs, but encouraged by the sound of lusty singing from within.

The church was crowded, which ended Ellen's hope of slipping inconspicuously into an empty back pew. She had to prowl the aisles before she found a place. The singing continued, but people were staring.

Too embarrassed to face the minister, Ellen surveyed the back of the seat in front of her, looking for a hymn book. She did not find one, but she found another object that made her forget her faux pas. It was an old-fashioned palmetto fan. She hadn't seen one of those since her visits to a Methodist grandmother in the Midwest. The fan was useful; the church was just as hot as she had expected it would be. None of the windows were open— they looked as if they hadn't been opened since the structure was built—and the whitewashed walls glared like the interior of a furnace. Wielding the fan vigorously, Ellen thought she had never seen so barren a place. There were no pictures, no hangings, no carving on pews or pillars. It was a light, bright room, but the absence of color was somehow depressing, and it was even smaller than she had thought. The worshipers, who filled the church, could not have totaled more than sixty or seventy people.

The hymn ended and a hush fell over the congregation. A voice from the pulpit announced, "Number sixteen, brothers and sisters." Ellen looked up.

The word that came to her mind was "meager." He was a scrawny little man who looked as if he had been hastily put together out of leftovers that weren't quite enough to make a whole person. His hair was scanty, his features were small and pinched. All his strength seemed to have gone into his voice. It was not a pleasant voice. Strident as well as booming, it reminded Ellen of something, though she could not think what.

A tinny piano struck up a tune Ellen knew, and she prepared to sing with fervor. She liked the old hymns with their bouncing rhythms, which contrasted pleasantly with the often pessimistic lyrics. After the first few words, she realized that although the tune was familiar, the words were not. The woman on her left had a piercing soprano and Ellen was able to make out the words. They were appalling. It was hard to decide which was worse, the limping meter and forced rhymes, or the sentiments expressed thereby. One verse lodged in her mind because it was the quintessence of awfulness:

> The scarlet woman he sends down
> To the hot fires of Hell
> The sinner gets to know the weight of His hand.
> You'd better learn to know it well.

After this Ellen could hardly wait for the sermon.

She only heard the first ten minutes. She listened in a mounting disgust; there was nothing even remotely funny about the hoarse tirade from the terrible little man on the pulpit. It was full of hate: hate for the Jews, who killed Jesus—for the blacks, the sons of Ham, whom God had doomed to perpetual servitude—for the godless Communists—for the popish worshipers of false gods—for the heathen, who rejected God—and for the pagans, who had never been allowed to choose, for if God had thought them worthy, He would have shown Himself to them!

Finally Ellen isolated the memory that had haunted her. She was too young to remember the screaming orator of Nuremberg and Berlin, but she had listened to records. To compare the pastor with Hitler was to credit him with more power than he possessed, though Ellen felt sure the minister would have enjoyed that power—to wipe out dissenters as his ruthless God had destroyed the cities of Canaan. "He smote it with the edge of the sword, and all the souls that were therein. . . ."

Ellen had no desire to offend anyone, but she would not condone such trash by sitting still and listening to it. Quietly she rose and walked out of the church. She knew that every single member of the congregation saw her go, and that the burning eyes of the pastor followed every step.

Oddly shaken, she sat in the car for a few minutes to recover her composure. She was disturbed, not so much by the encounter with a mind both violent and irrational, but by the realization that her safe, sane world was only one of many worlds. She had labored under the absurd but widespread delusion that the attitudes of her circle were those of the majority of humanity. For years she had lived in a world of superficial tolerance and good breeding. It had its faults; hypocrisy was one, certainly, and another was a kind of cynical indifference to the absolutes of both good and evil. But it was a stable world in its mediocrity and its studied pretenses. It was predictable. Surely she had been naive, though, to think of it as the normal world. In the strange universe she had glimpsed today, anything was possible.

She drove home singing "Love Lifted Me." Now there was a hymn! It moved like a march and it offered hope to the most miserable of sinners. Love was a word Mrs.

Grapow had probably never used; to her it was doubtless a dirty word like s-x.

As she drove between the mammoth pines, Ellen felt as if the boughs were a comforting green curtain, shutting her off from the town. Her pretty old house sprawled like a sleepy cat in the sunlit clearing. Ellen thought of the woman who had once owned it with a new sympathy. If the Earthly Church of the Wrath of God had disapproved of Mary Baumgartner, that was a strong point in Mary's favor. She ought to be canonized, Ellen thought with a wry smile, as she stripped off her soaking gray dress and headed for the shower.

For the rest of the day Ellen busied herself about the house, but she was not displeased when, about sunset, she heard a car drive up. As she had expected, her visitor was Norman. He peered at her through the newly repaired screen door and asked humorously,

"Is it safe to come in?"

"Safe? Oh—just a minute."

Ellen turned in time to scoop up Ishtar, who was coming down the hall. It was uncanny how the cat could sense Norman's presence; she had been peacefully sleeping in the living room. This time Ishtar did not protest as she was thrust ignominiously into the cellar, but the look she gave Ellen held more contempt than any human face could express.

They sat on the porch and drank sherry. The trees cast long lavender shadows across the thick grass, and the scent of roses strengthened as evening drew on.

"I'm so glad you came," Ellen said. "This is the only time of day when I have to fight loneliness."

"You must miss your family. I hope they write to you."

"Oh, yes. Even the boys are good correspondents. Sam, the oldest, is working in Boston this summer. Arthur is a counselor at a boys' camp; he's our athlete. The youngest, Phil, is camping in Canada. I can't say his postcards are always welcome. He hints at the most terrible disasters. He writes things like 'I got my wallet back, with some of the money,' and 'The police in this town are real jerks.' By the time I get the card, the crisis is long past, but I spend hours wondering what happened."

"What about your daughter? Will she be joining you soon?"

"No, she's going to visit friends after her tour is over. She'll spend a week here in September before she goes back to school."

"You're really breaking the umbilical cord, aren't you?"

"Maybe I'm being a little brutal," Ellen admitted, "but it's harder on me than it is on them. I miss all of them; they only miss me—if they do miss me!"

"It sounds as if you did a fine job with all of them."

"I had help."

"Yes, your brother-in-law." Norman held his glass up, as if admiring the sunlight sifting through the amber liquid. "I think I know of him. Didn't he write an article for *Foreign Affairs* a couple of years ago?"

"Yes. What a memory you have."

"It was a memorable article. One of the few I've read that made sense of the Middle East mess without pomposity or scholarese."

"He's always getting into trouble for speaking his mind." Ellen smiled reminiscently. "His letters are so funny. He's discreet, of course—never mentions names—but as he says, he's used to having an appreciative audience and now he has no one to dump his frustrations on. I keep thinking I ought to burn some of those letters."

"Hang on to them. They may be valuable historical documents."

"Jack suggested I keep them, too, but not because he has such a high opinion of their historical value. He says that after he retires he plans to write one of those spicy scandalmongering autobiographies. He's looking forward to being visited by beautiful veiled ladies offering him handsome bribes to suppress his memoirs."

Norman laughed.

"He must be quite a guy."

"Oh, he is! He has a silly offbeat sense of humor, and yet he's the most reliable, solid—" Ellen stopped, flushing. "Heavens, Norman, you mustn't let me run on like this. I must be boring you."

"No, you're not. You're giving me an excellent picture of yourself and the way you've lived all these years. I feel guilty. I should have realized how hard it would be for you to be alone with only yourself to rely on, after such a sheltered life."

Ellen gave him a long, level look.

"Aha," she said. "I get it. Don't tell me the news has reached you already? You warned me about the church, but honestly, Norman, I simply could not sit there and listen to that—that—"

"I know the word you're groping for. Good God, Ellen, I don't blame you. I haven't been inside that so-called church since I was a kid."

"The minister—"

"Hank Winckler. He's a local boy. I've known him since first grade, and he was a pain in the neck then. He's a bad case, but he didn't make the church; it was the other way around."

"How did it originate? I've heard of some strange sects, but this one is new to me."

"You probably know the western part of Virginia was settled by two main groups—Scotch-Irish and German. The German settlers were mostly Lutherans, but there were other sects—Mennonites, Dunkers and Sabbatarians, Moravians, Separatists. In the early eighteenth century the Blue Ridge and the Valley were really the back of beyond. There were no resident ministers, and the itinerant types might visit a given settlement once a year—or less frequently. For the most part the local congregations were run by laymen. All sorts of strange ideas flourished in the isolated mountain villages."

"Yes," Ellen said. "I've read about the quacks who established themselves out here in the early days. Empiricus Schmidt, who was a dentist and a self-ordained preacher—"

"That's right. Most of the quacks were soon run out of town—like Carl Rudolph, who called himself the 'Prince of Wurttemberg' and seduced the farmers' daughters in between sermons. I suspect something of the sort happened here, only this time the rogue succeeded in establishing himself. There is mention of a man named Jacob Schnell. Nothing more is known of him; he certainly wasn't a legitimate minister of any German denomination. Perhaps he wasn't a quack, but a genuine religious fanatic with a lot of sick ideas. Even the accepted theologies of that era seem fanatical to us today. Intolerance, bigotry, and persecution were the norm."

"How can anyone in this day and age believe such stuff?"

"Not many of them do," Norman said reasonably. "People break away, especially the young ones. But there is a coterie here in town that sticks to the old ways, and they carry considerable weight. Poor old Hank is a fool, but he wouldn't last long if he weren't backed by people like Mrs. Grapow."

"Well, I appreciate your efforts to help me, but don't bother. I'm not breaking loose because I'm unchaperoned. If Jack had been there, he'd have walked out long before I did. How is Tim?"

Norman accepted the change of subject with a grin.

"Raising general hell. One of the reasons why I stopped by was to ask if you could come over on Wednesday. I can't keep him in much longer, and I do want you to talk to him."

"Fine. What time?"

They settled the details and then Norman left.

Ellen let the cat out and prepared a light supper, but the visit had left her feeling nervous. She was vain enough to believe that Norman genuinely enjoyed her company, and it was nice to think they were on such casual terms that he felt free to drop in, but she had the impression that he was genuinely concerned about her most recent escapade. What was wrong with this town, anyway, and who was Mrs. Grapow, that she could worry a man like Norman? The woman was taking on cosmological dimensions; Ellen visualized her looming over the town like a vast black colossus.

Partly as an act of defiance, she decided to read in bed that evening instead of staying downstairs, as had been her recent custom. She had discovered a box of books that had belonged to Penny in her younger days and was now happily reading her way through Louisa May Alcott, Noel Streatfeild, and L. M. Montgomery. Nothing could be more soothing than the innocent prewar adventures of Anne of Green Gables; Ellen was fully absorbed in them when the shadow came again.

This time, being half prepared, she did not panic. She knew better than to turn her head. Staring straight ahead at the snoring, upturned shape of Ishtar, she "saw" the thing distinctly, at the outermost periphery of vision.

It was a woman's shadow. Her hair was unbound and her full skirts were those of an earlier era. The pose was not menacing; it suggested weary resignation. The shadow arms blended into the shape of the body, as if they hung loosely from the shoulders. The featureless head was bowed.

None of Ellen's other senses was affected. She felt the warm night air against her skin and heard the normal night sounds. She saw the cat's silky flanks heave in and out as she breathed. The room smelled of Ellen's perfume; blended with it were the rich flower scents from outside and hints of old timber, fresh paint, and lemon furniture polish. The room was normal. Everything was normal—except for the single impossible shape on the edge of sight.

Ellen waited. Nothing happened. The shadow did not move or change, but finally Ellen's staring eyes rebelled. She blinked; and in that split second the thing was gone. It did not come again, though Ellen read for another half hour in a conscious attempt to recapture the conditions that had produced it originally.

Eventually she turned out the light, marveling at the fact that the darkness held no fear. That was the most mystifying thing about the phenomenon—that it produced no sense of horror or cold. She remembered the occasional night fears of childhood, when it became an impossible choice as to whether she would turn her unprotected back toward the gaping window or the open door. Often she had stayed rigid on her back trying to watch both apertures, and finding demons in every moving shadow. There was no such aftereffect now. Her initial panic had been the result of shock and surprise, not a condition inherent in what she saw.

But if that was an optical illusion, Ellen thought drowsily, it's the damnedest thing I've ever seen.

Eight

It was several days before Ellen got back to town. She made herself go when she realized that she was inventing specious reasons for shopping at the supermarket in Smithville instead of the village store. She would not be intimidated by Mrs. Grapow.

There were no friendly nods from the loungers on the porch that morning, but Ellen scarcely noticed. She was nerving herself for the meeting with Mrs. Grapow, and resenting the woman even more because she felt the need of moral support.

The storekeeper was in her accustomed place behind the counter. Ellen wondered if she always stood there, staring blankly into space, even when there were no customers to be served. Didn't she read, or crochet, or do crossword puzzles? What was she thinking about? Did she think, in the true sense of the word, or did she function like a robot programmed by the more barbaric heroes of the Old Testament?

Ellen gave her order and Mrs. Grapow collected the items with her usual efficiency. Then she leaned forward over the heap of groceries and said slowly,

"Saw you in church Sunday."

"Oh? I didn't see you."

"I play the piano."

Ellen tried to picture Mrs. Grapow as a pig-tailed child taking piano lessons, but her imagination rebelled; she could only visualize a miniature, reduced version of the woman's present form perched on a piano stool. It was a dreadful picture.

"That's nice," Ellen said weakly.

She took out her wallet. Mrs. Grapow didn't speak, nor did she move to take the money Ellen offered her.

Ellen knew what she was doing. The technique was more subtle than she would have expected from Mrs. Grapow. It was also effective. Ellen had to fight an impulse to babble, to explain herself. With an effort she remained silent, and finally Mrs. Grapow said,

"You left early."

"I felt sick," Ellen said, with perfect truth.

"It wasn't polite to walk out like that."

"It would have been even ruder to be sick right in the middle of the aisle."

Ellen was pleased with her replies; so far she had spoken the exact truth, but she had avoided pejorative comment. Mrs. Grapow was not deceived. Her face darkened.

"Heard what happened to Klaus Roth?"

"No," Ellen said, surprised by the change of subject.

"Got hit by a car."

"How awful!" Klaus was not one of Ellen's favorites among the young people. A weedy, dark-haired boy, he talked of nothing except his cherished car and the speed it was capable of attaining. But of course she was sorry to hear of his misfortune and she said so, adding, "I hope he wasn't hurt badly?"

"Car just grazed him," Mrs. Grapow admitted. "He's mostly bruised. Point is—you told him it would happen."

"I told—"

For a moment Ellen was too stunned to think clearly. Then she remembered the fortune-telling session and laughed aloud.

"I told him to watch out for danger on four wheels! I was thinking of that jalopy of his—drag racing and so forth. . . ."

There was no answering amusement in Mrs. Grapow's face, not even the unpleasant smirk that passed for a smile with her.

"Joyce is going to that dance with Steve," she said.

"Naturally. I knew—"

"Yes, you knew. You told 'em that, too."

"It was only a game," Ellen said. "The kids didn't take it seriously, any more than I did. No sane person would."

"What about Klaus?"

"Coincidence."

"The people in this town wouldn't like any more coincidences."

"Then it will be unfortunate for them if any occur, won't it?"

Ellen slapped a twenty-dollar bill down on the counter. She wanted to get away from the store and its horrible owner. Her temper was rising. There was no point in trying to explain herself to Mrs. Grapow. The woman was beyond reason.

Mrs. Grapow rang up the sale and fumbled maddeningly with the change.

"That house isn't healthy for the likes of you," she said. "You better get out before it's too late, or else change your ways."

"What on earth are you talking about?"

"The witch. She's still there. If you let her in, she'll take possession of you."

Once again Ellen's normally glib tongue was paralyzed by anger and disbelief. Mrs. Grapow counted the change into her hand.

". . . nineteen, twenty. There better not be any more coincidences, Miz March. We don't like the devil walking up and down in our town."

Ellen's fits of temper were usually short and mild. Occasionally, however, she was seized by a rage of majestic proportions, prompted, most often, by injustice or cruelty to someone else. Such a rage gripped her now, and even Mrs. Grapow retreated at the sight of her white face and blazing eyes.

"How dare you speak to me like that! Possessed! I wish I could be. I wish I could learn a few good hearty curses; I'd put a hex on you and your ghastly church! I'd rather have Mary Baumgartner around—dead or alive!— than exchange another word with you. You're an ignorant, rude, bigoted, superstitious woman!"

Seizing her bag of groceries, she stormed toward the door. She thought of another telling comment, and whirled to deliver it; but the sight she saw stopped the words in her throat.

Mrs. Grapow had fallen back against the shelves. Her face was distorted by a look of mingled terror and malevolence. Both arms were extended, as if to ward off some imminent peril, and the fingers of her right hand were rigid in a gesture Ellen recognized.

ii

Wednesday was Ellen's day for writing to Jack. He counted on hearing from her; once before he had cabled when she missed a week.

When she sat down at her desk after lunch, she was not

consciously worried about the morning's encounter. It was almost like automatic writing, the way her hand proceeded to inscribe all the details of the conversation with Mrs. Grapow.

When she had finished four closely written pages, she reread them. The catharsis of writing had relieved her mind, and she was surprised at the hysterial tone of her description. She tore the pages across and dropped them into the wastebasket.

The second letter was much better. It contained a witty, lighthearted account of her growing reputation as the local witch, and a description of Mrs. Grapow that would amuse Jack, with his fondness for strange characters. She had already written about Tim, and had received a characteristic response from Jack, warning her against overoptimism. Rereading this comment, Ellen made a wry face. No doubt it was flattering to have all the men of her acquaintance want to protect her, but it was also rather insulting. She dashed off a poignant description of Tim's rescue of Ishtar. That would show Jack she wasn't being overly optimistic.

In the late afternoon she got ready for her encounter session with Tim. Since Norman wanted the meeting to appear unpremeditated, she planned to go by the path through the woods and "drop in" at the prearranged hour. With Ishtar watching from the foot of the bed, she put on slacks and a pale-blue cotton shirt and scraped some of the mud off her walking shoes. She didn't polish them; they would be muddy again before she reached her destination. It had not rained for almost a week, but there were boggy spots in the deep woods that never dried out completely.

It was still breathlessly hot, though the sun was far down the west. The rich amber sunlight made the leaves glow like emeralds. The woods were lively with bird and animal noises. A blue jay's harsh squawk sounded, and a squirrel answered with an irritable chatter.

Ellen crossed the stream on the stepping stones she had placed the first time she came this way. The stream was just a little too wide to jump, as she had discovered when she tried it. The fallen leaves were damp; her feet made hardly any sound as she walked on.

She was lost in a pleasant daydream in which Tim became a minister or missionary, when a sound gradually penetrated her absorption. At first it had been lost among the chorus of bird and insect chirping that filled the woods, but it was too painful a sound to remain obscured, and she was approaching it. Her heart gave a sudden leap. The sound was a high-pitched, piercing shriek, like that of a factory whistle, but it came from a living throat. No machine could express such anguish.

Ellen started to run.

The sound grew louder as she went on. It was intermittent now, as if the injured creature were becoming weaker, but its quality was not diminished.

A sudden turn in the path brought her to her goal. She stopped, sick and staring.

The place just ahead was not so much a clearing as a widening of the path. An ancient rotted oak had toppled, crushing lesser growth as it fell. Sunlight poured down into the little glade.

Tim knelt in the middle of the path and before him was something—Ellen's horrified eyes refused to see it clearly —something furry and bloody, from which came the weakening cry. Ellen was just in time to see Tim's lifted arm strike down. At the same instant the boy saw her. He gave a great start, but the heavy stone he held did not miss its target. There was a final scream, and then silence.

Ellen wasn't the fainting type, but she had come close to it once before when she saw Phil bumped off his bicycle by a speeding car. She felt the same symptoms now—

the lightness of her head, the darkening of peripheral vision, and the abnormal clarity of the object she was staring at. She could see the stiffened muscles of Tim's bare arms and the scabs of mosquito bites and poison ivy. His head was raised and his blue eyes shone with a red core. The tendons stood out in his thin brown throat. He looked like a minor sylvan deity, a faun or satyr—some creature not quite human.

Ellen turned her head, fighting nausea and dizziness. When the spasm passed, Tim was gone.

Ellen's desire to turn and run for home was almost overwhelming. However, she was closer to Norman's house than to her own, and there was no use in hiding like a hurt child from unpleasant truths. Norman expected her; if she didn't appear he would call, and then the story would have to come out. She might as well go on and confess her error. He had been right, and she had been tragically wrong.

Her eyes averted from the twisted furry lump in the path, she went on.

Norman answered the door. He took one look at her distraught face and caught her by the shoulders. She almost wept then; it was good to have a man's hands supporting her. But the walk had calmed her, and the brandy Norman prescribed finished the job; she was able to tell her story fairly calmly.

"I see," he said, when she had finished. "Forgive me, Ellen, I know it was a horrible shock, but I can't help being relieved. It could have been so much worse. When I saw you, I thought . . ."

She didn't ask what he had thought. Now she knew some of the horrors that haunted his mind.

"Where is he?" she asked.

"God knows. He saw you, didn't he? Then he won't be back, not while you're here. Thanks, Ellen. It was a good idea, but it didn't work."

"You don't think I'm giving up, do you?" While Norman stared, Ellen finished her brandy. "You must get him to a doctor, Norman. We'll have to think of something else, that's all."

A slow, reluctant smile curved Norman's mouth.

"You're a courageous woman, aren't you?"

"Not courageous, just stubborn." The brandy had done its job too well; Ellen felt relaxed and mildly depressed. "It seems as if everything has gone wrong lately, Norman. I'm not doing any better with Mrs. Grapow than I am with Tim. And I used to think tact was my strong point!"

"I've been hearing about your latest exploits," Norman admitted. "Whatever possessed you to make those crazy predictions?"

"It was all in fun. In Washington, lots of people go to fortune-tellers."

"But they don't take it seriously. Our simple little community doesn't play such games."

"I'm beginning to realize that. I guess I'd better keep my mouth shut from now on. But I won't go to church!"

Norman laughed, but shook his head.

"Maybe you ought to get out of town for a few weeks. This will die down if you aren't around to be bullied."

"You're the second person who has suggested I leave town. Is someone plotting a murder or a revolution or something, that you all want to get rid of me?"

Norman's face changed.

"Who else suggested it? Mrs. Grapow. . . . Why don't you visit your daughter? She's in New York now, isn't she?"

"Cleveland. She's with the Emerson's—he's the writer friend of Jack's, the one I told you about. They invited me to come. . . ."

"Then why don't you?"

"Because Mrs. Grapow wants me to."

"You are bullheaded," Norman said, smiling. "How about another drink on the strength of it?"

Ellen refused more brandy, but accepted Norman's offer to drive her home. She did not want to pass the dead animal on the path.

That night the shadow came again in the middle of Chapter Four of *Ballet Shoes*. Ellen watched it for twenty seconds, counting them off, before the inevitable flicker of her lids dismissed it.

Sleep was longer in coming than usual. Ellen was chiefly concerned about Tim, but the shadow was beginning to get on her nerves, too. Why doesn't it do something? she thought irritably, as she pounded her hot pillow. It doesn't even move; it just hangs there.

She was drifting off to sleep before the implications of the verb struck home.

iii

The heat wave continued. It was the first bad one of the summer, and Ellen, who was accustomed to air-conditioning, found that she had to readjust her schedule to suit nature in the raw. By midday she was only fit for a cold shower and a nap in her darkened room.

She had intended to have her eyes checked, but the thought of the baking streets of Washington discouraged her. So she sat and embroidered and did her gardening early in the morning and read until her eyes ached. Tired as they were, she saw no more shadows. Her dreams were uneasy, though, haunted by the echoes of faint animal cries. On a night of still moonlight they woke her and she lay shivering for a few moments, until she realized that the soft sounds were coming from Ishtar.

The cat was a dark shape against the moonlight that silvered the window's rectangle. She didn't stir, even when Ellen came to see what was going on. She put her hand on the cat's hunched back and felt a ridge of stiffened hair, but Ishtar didn't seem alarmed, only wary and curious. Down in the yard, a small white shape jumped from a fence post and ran into the woods.

Ishtar yawned.

"So you saw it too," Ellen said softly. "That makes me feel better, somehow. . . . Poor thing, I hope it has a home."

After a week of solitude she was bored with her own company, but not so bored that she was moved to seek companionship in town. Norman was away, Martha informed her when she called. Ellen wondered whether he had gone to Washington or Charlottesville to seek medical help for Tim. If I were in his shoes, she thought soberly, I wouldn't dare leave town with Tim on the loose. It must be terrible to go through the days never knowing when the next irate call or piece of disastrous news would come; always braced for a blow, expecting the worst— and getting it.

She was in the kitchen preparing lunch when she heard the doorbell ring. She hurried to answer it, not ill pleased at the thought of company, though she wondered who it could possibly be.

Her wildest speculations could not have prepared her for the actuality. The face peering through the screen door belonged to Prudence Muller. Trying to conceal her surprise, Ellen invited the girl in.

"I thought you were working," she said.

"It's my lunch hour."

"Oh, yes, you work at the drugstore in town, don't you? I hope you didn't walk all the way out here in this heat."

Prudence mumbled something about a bicycle. Her face was scarlet with heat and exertion. Her eyes dropped away from Ellen's and she began picking nervously at a loose thread on her skirt. She was obviously ill at ease, and Ellen felt an echoing uneasiness, mingled with pity. The girl was so hopelessly unattractive. The sight of her made Ellen's maternal instincts itch; if Prudence had been

her daughter she would have prescribed a dermatologist,
a diet, and some decent clothes, just as a start. Penny had
never looked that bad, even in the worst stages of puppy
fat and pimples. Prudence was a hopeless case; her personality was as limp as her stringy hair.

"Can I do something for you?" Ellen asked kindly.

"I want a potion."

Prudence was sitting on the edge of the chair. She
leaned forward, and for a stricken moment Ellen thought
she was going to drop to her knees. Misunderstanding Ellen's silence, she went on eagerly,

"I've got almost ten dollars. Nine seventy-five. If that
isn't enough—"

"Wait. Stop."

Ellen stood up. If she hadn't moved, she would have
screamed or smashed one of the fragile glass ornaments
on the table beside her.

"Let me get this straight. I can't believe. . . . What sort
of potion is it you want, Prudence? I'm not a doctor."

"A love potion. Like the one you gave Joyce, so Steve
would stop being mad at her. The dance is tomorrow
night; I've got to—"

"My God," Ellen said.

She had believed, after her years of working with disturbed children, that nothing would ever surprise her
again, but now she was at a loss. She didn't know how to
deal with this. With a silent prayer for guidance, she knelt
by the chair and took the girl's clenched hands in hers.

"Did Joyce tell you I gave her a—a love potion?"

"She wouldn't tell me anything that would help me. She
laughed at me. They all laugh at me, all the time. But I
know." Prudence looked at Ellen. She didn't turn her
head, and the sidelong roll of her eyeballs was ugly and
sly. "I know about you," Prudence said.

"Prudence, listen to me. You are making a terrible

mistake. You go to church, don't you? You must know better than to believe . . ."

"Samuel went to the witch of Endor."

"That was Saul," said Ellen sharply. "And you know what happened to him."

"I don't care what happened to him, it would be worth it." The girl's voice rose. "If ten dollars isn't enough—"

"I did not give Joyce a love potion," Ellen interrupted. "It was obvious that she and Steve were fond of each other. I guessed they would soon make up, and it was a lucky guess. That's all there was to it."

"You like her, and you don't like me," said Prudence. "That's why you won't help me."

"My dear child, I'd like to help you. I'll tell you what; there's a certain kind of makeup that my daughter used to use for her skin. I'll get some for you next time I go to the city."

"I have to go to the dance tomorrow night," Prudence said. "I have to have a potion, nothing else will work in time. I have to go with—"

She stopped speaking and a darker red stained her plump cheeks. Ellen felt so sorry for her she was tempted to go along with the fantastic request. A harmless mixture of sugar or baking soda. . . . The psychological effect of such faith was undeniable, it might give the girl the confidence she needed.

But Ellen was too experienced to succumb to the temptation. The trick wouldn't work because Prudence needed more than a psychological boost. She needed a whole battery of experts working full time. And the effect of such a procedure on Ellen's questionable reputation in town . . .

"There is no such thing as witchcraft," she said firmly. "I couldn't give you a magic potion if I wanted to."

"I have ten dollars in my bank at home," said Prudence, "For twenty dollars would you do it?"

"Not for twenty or fifty or a hundred. I can't, Prudence, why don't you understand? Look, come out some evening and I'll show you how my daughter does her hair and—"

Prudence wrenched her hands from Ellen's grasp. She stood up so suddenly Ellen almost fell over backward.

"Witch!" Prudence screamed. "Dirty old mean old witch! I'll get even with you, I'll fix you! Just wait! I'll tell them all you hurt me. I'll get you—"

"Out," said Ellen, in a voice she seldom used. "Get out of here. And don't come back until you are ready to apologize."

Sobbing, the girl ran from the room. Ellen heard the door slam.

Her second visitor came late in the afternoon. By this time Ellen had locked the downstairs windows and doors and was sitting in the kitchen distractedly eating bread and cheese. She had been too upset to eat lunch.

When the bell rang, she peered out of the kitchen window instead of going to the door. I'll be acting like a witch if this goes on, she thought morosely, as she squinted to see between the boughs of the dogwood tree. She couldn't see the front door, but she recognized the antique truck parked in the driveway.

With his punctilious courtesy Ed had retreated after ringing the bell and stood waiting on the front steps. He declined her invitation to come into the house.

"This is pleasant," he said, with a glance around the screened porch with its wrought-iron furniture and bright weatherproof cushions. "I will sit here, if I may."

"Wouldn't you like to see what I've done to the house?"

"No," Ed said calmly. "I am not interested in interior decoration. You should not invite strange men into your home, Mrs. March. This is a censorious community."

"So I am learning." Ellen couldn't help smiling; censorious was a mild word for the town if it could suspect improper "going-ons" between herself and Ed. "May I get you something to drink?" she asked.

"Thank you, I drink only water and I have had enough of that for the moment. But do not restrain yourself on my account. I do not judge the habits of others."

"I could use a drink," Ellen admitted. "But I won't have one. I suppose you know what happened today? Is that why you came?"

"That is one of the reasons. However, I have been remiss. I have neglected my obligations toward you. I have allowed personal disinclination to keep me from my duty. I am a selfish man."

"You're a very good man," Ellen said. "Stop berating yourself."

Ed shook his head. He looked like an Old Testament prophet, with his long gray beard and rough clothing. They were certainly an oddly matched pair, and yet Ellen felt as comfortable with him as she did with Norman. She could even follow his somewhat oblique reasoning, and knew that his disinclination to seek out her company was a compliment rather than the reverse. The illogical empathy between them threatened his self-imposed isolation.

"I am not a good man," he said irritably. "Good and evil are emotionally laden terms, Mrs. March. I am a rational man, and reason tells me that I must behave in a way that accords with my admittedly high opinion of myself. It is conscience—if I may use an inaccurate but convenient term—which has brought me here today. I don't like what is going on in town."

The sudden descent from Emersonian prose to colloquial comment made Ellen laugh. She did so unrestrainedly, knowing Ed would understand. His beard twitched in the manner that indicated an underlying smile, but he shook his head at her again.

"That is the core of your problem, Mrs. March. You

laugh too easily, at matters other people regard with deadly seriousness. Are you not aware that a sense of humor is dangerous?"

"Whom have you been talking to?" Ellen asked resignedly.

"I have heard absurd stories from several people. Today I encountered something more serious—a hysterical verbal attack from Muller's idiot daughter."

"I guess I'd better give you my version." Ellen told him what had happened. She added, "I suppose Prudence accused me of hexing her, or something."

"That was the gist of the accusation."

"What did you do?"

"I addressed her and the others who were listening to her. My speech was, momentarily, very effective."

Ellen had a sudden vision of Ed orating, with his gray beard waving like that of John Brown.

"I believe you," she said.

"But only momentarily. The voice of reason is feeble against human stupidity, and the Muller family, collectively and individually, represent the quintessence of feeblemindedness." Ed leaned forward; a very human curiosity softened his austere face. "What on earth did you say to those silly children?"

"I can't remember details! It was a pack of nonsense— vague promises and guesses. That's the whole point of fortune-telling. The customer remembers if some event occurs which he can twist into confirmation of a prediction. He conveniently forgets the incorrect guesses, and only remembers the ones that come true. And he doesn't remember those accurately; his memory is colored by later events and by a lot of wishful thinking."

Ed nodded.

"I am familiar with the psychology of the problem. The Muller girl is an excellent example of what one might call the Cinderella syndrome. Only magic can give her what her heart desires; she therefore finds magic in what is only a matter of elementary character study, and demands a fairy godmother for herself. However, I must say that your level of accuracy is higher than the statistical average one might expect."

"Not so high," Ellen protested. "Joyce and Steve and the dance was a sure thing; it wasn't even a guess."

"Still it counts as one. Number two was the vehicular accident—no, you need not explain your reasoning to me, I can follow it. That does not alter the fact that our fellow citizens interpret it differently. Number three was the gift to Sue Ann—"

"What gift?"

"It came only yesterday; perhaps you are not aware of it. Did you not tell the girl she would soon receive a valuable gift from an unknown admirer?"

"Oh, Lord." Ellen dug her fingers into her hair and tried to think. "I said something about gifts. Her birthday is in a few weeks; she was talking about it."

"The gift was a pendant, with what is apparently a pearl of some size," Ed said coolly. "She found the parcel in her mailbox yesterday. Number four—"

"Oh, no!"

"A letter to young Charles Yates informing him that Harvard College has found a place for him after all. He had been rejected by all the institutions to which he optimistically applied, and was planning to attend the local teachers' college."

"I never told him anything like that," Ellen exclaimed.

"Now it is you who fail to understand the psychology involved. There are only two possible explanations for Charles's admission to Harvard. Either all the members of the admissions committee have gone insane simultaneously, or some strong supernatural influence has been brought to bear on them. Of the two, witchcraft seems the more reasonable explanation. With such a miracle, and the force of the other predictions, it is not surprising that

Charles should 'remember' a prognostication that was not made."

"It's ridiculous!"

"It would be ridiculous in any town but this. Mrs. March, I believe I warned you not to go to church. Having gone, however, you ought to have stayed."

"I can't feel guilty about that," Ellen said.

"Guilty, no. Cautious, yes. Winckler came to call on me once," said Ed reminiscently. "A ministerial call, to tell me of the evil of my ways. He did not come a second time."

"What did you do to him?"

"I threw him into the lilac bush. It was a sacrifice, for it damaged the bush—my favorite white lilac. But I did not wish to risk actual damage to bone or vertebrae."

Ellen laughed. Then she stopped, struck by a sobering thought.

"Do you suppose he'll call on me? I can't throw him out bodily."

"Don't let him in," Ed advised. He rose. "I have over-stayed my time. This is foolishness, Mrs. March, as you and I know. But stay away from those unstable children —including young Tim."

"For a self-styled hermit, you know quite a bit of gossip," Ellen said severely. "Tim is a sick boy. He needs help."

"We cannot help others," Ed said. "We can only help ourselves."

With these pessimistic words in her mind, Ellen was glad to find a sheaf of letters when she walked down to the mailbox. She settled down on the porch with the cocktail she felt she deserved, and began to read her mail.

Penny's letter was a brief scrawl. She was having a marvelous time, but she was homesick. "Can you believe yawning at the 'Mona Lisa'?" she wrote. "I love museums, but I've had too much of a good thing. I was getting tired before I left Europe, and now I'm so close to home, it seems unbearable that I can't be with you. I may cut my so-called vacation short."

There was a postcard from Phil, whose humor was of the bucolic variety; this gem featured an outhouse and a fat lady. The message ran, "Having a great time. Glad you aren't here, you'd hate it. I got forty mosquito bites last night. Love, Phil. P.S. I miss you."

The P.S. was scrunched into a corner upside down. Phil didn't want the United States mail to know of his lapse into sentimentality.

Ellen saved the best for last. With a luxurious sigh she opened Jack's bulging letter with its gaudy foreign stamps.

"The cooking in this place is terrible," he wrote. "No fudge cake, no lemon meringue pie, not even a tunafish-and-noodle casserole. I live on rubbish like *boeuf bourguignonne* and *coquilles Saint-Jacques.* I've been grousing so much they are talking of sending me home. Seriously—I have to go to Washington next week for conferences; am counting on at least one meal at 'our place.' "

Ellen smiled. "Our place" was the Howard Johnson's in Bethesda, hallowed by many forgettable meals with the young, who considered that chain the ultimate in gourmet food.

As she read on, through descriptions of embassy parties and luncheons with local dignitaries, she thought Jack's humor seemed a little forced. She knew him too well to miss the undercurrent of mild depression. It was typical of their relationship that, at the end of the letter, he should accuse her of the same thing.

"If you're lonesome, I wish to hell you'd break down and admit it. I get the feeling something is bothering you, Ellen. Your little town sounds like quite a place—fine to visit, but are you sure you want to live there? As for your young delinquent, the more I think about him, the more he worries me. I know you hate my being protective, but I can't help it. A boy like that can be dangerous, all the more so if he likes you. You know how readily these attachments can turn perverse. Do me a favor—just because I ask 'you to—talk to Jim Bishop, or Doctor Frank, or one of your other buddies in the psychiatric business before you go any farther with this boy. I'm not ashamed to admit caring even if you are."

Ellen lifted her eyes from the letter. It was dusk—the saddest, most beautiful time of the day. The shapes of the pines stood out black against the pale translucent blue of the evening sky. From the depths of the woods a bird called with infinite melancholy. And on the gatepost, barely visible in the declining light, sat a small white shape.

Ellen picked up her letter and her empty glass and fled indoors. She turned on all the lights and prepared a meal. Jack's letter had hit home with an accuracy he had not intended. She missed him so desperately she could only endure the loneliness by never admitting it; but as she glanced around her pretty kitchen she thought wistfully how much she would enjoy this place if she had someone living with her. Jack would laugh himself sick over the town's nonsense, and then deal with it, with the mixture of bluntness and tact that was his hallmark. He would scoff at shadows. . . .

And she had better sit down right now and answer his letter before he got any more worried. His comments about Tim had been full of insight; no doubt he would be relieved to learn that she had come to the same conclusion and meant to follow his advice. She must write Penny, too, or the girl would be arriving on her doorstep. Ellen didn't want that, not now. Not while all this foolishness was going on. . . .

She wrote both letters that night. Next morning she went out to mail them, despite the fact that it was raining. She drove into town even more slowly than the wet pavement made expedient, but it was not until she pulled up in front of the store that she realized how reluctant she was to be there. Only her innate stubbornness got her out of the car.

The chairs on the front porch were unoccupied. Breeze-blown rain pattered the empty seats. The whole town seemed deserted. Ellen knew the weather accounted for the absence of loungers and pedestrians, but the overall effect was disturbing, as if the town had withdrawn, turning its back on an unwelcome intruder.

As she stood on the porch closing her umbrella, the window shade behind the glass panel of the door was pulled down. Ellen distinctly heard the sound of a key being turned in the lock. It cracked like a rifle shot.

Incredulously she stared at the door, and saw the shade move. It was dark inside; but she knew Mrs. Grapow was there, peering out at her.

Ellen felt her cheeks burning. Wild images of violence churned in her mind; she wanted to break the glass with her umbrella and pound on the door, shouting.

But dignity and common sense dictated the only possible response. Slowly and deliberately Ellen put up her umbrella and got back into the car.

She drove away in a daze of anger and disbelief, with no particular destination in mind. At noon she found herself turning off Route 29 onto the Washington Beltway. She stopped at a gas station to make a call. It produced the result she had hoped for but hardly dared expect; Jim Bishop had a schedule crowded with patients and usually didn't eat lunch. It took her almost another hour to reach his Connecticut Avenue office, but the normal Washington traffic was relatively soothing after her recent adventures, and Jim's bear hug of greeting made her spirits rise.

He was a big bear of a man, with a busy brown moustache and thick dark hair. He refused to grow a beard because he said he didn't want to look like a psychiatrist.

"We only have half an hour after all," he said apologetically, indicating his couch with a gesture and grinning when Ellen refused it in favor of a chair. "Damn. I never can get you on that couch, can I?"

"Ply me with liquor," Ellen suggested, fluttering her eyelashes.

"I tried that, remember? You remain depressingly perpendicular through all attempts. Hope you like chicken salad sandwiches," he added, as his secretary appeared with a paper bag. "We haven't time to go out. One of my neurotics had a crisis this morning and I had to fit her in."

"I'm grateful you could give me this much time," Ellen said, with a nod of thanks to Miss Bates.

"I take it this is a professional call?"

"Sort of. What kind of label do you attach to someone who sees shadows?"

"Normal," said Jim promptly. "Who sees shadows, you? So do I, all the time. You'd be in trouble if you didn't see them."

He took an enormous bite of sandwich and Ellen told him about her optical illusions. She went on to describe Tim; and Bishop, who had been smiling at her symptoms, sobered.

"Go see an ophthalmologist and don't bug me with your eye problems. Your boy is something else. You say he's had treatment? Not from me."

"How can you be sure, I didn't mention his name."

"You wouldn't, Mrs. Propriety. But you've given me enough clues. If I had had him as a patient, I'd remember."

"I know you don't have time now to take him on."

"Wish I did. I can give you some names, of course, but that isn't the problem, is it? Why isn't the uncle doing this instead of you?"

"He's done his best. He gave up a few years ago after seeing Abrahamson and a few others. I'm trying to encourage him to try again. . . . And stop grinning at me, Jim, I know perfectly well I'm a busybody, and I don't care. Honestly, what do you think?"

"If it were anybody but you, I'd hem and haw and talk about professional ethics, and vague descriptions. However . . . yes, I think the boy needs help. Professional help," he added, fixing Ellen with a stern eye. "You are one of my favorite amateurs, I admit; but you keep your dainty hands off the kid. Remember Roger?"

"It would be hard to forget him."

Roger had appeared at her front door one night brandishing a knife and accusing her of betraying him with another man. Ellen always maintained that the poor boy —who was sixteen and weighed over two hundred pounds —would never have hurt her, but she didn't have the chance to find out. Jack had promptly disarmed Roger, who collapsed into a sobbing heap and was removed to the nearest psychiatric ward.

"I won't waste jargon on you," Jim went on, punctuating his remarks with jabs of the big smelly cigar he allowed himself after a meal. "You know as well as I do that the potential for violence is there. If you can persuade Uncle Whoever to call me, I'll recommend a good man. Or—hell, you've got me curious. I'll see the boy, if only for a diagnosis. Okay?"

The buzzer on the desk had sounded twice. Ellen rose.

"You're a doll. Thank you, Jim. Now you can go to your neurotic."

"I'll put her off, if—" Jim gestured toward the couch. Ellen left, laughing.

She spent the afternoon in Chevy Chase shopping and emerged from Saks in the middle of rush-hour traffic with a pale-pink chiffon "at-home" gown. It would be totally out of place in her Early American living room, and it had cost far more than she could afford to pay. She felt much better for having bought it.

Her visit with Jim or her frivolous purchase, or both, had had a therapeutic effect. Sitting in the car and watching the drizzle mist on her windshield, she could admit how reluctant she was to return to Chew's Corners. Just for that, she told herself, you can go home right now, through the worst of the traffic.

The crawling pace of cars on Wisconsin Avenue didn't bother her; she rather enjoyed having so many anonymous disinterested people around. It took almost an hour to get onto the Beltway and around to the exit, but then the skies began to clear, and by the time she neared home the sun was setting in an angry blaze of cloud and color. The rain had cleared the air. It was beautifully cool, and Ellen sang as she drove along the quiet country roads.

Her good spirits received a slight check when she found muddy footprints on her front porch. The prints were those of a man—a stupid man, for he had been unaware of the betrayal of his steps. There was a big patch of mud by one of the windows. It conjured up a singularly unpleasant picture. He had stood there for some time trying to see in and moving his feet restlessly, like an animal pawing the ground.

Nine

The next day was the kind Virginians brag about and seldom enjoy. The fresh breeze was heavy with the scents of summer, and the sun was as golden as the heavenly gates. Ellen bounded out of bed just in time to grab Ishtar, who was crouching in front of her new pink dress, eyeing it speculatively as the breeze lifted the trailing sleeves.

Ellen understood the cat's interest; for a moment the dress had looked alive, as if some invisible woman were wearing it.

She hung it in the closet and closed the door, wondering what insanity had prompted her to buy such a fragile dress when she owned a Siamese cat. Ishtar's claws weren't even clipped. The first time Ellen had tried to clip them, Ishtar cried. Ellen had never seen tears oozing out of an animal's eyes, and the sight completely demoralized her—as it was no doubt meant to do. Ishtar had walked arrogant and sharp-clawed ever since.

151

After breakfast Ellen rolled up her sleeves and started cleaning house. She had rather let things go during the sultry heat wave. The doorbell rang while she was cleaning the refrigerator. As soon as she saw the man at the door, Ellen felt sure he had been responsible for the prowling footsteps. It would be quite in character for the Reverend Hank Winckler to peer in windows. He must have been disappointed not to find an orgy going on within.

"Good morning," she said, standing squarely in the doorway. "Is there something I can do for you?"

"A pastoral call," mumbled Winckler. "Long overdue . . . meant to come before. . . ."

Stripped of his pulpit, he had lost most of his arrogance, and the chief impression now was one of slyness. His mean little eyes darted from side to side, as if trying to see past her.

"I'm sorry I can't invite you in," Ellen said. "But that would be improper, wouldn't it?"

The look that came over the thin face made Ellen dislike the man more than ever. What a dirty-minded little rat he is, she thought. But so far he had not said anything offensive, and it was hard for her to be rude without provocation. With a sigh she stepped forward, closing the door behind her.

"I'm very busy this morning," she said. "But for a few minutes . . . I suppose I ought to explain about what happened in church last week. I was taken suddenly ill."

It was not a very gracious apology, but it was the best she could do; it had cost her an effort to say that much. Winckler seemed to find it satisfactory. He smirked. He had already seated himself. Ellen took a chair as far from his as she could get, and pulled her skirt down over her knees. Winckler's eyes, frustrated, moved to her face. "I trust we will see you in church this week," he said.

"I think not. I respect the beliefs of others, but I practice my own."

"And what are your own?"

"I'm a Presbyterian," Ellen said, suppressing her annoyance.

"The nearest Presbyterian church is in Smithville."

"I know."

Winckler took a deep breath and seemed to swell.

"It is a nest of vipers and a hotbed of sinners."

"I'm sorry you think so," Ellen said.

"It will not give you what you need."

"And what is it I need?"

Winckler was not clever enough to note the change in her voice, nor would he have heeded its warning if he had. He leaned forward, his eyes devouring her face.

"Prayer. Penance. Repentance. The mortification of the flesh . . ."

The way his lips lingered over the last word solidified Ellen's mixed emotions into a hard wall of dislike. She rose. She still had control of her temper, but she could feel it slipping.

"I appreciate your concern, Mr. Winckler, but I am in no need of any of the things you suggest. And now, if you will excuse me . . ."

Winckler came toward her. He had a funny skipping walk that reminded Ellen of the movements of a multi-legged insect. Instinctively she shrank back as he thrust his face toward hers.

"Now, dear lady, don't be distressed. I know what they are saying, and believe me, I discount such talk. Mrs. Grapow is a good, devout woman, but she doesn't understand certain things, certain temptations . . . eh? It's not too late for you to cast off the Devil and seek the Lord. I'll help. I'll come at any hour of the day—or night . . . mortify the flesh. . . ."

He put his hand on Ellen's arm. His palm was hot and moist. Ellen pulled away from it.

"I think you had better go," she said.

"Now, don't be hasty." The little eyes leered. "You're

already in trouble here, dear lady. Not that I blame you," he added, belatedly sensing Ellen's mounting anger. "This sinful house is the villain. It needs exorcism—needs to be burned and sown with salt. . . . Not your fault, no, but you need my help. Prayer, that's the thing. And a few words in the right ears, eh? I can help you a lot, you know."

His hand went out again. Ellen turned and marched to the porch door. She flung it open.

"Get out," she said icily, "or I'll call the police."

From Winckler's expression she deduced that he was not wholly unacquainted with such threats. He obeyed, but on the stairs, with the screen door between them, he turned for a final word.

"You'll regret this! We don't take kindly to women like you. This is a God-fearing town, and—"

Ellen's control snapped.

"Get out of here!" she shouted. "And don't come back! If I see your hypocritical face around here again, I'll—"

Beside herself, she stooped and picked up a heavy flowerpot.

Winckler's face paled. He scuttled off down the path and disappeared from sight.

Shaking with rage, Ellen stormed back into the house and slammed the door. She was still pacing the floor and swearing when the bell rang again. Ellen marched to the door and flung it open. She was almost hoping it was the minister; she had thought of a lot more she wanted to say. But the visitor was not Mr. Winckler. It was her daughter.

The following minutes were chaotic. When Ellen had recovered sufficiently to detach herself from the enthusiastic young arms, she was so full of questions she hardly knew where to start. Instead she exclaimed,

"Oh, darling, how awful you look," and embraced Penny again.

"Thanks a lot! These are my seeing-Europe jeans—don't you get the significance of the patches? A remnant from Paris on the left knee, a scarf from Florence on my seat—"

Ellen held the girl off at arms' length.

"What a tan! You look like a gypsy. How long is it since you washed your hair? Where did you get that awful T-shirt? Is it supposed to be gray? Your toes are sticking out of those sneakers! You've lost weight. Oh, you look beautiful!"

"That's better," Penny said. She was grinning, but her eyes were suspiciously bright. "Hey, cut the maternal raptures for a minute and thank Ted for bringing me here."

Confusedly Ellen shook hands with Ted, a tall, freckled redhead. She was used to the succession of more or less anonymous boys who brought Penny to various places and then were dismissed when her needs were served, nor was she surprised when Ted refused her invitation to come in. These kids thought nothing of driving several hundred miles to pick up or deliver a friend, and most of them were wary of parents. In this case though, Ted's withdrawal might have been due to tact. As soon as he had left, mother and daughter fell into each other's arms again.

It was not until some time later that Ellen really got a grip on the conversation. Penny's battered suitcases had been carried upstairs. They were sitting in the kitchen and Penny was devouring everything in sight, with Ishtar purring like an engine on her lap and making grabs at the unguarded scraps of food.

"Haven't you got any cookies?" Penny asked pathetically. "All through Europe I dreamed of your seven-layer cookies."

"If I'd known you were coming . . ." Ellen said. "Which brings up a subject you've been trying to avoid. What's the idea of disrupting all our plans and dropping in like this?"

"It's terrible the way you hate me," Penny complained.

Ellen was already on her feet collecting ingredients. She put a stick of butter to melt in a baking pan and smiled at Penny.

"Cookies for lunch."

"I'm having lunch," said Penny, reaching for the last piece of cheese and feeding a sliver of it to Ishtar. "Oh, gol, it's good to be home. Europe was wonderful, Mom. I mean, it was really wonderful. But this is better. You and Ishtar and this great house—"

"And the cheese, and the cookies—"

"I got so lonesome," Penny said soberly. "The Emersons were swell, but. . . . I saw Jack in Rome last week."

Ellen dropped a package of butterscotch chips and bent to pick it up. Luckily she hadn't opened it yet. She did so, and finished putting her cookies together before she spoke.

"What was Jack doing in Rome?"

"Some kind of meeting," Penny said vaguely. "Seeing him just made me more homesick. Gosh, Mom, don't you miss the guys? But I guess maybe you do enjoy the peace and quiet, like Jack says."

"Your grammar is terrible." Ellen put the cookies in the oven and set the timer. "What else did Jack say?"

"Oh, he bawled me out. You know his lectures. He said I was selfish, and that I ought to let go of you as gracefully as you let me go. He said it was even harder for you; but you didn't whine about it. Was it hard, Mom?"

Ellen put her arms around the slim shoulders.

"Does that answer your question?" She straightened. "Enough of this mush. I will conquer my emotions by unpacking your suitcases."

"That'll do it," said Penny calmly.

"Do you mean you haven't done any washing since you got back?"

"Mrs. Emerson tried to talk me into it, but I resisted." Penny rose with one lithe movement, scooping up the cat and depositing her on the empty chair. "Now wait a minute, I'll do my own unpacking; some of the things in those bags will turn your hair gray."

They raced each other up the stairs, laughing.

The suitcases were almost as bad as Penny had predicted. Ellen made a show of carrying various dingy garments to the hamper with her nose in the air while Penny fished out miscellaneous gifts wrapped in tissue paper. She had presents for everyone. The prize was a particularly hideous tie with a colored representation of St. Peter's, for Jack.

"The dome is done in luminous paint," said Penny, contemplating this atrocity proudly. "It glows in the dark."

"Jack will love it."

"He'll wear it, too."

"I know. . . . Why didn't you give it to him in Rome?"

"I didn't get it till just before I left. Anyhow, he'll be home next week. Didn't he write you?"

"Yes."

"He said he'd call the minute he got in. He wants us to come into Washington and have dinner with him."

"Us? So you were planning this even then?"

"The idea had occurred to me. . . . I'm going to wash my hair, okay?"

Since this process usually took an hour or more, Ellen had time to put together one of her daughter's favorite lunches. She had no illusions about Penny's ability to eat again. She was cutting the cookies into squares when the phone rang.

"Norman! I'm so glad you're back."

"You sound glad. How flattering."

"Well, there is another reason for my mood. My daughter just arrived."

Norman laughed.

"I know."

"How?"

"The whole town knows. Did you think those loafers at the store would miss a pretty girl in a bright-red convertible? Somebody recognized her, from when she was here before. I'm glad she's here, Ellen."

"So am I," Ellen admitted. "I want you to meet her, Norman."

"Just what I had in mind. What about dinner tomorrow night? I know you two will have weeks of conversation to catch up on, or I'd suggest tonight."

Ellen accepted with pleasure. After she hung up, she remembered Tim. Frowning slightly, she went on with her cooking. She had meant to tell Norman about her visit to Jim Bishop; it might have been interpreted as unwarranted meddling, and she wanted to be candid with Norman. There was another problem. What should she tell Penny about Tim? She tried to remember what she had said in her letters, but with so many correspondents it was hard to recall what she had said to each one. She had, of course, mentioned Tim to Penny, but she was fairly sure she had not gone into detail.

She forgot about Tim when Penny burst into the kitchen with her wet hair spraying drops and exclaiming rapturously at the sight of her favorite food. For the rest of the day and far into the night she talked, and ate, and talked again, describing her European adventures. Ellen didn't have a chance to tell about *her* adventures, even if she had been inclined to do so.

Penny was already up and out when Ellen rose next morning. She went to the kitchen and was making coffee when her daughter wandered in. She was wearing the jeans again, and the sneakers; with them went a long-sleeved Greek shirt of unbleached cotton. Studying the slim figure and bright face fondly, Ellen decided Penny would look beautiful in anything—even those jeans.

"Who does the white cat belong to?" Penny asked, leaning against the stove.

"When did you see it?"

"Just now. It was sitting on the fence, but it ran off as soon as I came around the house. You've been feeding it, haven't you? Don't deny it, I know you."

"I put some of the dry cat food in a bowl out by the fence," Ellen admitted. "I don't know who the animal belongs to, but it seems wild; it must be hungry."

"It looked fat and complacent to me."

"Well, something eats the food. I don't think squirrels or rabbits like that sort of thing."

"Oh, bah. I was hoping I'd seen your ghost."

"Ghosts don't come around in the daytime."

"Since when did you become an expert on the habits of ghosts? I thought you'd have found out all about Mary by now, and you don't seem to have done a thing. Maybe I'll run into the library and do some research."

"Library, indeed. The bookmobile calls once a week at Chew's Corners. Here, eat an egg. I know you don't want it, but eat it anyway. You're too thin."

"Where is the nearest library?"

"Front Royal or Warrenton I suppose. At least twenty miles away."

"A mere fifteen-minute run in the auto," said Penny, her eyes twinkling.

"Now the truth comes out. You just want to use the car."

"I haven't driven for a month. And I'm dying to explore." Penny finished her egg in two bites and pushed her chair back.

"Okay, but be back by one, or I'll worry. And—"

"I know, I know. Drive carefully, lock the car doors, don't pick up any hitchhikers!"

Ellen watched her leave and then turned from the window with a queer sense of foreboding. Penny was a better driver than she was. Thanks to the boys, she could handle a car in any weather and change a tire faster than the average mechanic. No, it wasn't the car that worried her. It was the town.

As she worked in the kitchen, wiping up spattered bacon grease and bread crumbs, she knew she ought to have warned Penny about what she might encounter in Chew's Corners. They had had lots to talk about, but she could have made time for that subject.

She moped around the house, getting more and more nervous as the hours passed. Of course it was silly to worry. Nothing dangerous or harmful could happen to Penny. But it would be a blow to the child if she ran headlong into a cold stone wall of disapproval. She was such a friendly, outgoing girl. . . .

As always, she underestimated her young. When Penny returned, well before one o'clock, she looked calm, if rather sober. Ellen thought she had not stopped in town after all. But the girl's first words dispelled this hope.

"What have you been up to?" she asked, flinging herself into a chair. "Seducing somebody's husband, maybe?"

"What do you mean? What happened?"

"That old witch at the store refused to wait on me."

She saw Ellen wince, and began to laugh.

"Sorry, Mom; the word was ill chosen, wasn't it?"

"What did Mrs. Grapow say to you?"

"Nothing that would bring a blush to my maiden cheek."

"Penny. What did she say?"

"Among other things, she called me 'witch's brat. . . .' Now, mom, why are you looking like that? I think it's hilarious. I couldn't help laughing."

"Mrs. Grapow doesn't like to be laughed at."

"I noticed. She turned the weirdest color. Then she told me they didn't want people like us around here."

"Oh, Penny—"

"It upset me for a minute," Penny admitted. "But it was educational, you know? Now I understand how members of minority groups must feel when people spit at them for no good reason. Are you going to tell me about it, or are you still trying to protect your baby daughter from the facts of life?"

"I'm sorry," Ellen said seriously. "I had hoped you wouldn't have to encounter this, but you're quite right; I am being overprotective. It's a hard habit to break. Sit down and eat your hamburger and I'll tell you the whole story."

Her description of the fortune-telling episode fascinated Penny so much she almost forgot to eat.

"But that's fantastic. Why have you been hiding your talents from me all this time?"

Ellen slapped a plate of cookies down on the table.

"Stop it. My sense of humor on the subject is getting pretty jaundiced."

"I suppose it is." Penny looked thoughtful. "All the same, Mom, that's an impressive list of coincidences. There's something funny about the whole thing."

"I don't see anything funny about it."

"Funny-peculiar, I mean. Maybe I'll talk to some of those kids."

"I suppose you'll have to meet them eventually."

"We can't hide in the house the rest of our lives. That's what you've been doing, isn't it?"

"I guess so," Ellen admitted. "And you're right; I can't go on doing it. This will all die down in time, I'm sure."

"If you don't go on practicing witchcraft. Mom, don't get mad, but—you haven't seen anything—here in the house, I mean?"

"No, of course not."

"Oh." Penny looked disappointed. "I didn't find out anything about Mary at the library."

"Then you did go to the library."

"Would I lie to you? Sure I went. It was a bust, though. I did find out a few things about Chew's Corners, but not from books. There was this boy—"

"There always is."

"Mo-ther! It was very proper. He works at the library, that's how I met him. When he heard where I was from, he was very interested. We sat on the steps for about half an hour—he was taking his break, you see—and he told me things."

"What sort of things?"

"Mostly about the church," said Penny, reaching for a cookie. "It's a *cause célèbre*—is that the word I want?"

"I doubt it."

"Well, you know what I mean. Everybody around here knows about it. It sounds really wild. I can hardly wait to go."

"You'll have to contain yourself. I'm afraid. Neither one of us is going back to that place."

She told Penny about her one unfortunate visit. She tried to make a funny story of it, but Penny was not deceived. Knitting her brows, the girl said,

"It sounds horrible. I wish I'd been with you."

"I'm glad you weren't. You wouldn't have walked out in silence."

"No," said Penny significantly. "Well, if you're going to deprive me of that pleasure, I'll have to find other means of entertainment. There was a blond boy in town, unloading boxes at the garage. . . ."

She grinned at her mother. Ellen's heart gave a sudden bound and then subsided. Tim wouldn't be working at the garage.

"That must have been Steve. He's taken."

"Are you challenging me? No, sit still, I'll clear the table. I plan to assume my rightful place as the mature daughter of the house."

"Sounds great. What are you planning for this afternoon? The kitchen floor needs—"

"I'll make some more cookies," said Penny, taking the last one off the plate. "What are we going to have for dinner?"

"We are dining out. I told you about my neighbor, Mr. McKay."

"Oh, good. That saves me the trouble of planning an encounter. I promised Jack a report as soon as possible."

"You're terrible," said Ellen helplessly.

"Worse than you think. Hasn't Mr. McKay got a nephew?"

"Yes. The local delinquent."

"You mentioned him. He sounds fascinating."

"I made him sound too fascinating," Ellen said grimly. "Since we're letting our hair down, I might as well go all the way."

She told Penny about the tortured animal. She did not expurgate the story, and the brutal details had the desired effect; but she felt a pang as she watched the amusement fade from Penny's ingenuous face.

"Mom, how awful."

"It was."

"Awful for you. . . . Really, when I think of me and Jack in Rome getting sentimental about your quiet, peaceful life in the country. . . . What a place this is!"

Ellen said no more. She did not intend to forbid Penny to associate with Tim in so many words; like the old story of the children and the beans in the nose, suggestion sometimes brought on the very result you wanted to avoid. She rather thought she had accomplished her purpose effectively, and was sure of it when Penny took only ten minutes to get ready for their dinner date, instead of the hour she spent when there was a young male in prospect. She looked very sweet and pretty, though, Ellen thought; in deference to her mother she was wearing a dress instead of the inevitable jeans. Jack had once innocently mistaken this garment for a bathing suit; it had narrow straps, a puckered bodice, and a skirt that barely covered the matching panties, so his error was understandable.

"Let's take Ishtar," Penny said, as the insinuating animal wound itself around her ankles, purring throatily and trying to look pathetic. "She doesn't want to be left alone."

Ellen scowled at the cat, who had flung herself down on her back, with her pale stomach trustingly exposed.

"It's almost as if she knew where we were going. Didn't I tell you about Norman's ailurophobia?"

"Norman's what?"

They started along the path while Ellen explained. Penny found the whole thing quite amusing, but forgot her contempt for elderly weakness as the woods cast their spell.

"I can see why you love it," she said softly, pointing out a cardinal sitting on a twist of feathery foliage.

The comment was a bit ironic, for they were approaching the spot where Ellen had found Tim torturing the animal. Naturally she made no reference to it, but she had to force herself to walk briskly past the spot without stopping or turning aside. A quick glance had told her that the path was empty; not even a bloodstain remained. But of course, she reminded herself, some scavenger must have removed the body long before.

Penny's first sight of Norman's house produced a one-word appraisal.

"Ostentatious," she remarked.

They were halfway up the drive when a sudden cacophony of barking made Ellen start. The dogs really did make the most diabolical sound!

"The Hound of the Baskervilles," exclaimed Penny, echoing her thoughts. "Of course. I should have known nothing in this town would be normal. Does Mr. McKay have long, sharp white teeth and hair on the palms of his—"

Ellen answered with a scream. Around the corner of the house, howling furiously, came the dogs. They ran straight at the two women.

Ellen grabbed at Penny, with some idea of pushing the

girl behind her. The dogs were not greeting guests, they were ready to attack. Penny stood like a rock. Only her arms moved. One went out, fist extended. The other encircled her mother.

The dogs were only a few feet away when a shout stopped them both so suddenly that they spun absurdly on their haunches. At least they would have looked absurd if it had not been for their gaping mouths and sharp teeth. They sat still, panting, and Norman came running down the hill toward them.

"Are you all right, Ellen? My God, I was scared. I don't know how they got loose; I fastened the chains myself an hour ago." He turned to Penny. "This is a fine welcome, child. Do forgive us."

"I'm not afraid of dogs." Penny said calmly. "They are handsome specimens."

"They wouldn't have hurt you," Norman assured her. "They know your mother, and as soon as they recognized her . . ."

The argument didn't even convince him; it would have taken a very nearsighted dog with an atrophied sense of smell to fail to recognize Ellen long before his shouts had stopped the animals.

Norman sent the dogs back to their kennel with a sharp command and escorted his guests to the house. He offered Penny a glass of sherry, which she politely refused. She did not refuse the hors d'oeuvres Martha brought in, but her compliments failed to win a smile from the cook. One glance at Penny's skirt length was all Martha needed; Ellen could practically read her mind.

Deliberately, Ellen took a back seat and let the other two talk. She was curious as to how they would react to one another, but she couldn't be sure of the feelings hidden under their facade of good manners. Penny was socially adept and naturally gregarious; she could talk to an Eskimo or a man from Mars, with gestures, if need be. Norman's poise was admirable; however, he was a little

too jolly and avuncular, a little patronizing. Ellen hoped
her daughter would be charitable about judging Norman;
how could he know how to talk to young people when his
nephew had no friends and he himself was virtually sub-
vocal?

Then Penny stopped talking in the middle of a sentence. Her eyes widened. A ray of sunlight falling on her
face made it look luminous—haloed. Following her gaze,
Ellen felt a sharp pain in that internal organ which is erroneously called the heart.

Tim's bare feet had left a trail of dust this time. His
shirt looked like the one Ellen had seen him wearing for
the past month. To Ellen's admittedly biased eyes he
looked like a big, dirty, disturbed adolescent. But his wide
blue eyes had the same hazed stare as Penny's, and Ellen
knew she was seeing a phenomenon she had read about in
a thousand novels, but had never really believed.

"What lady's that, which doth enrich the hand of
yonder knight? O! she doth teach the torches to burn
bright! . . ."

Such was her state of mind that she would not have
been surprised to hear Tim repeat Romeo's honeyed
words. His reaction was more prosaic—a mumbled "hi."
But Ellen was not deceived. The monosyllable fell on her
ears like the sound of a tolling bell.

"Hi," said Penny.

The sun was not shining on her face. It was lit from
within.

"Here's the young lady we've been looking forward to
meeting," Norman said heartily. "Penny, meet Tim. You
two are about the same age, I think."

Ellen stared at him in amazement. Had he missed the
miracle, that he could babble on so idiotically? Maybe *she*
was crazy! Looking at the young people now, she could
see nothing unusual in their behavior. Tim slouched to a
chair and fell into it. Penny took another smoked oyster.

The evening passed in a horrible haze for Ellen. One

emotion predominated—a growing annoyance with Norman. She could understand his good cheer, for Tim behaved with what was, for him, utter charm. He did not scintillate during dinner, but neither did he indulge in the jabs and insults that had marked Ellen's first meal at the house. Ellen would have found Norman's pleasure pathetic if he had not done everything possible to promote the rapport between the two young people. After dinner he suggested that Tim take Penny upstairs to show her his record collection; and then Ellen rose in the majesty of offended motherhood.

"We must be going. Penny is still short on sleep, and we have an early appointment tomorrow."

Her tone dripped icicles. Norman quailed.

"Sorry. I didn't think—"

"Just a minute, Mom," Penny coaxed. "Tim said I could borrow an old Beatles album. It's one I don't have."

How the two had arrived at this understanding Ellen did not know; she had tried her hardest to overhear every word they said to one another.

"All right," she said ungraciously. "But hurry up."

Tim had not spoken. He didn't seem to be aware that there were other people in the room. When the two had disappeared up the stairs, Ellen turned on her host.

"Let's get one thing straight, Norman. I will not encourage a friendship between those two."

"So that's where charity stops," Norman said softly.

"With Penny—yes. I'm still interested in Tim. In fact . . ."

She was tempted not to mention her visit to Jim Bishop. It weakened her position and she knew it, but honesty had to be served. Her tone, as she explained, was mild and defensive.

"If anyone but you had done such a thing, I'd resent it," Norman said. "However, I've taken steps myself. I've persuaded a man in New York to see Tim. Couldn't get an appointment for a couple of weeks, but I'll get Tim up there then if I have to drag him. I can see how you feel about your daughter; but can you blame me for grasping at any straw? Something like this could be just what Tim needs."

"A guiding star?" said Ellen sarcastically. "I can see how you feel, too; we're an understanding couple, aren't we? But you still believe in fairy tales. It's only in fiction —Victorian fiction—that the love of a good woman redeems a bad man. If you think—"

She stopped at the sound of footsteps on the stairs. Penny had obeyed her mother's order to hurry.

Norman insisted on driving them home. Ellen couldn't talk freely with Penny in the back seat; she thanked Norman coolly and watched the car drive away before she followed her daughter into the house.

Penny was in the kitchen, foraging in the refrigerator.

"Want some ice cream?" she asked.

"After that dinner? No, thanks. I'll have a cup of tea, though."

"You and your tea."

Penny put the kettle on. Seated at the table watching her, Ellen was reassured. The glow was gone—if it had ever existed, except in her own mind.

"What did you think of him?" she asked guilefully.

"Your boyfriend?" Penny grinned. "He's what your generation calls a real catch, isn't he? That house! And that car! He must be loaded."

"Don't you think he's a little stuffy?"

"He's not used to people under thirty," Penny said. "If he'd had a houseful of them, like Jack, he'd know how to talk to them."

"He doesn't know how to handle young people. I've often wanted to see Tim's room myself," said Ellen craftily. "It might be indicative of their relationship, if you know what I mean."

"It's indicative of generosity, if that's what *you* mean.

Gosh, that guy has everything! Records and a great big hi-fi and his own TV and a posh guitar—you name it, he's got it."

"Really?"

"Uh-huh." Penny's back was still turned. "Too much stuff. Like Uncle Normie is trying to make up for some other lack."

"Now, Penny—"

"I know. Slick, superficial analysis. He's never been married, has he?"

"Who, Norman?" Ellen was a little bewildered by Penny's abrupt changes of subject. This was not the way she had meant the conversation to go.

"I think," she said slowly, "that he was in love with Tim's mother. He still speaks of her in a way that—well, I found it very moving."

"His brother's wife, eh?"

Penny's voice was muffled as she inspected the contents of the refrigerator, but her tone jarred Ellen.

"You needn't try to be cynical," she said sharply. "I may be mistaken. In any case I'm sure there was nothing improper about it. She didn't respond. Norman said she laughed at him. I found that moving, too. It accounts, to some extent, for his generosity to Tim. He wants desperately to win the boy's love."

"How noble," said Penny, her face still concealed. "Very noble. A lot of men would resent being laughed at by the woman they loved."

Ellen abandoned subtlety.

"What do you think about Tim?"

"He's got problems, all right."

"He was on his best behavior tonight. I think he took a fancy to you."

Penny turned, holding a bottle of milk. Her face was vivid with amusement.

"Mom, where do you get those gems? Took a fancy, for heaven's sake!"

"I'd be careful," Ellen said.

She hadn't intended to be so blunt. Penny's reaction was predictable.

"I can take care of myself," she said, with a toss of her head.

"The common delusion of youth—"

"What about the common phobia of mothers?"

Ellen was silent. There was no point in forbidding Penny to see Tim. Short of following the girl like a prison guard, she could not prevent a meeting, and she knew the charm of forbidden fruit. Her distress showed in her face; Penny leaned over suddenly and hugged her.

"Mom, believe me—there is nothing to worry about."

"Don't you find him attractive?"

"Oh, sure. But I'm a little too sophisticated to be swept off my feet by that blond Heathcliffe look. Didn't you tell me Norman has taken him to several psychiatrists?"

"Yes, some of the best. Abrahamson, for one."

"Mmm." Penny seemed to lose interest. "You know, I am tired. Mind if I play that record, if I do it quietly?"

Ellen's conscious mind was reassured by the conversation; but it is not surprising that her dreams that night followed a certain pattern.

She ran frantically through a darkness made hideous by the howling of the great dogs. It seemed that she ran for hours, groping and leaden-footed, knowing all the while that she would be too late. The dogs had their prey down on the ground when she finally found them. The scene was lit by a sickly glow, which emanated from the beasts themselves. Their bodies hid the thing they tore at; only two outflung arms and a great sweep of black hair were visible. But when the dogs disappeared, with the perversity of dream animals, Ellen saw that the victim's face was not Penny's. It was that of an older woman, someone she had never seen before. Ellen's dream mind knew the victim, though, and the horror and despair that gripped her were not lessened by the recognition. As she stood swaying over the body, the nightmare reached its climax. The eyes of the dead witch opened and she began to laugh.

Ellen struggled up out of the dream, but the laughter came with her. Still half asleep and limp with horror, she stumbled out of bed and ran across the hall.

Penny slept with a night light, a cracked plastic replica of Donald Duck, which she had cherished since childhood. Its faint light shone on her placid face and slender, relaxed body. Her slow breathing lifted the ruffles of the skimpy short nightgown.

But somewhere in the house something was still laughing.

Ten

Ellen was becoming adept at rationalizing the eccentricities of her house. The eerie laughter was simply an auditory hallucination that lingered after the nightmare that had produced it. Yet Ellen couldn't help regarding the laughter, and the dream, as warnings—not from the world beyond, but from that convenient hypothetical source, her subconscious.

She took steps. She filled the next days with as much activity as possible, so that Penny would not have time for many solitary excursions. She invited friends out for the following weekend. She didn't care much for the couple, and Penny despised their teen-age son; but every other eligible boy was on vacation.

Ellen knew she was fighting an enemy so tenuous she couldn't even be sure it existed. One moment of seeming magic, one look on a girl's face and a fleeting expression in a boy's eyes . . . and a crazy instinct that shouted down every sensible objection. Or was it fear instead of instinct —the common phobia of mothers, as Penny called it?

Not only was the enemy tenuous, it was strategically superior. Penny did go out alone. The very morning after the dream, when Ellen slept late, she came down to find a note on the bulletin board saying that Penny had gone for a walk. The girl came back with her legs scratched and her fingers stained by blackberries. She readily admitted that she had encountered Tim in the woods. The admission reassured Ellen, and so did Penny's questions, which tended toward the clinical rather than the romantic. She was even more reassured when Penny's interest turned from Tim to what she called the witch bit.

"It's time we got to work on those prophecies," she announced one morning at breakfast. "I want you to give me as résumé of what you said to those kids."

"What are you up to now?" Ellen asked curiously.

After a writhing struggle Penny produced a small notebook from the back pocket of her tight jeans.

"I am pursuing original research," she said, with dignity. "Try to remember exactly what you said."

Ellen obeyed, happy to encourage a relatively harmless interest. Penny scribbled industriously, her long hair falling about her face as she bent over the notebook on the table.

"Is that all?" she asked finally. "Okay. Now can I have the car?"

"Cherry pie for supper?" Ellen asked innocently.

Penny grinned.

"The cherries are finished. Black raspberries, maybe. How come you always know what I'm up to?"

"I thought of doing it myself," Ellen admitted. "Checking with the kids, one by one, to find out what really happened. But are you sure—"

"I'm not afraid of them," Penny said scornfully. "In fact, from your letters they sound like fairly nice guys. I thought I'd go to the orchard and look Joyce up first."

"I guess it can't do any harm. Actually, the idea is a good one. People are apt to be more restrained in their descriptions when they see someone writing it down."

"Exactly."

This time Ellen awaited the girl's return with more curiosity than trepidation. Penny had apparently found the orchard great fun; she came in staggering under an armload of fruit that made Ellen protest.

"We'll never eat all that! Are you planning to make jam?"

"Pies for the weekend. That creepy Morrie loves pie."

Humming, she began to unpack boxes of berries.

Ellen's curiosity got the better of her.

"Did you have any luck?"

"Depends on what you call luck. Joyce is nice. I like her. She sent you a message."

"Oh?"

"She said she wanted to come out and see you, but she was afraid it would cause more trouble. She's sorry about how things happened. But—" Penny turned from the sink, where she had begun to pick over her berries. Her eyes were grave. "She's scared, Mom. They all are. And in a way, I don't blame them. You know what the scariest thing is?"

"Prudence," said Ellen.

"Oh, that one." Penny dismissed Prudence with a contemptuous curl of the lip. "I stopped at the drugstore for a cup of coffee and got a look at her. She's just a common-garden-variety hysteric. Remember Beth Barnes?"

"The one you played with when you were four, who had screaming fits when you tried to take your own toys? I do. I also remember the Salem witch trials, and the hysterical young girls who swore away the lives of several people."

"Sure, they can be dangerous. But they are understandable. No," said Penny. "The scary thing is that letter Chuck Yates got from Harvard. You know he carries it around with him?"

"That's not surprising."

"The surprising thing is that he got it at all. After Joyce told me how dumb the guy is, I thought maybe someone was playing a joke on him. But he showed me the letter."

"And?"

"Regular letterhead stationery, from H.U. itself."

There was a queer note in Penny's voice—almost a tone of satisfaction. She went on.

"I haven't seen Sue Ann's necklace yet, but the others have. They described it to me. The pearl is real, her folks took it to a jeweler. None of the kids could afford such an expensive joke."

"You did accomplish a lot," Ellen said.

"That's why I bought all that fruit," Penny explained. "I had to to cool the guy who owns the orchard. He came out while I was talking to the kids and bawled them out for loafing. Hey, Jack is supposed to arrive today, isn't he?"

Ellen accepted the change of subject. She wasn't eager to continue the old one.

"Yes, I expect we'll hear from him tomorrow."

She didn't really expect Jack to wait that long, and she wasn't disappointed. The phone rang at about ten that night, and the first word, in the familiar voice, told Ellen that the weeks without him hadn't changed her feelings in the slightest.

"I'm at the airport," he explained. "Couldn't wait. What? Oh, sure, they sent a car; the chauffeur is pacing up and down in front of the booth right now, so I can't talk long. Can you come in for lunch tomorrow?"

"I'd love to. But aren't you going to be tied up for lunch? Would dinner be better?"

"Lunch and dinner would be best. But only if you'll stay overnight; I don't want you driving back so late."

"We'll make it lunch, then, and go on from there," Ellen said, abandoning good sense. "Penny's here, you know."

"That brat?" said Jack, who knew quite well from the heavy breathing that Penny was on the upstairs extension. "Well, if you can't get rid of her I expect you'll have to bring her along."

Jack had refused to go to Howard Johnson's, so they had agreed to meet at a favorite French restaurant in Georgetown. When they got into the city they were enveloped in muggy heat and exhaust fumes. Georgetown looked dusty and wilted. But the restaurant, on a side street shaded by trees, was pleasantly cool; and Jack was waiting for them.

He embraced both of them and made sarcastic comments about the effect of country living on their figures.

"I wish I could say the same for you," Ellen said. "You've lost weight, Jack."

"I don't mind being bald, but I won't be bald and fat. Ellen, Ellen—you are the best sight I've seen for weeks."

It took them most of the meal to catch up with family news. The boys were all happy and working hard. Jack hoped to meet Arthur in New York on his way back.

"Which is tomorrow," he said, his smile fading. "Some damn fool thing has come up, and I must be in Paris the following day. It means no dinner tonight, I'm afraid. Some jackass has called a meeting."

"You know all these Georgetown shops are bugged," said Penny solemnly. "Better watch what you say."

"I didn't mention the jackass's name."

"Oh, darn. I was hoping you'd be able to come for the weekend," Ellen said.

"Maybe I can run down for a few hours. I'll be back in Washington Saturday."

"Jack, that's terrible. You can't go racing around the world like that!"

"No sweat," Jack said cheerfully.

"Is something wrong?" Ellen asked.

"Just a minor diplomatic flap." He smiled at her. "It's not World War Three, my dear, if that's what you mean. Not nearly as interesting as your activities. What's the latest news? Raised any storms lately?"

Ellen sat back and let Penny tell the tale. It was an accurate, if somewhat sensational, account; Jack continued to smile as he listened with the concentration that was part of his charm. But he watched Ellen out of the corner of his eye, and when Penny had finished, he said,

"It's a weird situation, all right. Is the whole town crazy?"

"Oh, no," Penny said demurely. "Mom's new boyfriend is a very solid citizen."

"Now, just a minute," Ellen began.

"Quiet," Jack said severely. "I've been meaning to look into this. All right, Penny, let's have the facts—name, age, credit rating. . . ."

While Ellen expostulated, Penny gave a complete report, including a physical description.

"He's got lots of hair," she added maliciously. "Long and thick and wavy, the kind you like to run your fingers through. . . ."

"Probably a wig. The name is vaguely familiar. I don't know anything derogatory about him." Jack brightened. "But maybe I can dig up something."

Ellen rose.

"If you two are going to talk such nonsense, I'll leave you. Penny?"

"I don't have to," said Penny.

When Ellen came back, the two heads were close together. She was fairly sure they had been talking about her. There was no more time; Ellen suspected that Jack had put off an important meeting in order to see them. As she watched his broad back retreating down the street, to a corner where he could hope to get a taxi, a wave of desolation swept over her. No matter how often she saw him, the hours would be snatched from a life that no longer included her.

ii

Over Ellen's protests, Penny went to town next morning.

"I want them to get used to seeing me around," she explained. "And I've got a new technique with Mrs. Grapow. I walk into the store, take the stuff I want off the shelves, and put the money on the counter. She stands there mumbling at me and waving her arms. It's fascinating."

But she returned long before Ellen expected her, so excited that she let the screen door slam on Ishtar's tail. After the outraged feline had been caught and soothed, Penny turned to her mother.

"Guess what? Somebody broke into the store last night."

"Burglary?"

"Not exactly. There were four-letter words written all over the walls in purple Magic Marker. Also some upside-down crosses, and things like that."

"I suppose they think I did it," Ellen said wearily.

"That's one theory. Tim is also a hot favorite. Some people think it was both of you, in collusion."

"Of all the wild ideas—"

"You went to his rescue the day he got hit by the stone," Penny reminded her. "You know, this town is a seminar in mob psychology. I'm beginning to realize why they crucified Jesus. He was kind to the pariahs, the outcasts. He made the self-righteous stone throwers feel guilty, so they hated him."

"I'm flattered by the comparison," Ellen said, only half in jest. "Honey, please don't go to town again."

"I'm not in any danger," said Penny. Ellen looked at her sharply; had there been some emphasis on the pronoun? Before she could ask, Penny went on, "Who's the skinny little man who sounds like Hitler and looks as if he were put together out of bits and pieces?"

"You've been reading my mind. It can only be the pastor, Mr. Winckler."

"I thought so. He was holding forth on the porch of the store, to an admiring crowd of ten toothless old gents. I expected to hear them all yell '*Sieg heil!*'"

"What was he haranguing about? Me?"

"Yep. What happened? He made a pass, and you gave him a karate chop?"

Ellen gasped.

"If there's a witch in this family, it's you."

"Elementary psychology, Mom."

"You're so smart you worry me."

Penny's young face was grim.

"You haven't seen anything yet."

Ellen half expected an irate delegation of townspeople, headed by a Bible-bearing pastor; but the rest of the week passed without incident and Penny reported that the town was quiet. There was no word from Norman. Ellen wondered whether he was angry, but she didn't really care. She was in an odd state of mind. Once she had spoken of a mounting storm, of feeling it approach "in the air." She felt it now, like electricity on her skin. She dreamed nightly—exhaustingly. None of the dreams were as ghastly as the first one, but they were all disquieting, and the ones she couldn't remember, when she awoke the next morning, left the strongest sense of discomfort. The dreams she did remember had a common theme. She was trying to reach a place, or a person, in time to prevent some approaching tragedy.

Yet when she faced her real, waking worries, they seemed trivial. What was she concerned about? The antagonism of the townspeople was vexing and mildly inconvenient, but no more. People didn't burn witches in this day and age. As for Penny and Tim, that was even more ridiculous. She had no solid evidence that they had any kind of—what was the word the kids used?—relationship. And if they did, what of it? Tim wasn't the friend she would have chosen for her daughter, but Penny was sound. She had probably dated boys who had equally serious problems. God knows there were plenty of them these days.

So Ellen walked through the days waiting for something she couldn't define. The weekend began to look like an island of refuge. Friends from the real, sane world outside—and the hope of a visit from Jack.

On Friday she awoke late—a frequent occurrence, now that she was sleeping so badly—to find that Penny had gone out. The weather was cooler and slightly overcast; it felt refreshing after the muggy heat of the preceding week. Ellen decided to take a walk. She wasn't looking for Penny; it was simply that she hadn't been in the woods for some time.

As she crossed the lawn she heard a gun go off somewhere in the woods. It was not the first time she had heard gunfire on her land, though Ed Salling had assured her the legal hunting season was still some months away. She had posted signs, but she knew this was an inadequate measure, as were her unsuccessful attempts to catch the hunter in the act. The local people knew the terrain better than she did and could easily evade her.

Her failures didn't keep her from continuing to try, though. Aside from her concern for the animals, it was annoying to have people shooting off guns while she and Penny and Ishtar were within range.

As she stood looking at the trees, she heard another

shot. Ellen started to run. She was angry and spoiling for a fight, though she didn't expect to obtain that pleasure. When the third shot rang out, she ducked involuntarily; it sounded as if it had gone off right beside her. She ran on, making no attempt to move noiselessly; in fact, she began to shout. She didn't want to be mistaken for a game animal.

She saw the man among the trees before he saw her. His carelessness told her of his probable state even before he turned a red, sweating face in her direction. Yes, he was drunk. She was not surprised, for she had recognized the gross, fat body and filthy hunting jacket he habitually wore. It was Muller, the father of Prudence and Bob and the husband of the gray-faced woman she had met at the store. Ellen had seen him in town, identifying him by his state of inebriation and his resemblance to his son; and she had understood why Mrs. Muller's eyes had that look.

He stood staring stupidly at her, the shotgun wobbling in his hand. He's too drunk to hit anything, Ellen thought disgustedly; thank God for that. She advanced toward him, pushing branches and vines away as she moved. Muller turned. The muzzle of the gun pointed straight at Ellen.

Ellen knew something about guns. Jack refused to have one in the house, but the summer before he had taken them all to a rifle range and taught them how to load and fire several types of weapons. Even so, her act was foolhardy. She would never have done it if she hadn't been so angry. Muller's drunkenness was the last straw. Sober poachers were bad enough, but this sodden idiot was a real menace.

She reached out and grabbed the gun. Muller's reflexes were in poor shape; by the time he reacted, Ellen was several yards away, with the shotgun firmly in her grasp.

"Stand still," she said sharply. "I'm not used to this thing. It could go off."

Muller licked his lips. He was a revolting spectacle with his greasy, unshaven face and his fat belly wobbling above his belt.

"Whassa matter?" he demanded. "Tha's mine. Gimme it back."

"This land is mine. You are trespassing. I could have you arrested."

"Now you look here," Muller began.

Ellen shifted the gun to her shoulder. She had no intention of firing it; she had never handled a shotgun, and she suspected that the recoil would knock her off her feet. But Muller was too drunk and too stupid to figure that out. According to local gossip, he had one other interest besides cruelty, and as he studied Ellen's face she saw his expression alter.

"Nice pretty lady like you shouldn't shoot people," he mumbled. "Let's be friends, huh? Have a li'l drink together, talk nice. . . ."

He staggered toward her, his face made even uglier by what he clearly believed to be a seductive smile. One hand fumbled in his pocket. Ellen had seen the bulge and was not surprised to have her suspicion confirmed. He carried his bottle with him.

"Take one more step and I'll shoot," she said clearly. There was no point in being subtle with this clod; she added, slowly and distinctly, "You smell. You make me sick. If I ever catch you on my property again, I'll have you locked up. You won't be able to get liquor in jail."

Muller began to whine, pleading for mercy and mentioning his six starving children. Ellen ignored him. He was only dangerous when he held a weapon.

Dubiously she studied the gun. She didn't want to take it home with her; Muller might be inspired to come looking for it, since it was obviously dear to him. A sex symbol, no doubt. He was probably impotent without his gun. Nor was she willing to hand it back loaded. After some fumbling she located the breech and removed the shells.

She put them in her pocket and threw the empty gun into the underbrush, noting, with satisfaction, that it landed in a clump of poison ivy. Muller howled as if she had struck him.

"Now get out," Ellen said. "If you're off my property in ten minutes, I won't call the police; but if I hear another shot around here, I'll have you arrested."

Muller was pawing around in the poison ivy when she left.

After some thought Ellen decided to call the police after all. She did not mention Muller's name, feeling there was no point in rousing his hostility, but the state trooper knew Chew's Corners well.

"Probably Muller," he said casually. "Don't worry, ma'am, he's not dangerous. This isn't the first complaint we've had. He doesn't go back to places after he's been warned off. Too big a coward. I'll read him a lecture next time I see him."

"I wouldn't want him to think—"

"Well, sure, I won't say you called. Though there's nothing to worry about with Muller. Like I said, he's too chicken to hurt anybody."

Ellen sincerely hoped he was right.

Most days are mixtures of good and bad, but sometimes there are Jonah days, when trivial irritations pile up until they weigh more heavily than a catastrophe. Friday was such a day for Ellen. Penny didn't come back until afternoon, which would have rated a lecture in any case; her encounter with Muller then gave Ellen another cause for worry, so that by the time Penny arrived, her nerves were stretched to the breaking point. She shouted at Penny; and Penny, too well trained to shout back, stormed off to her room and spent the rest of the day there.

Jack called that evening to say he couldn't make it for the weekend. He hoped to get down to see them for a few hours on Sunday, but Ellen knew by his tone that the hope was a faint one. He sounded depressed, and only Ellen's disinclination to worry him kept her from crying into and onto the telephone. Without Jack, and in her present mood, the visitors were going to be an unmitigated bore. She tried to console herself with the thought that they were only coming for the day, not for the whole weekend, but it was a small comfort. Impulsively she reached for the phone and called Norman. He was at home, and accepted her invitation for dinner with seeming pleasure, although Ellen warned him that the other guests were not brilliant conversationalists.

The day ended with a repetition of the same dream that had begun her cycle of nightmares. If anything, the atmosphere of this dream was more agonizing than the first had been; the woods were darker, the howling louder, the anguished dread more intense. And when she awoke, sweating with terror, the house rang with the same echo of mocking laughter. It was too much for Ellen. She pulled the sheet over her head and cowered in bed until the laughter died.

iii

She awoke the next morning with a dull headache and a sour taste in her mouth. Penny was repentant and full of zeal; with her help Ellen got the cleaning and cooking done, so that she was able to receive her guests with relative goodwill.

By evening the headache was back. The Randolphs were not only boring, they were a pain in the neck. Betty was the daughter of Ellen's mother's oldest friend. She had ignored Ellen when the latter was a struggling young divorcee, but when Ellen moved in with Jack and the boys, Betty had suddenly become very friendly. Her husband worked for the State Department, which explained some of Betty's fondness for Ellen; but Jack consistently ignored Betty's hints. He told Ellen that Bob was an incompetent jerk, whom he wouldn't recommend for dog catcher. Their son was a chip off the old block, and Ellen privately agreed with Penny's abhorrence of the boy. Like his parents, Morrie was overweight and puffy from lack of exercise. He had fat, clumsy hands, and a paucity of conversational resources that was outstanding, even in his generally inarticulate peer group.

The Randolphs' idea of exercise consisted of a gentle stroll around the yard. They refused to enter the woods. All they wanted to do was sit on the porch drinking gin and tonic and discussing the latest disasters among their circle of acquaintances—alcoholism, divorce, delinquent offspring, and financial distress.

When Norman arrived, Ellen greeted him with more than her usual enthusiasm, and Norman responded gallantly. Betty's eyes narrowed as she considered Norman's clothes, his car, and his good looks; Ellen knew Betty would be on the telephone all the next day reporting Ellen's latest conquest, but she didn't care. She didn't even mind Norman's proprietorial air. It was natural for him to take on some of the functions of a host, opening wine bottles and preparing drinks. His ease of manner and conversation turned the evening into a qualified success, and she appreciated him all the more because her family had failed her. Jack had not come, and Penny sat like a lump in the corner, watching the adults as if they were monkeys in a zoo. She refused to entertain Morrie, but she helped serve the meal, which was praised by all parties.

Ellen could never remember how the conversation turned to the supernatural. Betty had been interested in the occult, before she took up Yoga and acupuncture; she could still talk learnedly of cusps and astrological houses, of discarnates and ectoplasm. Her husband scoffed at her hobbies, but Ellen sometimes wondered if he wasn't even more gullible than his wife. She had once seen Bob sneaking out of a palmist's establishment in Bethesda.

When she first saw the house, Betty had immediately pronounced it "just the place for a ghost." After dinner she brought the subject up àgain. Or *was* it Betty? Ellen wasn't following the conversation. She was counting the hours until her guests could be expected to depart, and thinking wearily of the stack of dirty dishes in the kitchen. Betty never offered to help with the cleaning up.

Then a name penetrated her absorption. Norman was telling the Randolphs about Mary Baumgartner.

Ellen studied the faces of the others: Norman's deceptively youthful features, moving animatedly as he gave the story the full treatment; Betty's wide-eyed stare; Bob's gaping interest—for he had forgotten his pretended skepticism, and looked like a medieval peasant listening to the miracles of the saints. Penny's face was a blank. She made no comment, and when someone suggested a séance, Ellen's was the only dissenting voice.

The Randolphs overruled her. Ellen gave in with a shrug, but as the laughing group trooped into the dining room, Ellen felt a premonitory quiver of uneasiness.

The dining room was one of her least favorite rooms. It was rather dark even in daylight, with its low-beamed ceiling and small windows. The windows were now wide open; it was still hot, although night had fallen.

They took their places around the oval table. Norman dimmed the lights. The boys had installed a dimmer when they added their finishing touches to the house. Ellen seldom used it; she didn't like the sickly half-light. "If I want atmosphere, I'll use candles," she was wont to say. But the light was effective for the present purpose. Its fading seemed to lower a barrier against the dark, which seeped foglike through the open windows.

"Wait a minute," Betty said. "We haven't decided on a procedure. What are we going to do, just sit around in a circle holding hands?"

"That's okay with me," said Morrie, leering.

"Now, Morrie," said his mother absently.

"I'm not the expert," Norman said. "I thought that's what people did at séances."

"Only if there is a strong trance medium present," Betty explained. "I don't suppose you . . ."

"Good heavens, no," Norman said.

"Then we need something like a Ouija board."

"There's no such thing in the house," Ellen said.

"No home should be without one," said Bob.

"Now, Bob. I don't suppose you have any alphabet cards either, Ellen."

"No."

"We could make some."

"It would take too long," Bob objected. He was as fascinated as his wife.

"I read about something once." Norman's voice had the polite detachment of a host trying to accommodate an unreasonable request from a guest. "You fasten two slates together so they can't be tampered with, and call on the spirits. Sometimes they will write a message on the inner surface."

"I don't imagine Ellen has any slates, either," said Betty critically. "Too bad, because the writing . . . writing, of course! How about automatic writing?"

"What's that?" Norman asked.

"You must clear your mind and relax," Betty explained. "Hold a pencil loosely in your right hand. If contact is made, the communicating spirit will use your hand to write a message."

"I don't think I like that," Norman said. "I am not keen on letting anybody, or anything, use my body."

"Amen," said Ellen heartily.

As she should have known, opposition only made Betty more stubborn.

"It's a marvelous idea. We must all try it. Ellen, paper and pencils——"

A rumble of thunder interrupted her. Ellen's skin prickled.

"I ought to close the windows," she muttered.

"Not yet; it's too hot. Haven't you got any paper?"

"I'll get it," Penny said.

"There's some stationery in the hall desk," Ellen said resignedly.

The pencils took longer to find; it is surprising how few households can produce half a dozen functional pencils. But Betty insisted that ball-point pens were inappropriate; the hand had to be relaxed and the pressure light.

Finally they were all equipped, and Norman went back to the light switch. He was smiling, and Ellen silently blessed him for his skepticism.

"Is this dark enough?" he asked, turning the switch. "I understand the spirits don't like much light."

"Turn it all the way off," Betty said. "It is easier to make contact in the dark. Anyhow," she added, with a belated flash of caution, "it minimizes the possibility of fraud if we can't see what we're doing."

"No," Ellen said, as Norman's hand moved the switch. But her voice was too low; it was drowned in the general exclamations, as the dark rushed in and covered them.

It was odd how the absence of light altered people and places. The room felt smaller. It even smelled differently to Ellen; under the lingering odors of good food and fresh furniture polish, she caught a whiff of something old and dank, like wet brick. As her eyes adjusted, she saw the others as featureless silhouettes, but there was nothing remotely familiar about any of the shapes. She gasped as a sulfurous glow of light momentarily illumined the faces; in that ominous glimmer they looked alien and diabolical. The light faded and was followed by thunder.

"Perfect atmosphere," said Norman's voice coolly. "Ellen, I'll bet you conjured up a storm for us."

Ellen didn't answer. There was a hoarse chuckle that could only have come from Morrie. He had sulked when it became apparent that he wasn't going to get a chance to hold Penny's hand. He seemed in a better humor now.

Maybe he was planning a joke—some stupid comment, purporting to come from the ghost of a distinguished dead man.

His mother knew him as well as Ellen did.

"No more talk," she said sharply. "And no jokes, Morrie. Relax and clear your minds. Relax. . . ."

Ellen had never felt less relaxed. She wanted to stand up and pound on the table and shout insults at the fools who had instigated this insanity. She didn't want to relax. She was afraid to. She was afraid of what her own hand might write.

As the silence lengthened, and small rustles and breaths of movement were magnified by the loss of sight, she sat wondering at herself. Had her beautiful, beloved house actually reduced her to this fearful belief in something that violated every tenet of ethics, religion, and common sense?

Someone was writing. She could hear the scraping of the pencil. Lightning flashed again, so much closer that it dazzled instead of allowing vision. She could not see who was writing. Automatically she counted seconds, and started convulsively when the thunder rumbled before she had barely begun. Her hand was tingling. She clutched the pencil. If relaxation would produce the phenomenon called automatic writing, then she would keep every muscle taut. The pencil felt as thick as a walking stick.

The room was alive with soft movement—rustling scraping, scuttling sounds. The curtains billowed out in a gust of wind. Lightning again—closer, brighter—thunder that crackled instead of rumbling.

"That's enough," Ellen said suddenly. "Stop. . . ."

"No, wait. I'm getting something." It was Betty's voice, shrill with excitement.

"Please, Mom. Just a minute." That voice was Penny's. Ellen didn't like the sound of it. She was about to rise when lightning and thunder came together in a monumental explosion.

For a dazed moment Ellen thought the bolt had struck the house. She got to her feet and went groping for the light switch. She had lost her sense of direction. The room seemed to be filled with people, moving, fumbling as she was. Wind rushed through the open windows, sending papers flying and bringing the first sharp sting of rain. From the nether depths came a ghastly, inhuman howling. Ellen ran into someone, who recoiled with a yell. Then her outstretched hand encountered a door frame. A moment later she found the switch, and light came.

Her hand holding the knob as if it were an amulet, Ellen surveyed the rest of the party. They looked like the victims of a shipwreck or earthquake—dazed, blinking, pale.

Norman was the first to recover.

"Good Lord," he said, passing his hand over his eyes. "I've read about panic, but I never thought. . . . You were right, Ellen, that was a stupid thing to do."

"That howling," whispered Betty, hands clasped over her heart. "Something came . . . something horrible . . . listen to it. . . ."

"Ishtar doesn't like thunder," said Penny. She was still seated at the table.

"Oh," Betty said flatly. "The cat."

"I'm afraid you'll have to ignore Ishtar," Ellen said. "It's starting to rain hard, and my curtains are going to fly out into the night any minute."

The activity of closing windows and mopping up puddles restored everyone to normal. Bob was assiduous in helping, but he didn't fool Ellen; she had seen him and his son halfway out the door to the kitchen when the lights came on. Rats deserting the sinking ship, she thought disgustedly, and then smiled and offered brandy all around.

"Good idea," Bob said enthusiastically. He went to the bar.

"That was fascinating," said Betty. "I'm sure I felt an entity." She looked defiantly at the door. Ishtar's yowls had subsided, but an occasional roar still echoed, to inform them that she was not to be tortured without putting up a fight. "Something besides that damned cat."

"Pure suggestion," said Norman; but he sounded less confident than usual.

"I wrote something," said Morrie, with his inevitable giggle. "I mean, like, my hand did."

"I'll bet it did," Ellen said. She caught Penny's eye and smiled reluctantly.

"We forgot the papers," Betty said. "My goodness, they're all over the floor. That wind was terrible. Let's see what we got."

She collected the papers. Bob had abandoned spiritualism for spirits and hovered near the bar, but the others gathered around the table.

"Someone was doodling," Betty announced, holding up the first sheet of paper. Incredulously, Ellen recognized the agitated stick figures and formalized trees she produced when she was talking on the telephone. She had not the slightest recollection of having moved her pencil.

After one glance at the next sheet, Betty flushed angrily and crumpled it in her hand.

"Morrie, that is not funny!"

"Let's see," Norman said.

"Not on your life. Morrie, if I've told you once, I've told you a thousand times—"

"But Mother, I don't know what I wrote," Morrie said innocently. "It was automatic writing."

The next sheet had a drawing. The outlines were rough, which was understandable for a sketch done in the dark, but it was identifiable as a naked female figure.

"Done by the ghost of a dirty old man?" Ellen suggested drily.

All eyes turned toward Bob, who came ambling over, glass in hand, to see what they were looking at. He glanced at the drawing.

"What is it?" he asked. "Looks like pop art."

His voice sounded genuinely puzzled.

"This is a funny one," Betty said, "Look at this."

She put the paper down on the table so they could all see it.

The entire sheet was covered with sprawled, looping letters. The writing was fiercely black; the pencil had pressed so hard it had torn the paper in two places.

"He will do it tonight," it read. "Watch out, he will do it now. Quick, quick. He will do it tonight. He will—"

Ellen had always suspected that Bob was one of those people who can't read unless they move their lips. He read the message aloud.

" 'He will do it tonight.' You're right, Ellie, it is the ghost of a dirty old man."

Morrie echoed his guffaw, but no one else laughed. Suddenly, without a word, Norman turned and ran from the room. Ellen had a glimpse of his face; it was taut and pale. She heard the front door open and close before she could recover from her surprise. Then she ran after him.

"Norman—"

He was gone. The taillights of the car flared and then disappeared as he drove, too fast, down the driveway and out of sight.

"He tore out into the rain without his hat or coat," said Betty, behind her. "What was it, Ellen? The message was meant for him, but what did it mean?"

"Nothing. It meant nothing. Betty, if you ever suggest another séance—"

"It wasn't my idea," Betty said. She added, with a malicious glance at Ellen, "It might not mean anything to you, dear, but if it sends a man rushing out into a storm. . . ."

The Randolphs were disinclined to tackle a three-hour drive in a raging thunderstorm. Ellen didn't blame them, but she offered hospitality for the night with grudging reluctance. All she wanted was to get them out of the house so she could collapse in peace.

However, it was distracting to bustle about, changing

sheets and making up the cot in the study for Morrie. Penny insisted that her mother take her bed, but Ellen refused; the living-room couch would be good enough for her. She rather doubted that she would sleep.

She did not know what the bizarre message meant, if it meant anything; but she knew what Norman thought it meant, and once again she had a glimpse into his private hell that made her ache with sympathy. She only hoped he didn't kill himself, driving like a maniac on slippery roads, to find Tim. There was no cause for alarm, of course. Tim wouldn't pick a night like this for any of his unpleasant tricks. Norman would find him in bed asleep and would realize that his alarm had been causeless. All the same, Ellen had to fight down a desire to telephone.

The rest of the evening was a series of petty, prickly annoyances. Betty wouldn't go to bed; she insisted on having a cup of tea and rehashing the séance. When Ellen let Ishtar out of the cellar, the cat bit her. At some point in the proceedings, Penny disappeared. Ellen didn't realize she was missing at first; she was merely annoyed because Penny was not on hand to help her find clean towels and sheets. When she realized Penny wasn't watching television with Morrie, she flew into a panic. She was on the verge of silent hysterics when she heard a door close. Going to the kitchen, she found Penny trying to get out of her wet clothes before anyone saw her.

"Where have you been? You're soaked!"

"Just for a walk." The wind had whipped color into the girl's cheeks, and her eyes glittered. With her long hair plastered to her head by rain, she looked like a drowned witch. "I love being out in storms."

"Didn't you know I would worry? Of all the thoughtless, inconsiderate. . . . The dogs might be out!"

"They are out," said Penny, in the oddest voice. "I heard them. Mom, stop getting uptight. I can't stand that awful Morrie; I had to get away from him. What are you so worried about?"

Before Ellen could answer, Penny had walked out of the room, leaving a drenched raincoat in a puddle on the floor. Ellen picked it up and stood there holding it. The steady drip of water echoed in her head like the Chinese water torture.

Eleven

Ellen was awakened by the sound of Morrie's snores. Squinting apprehensively at the new day, she saw that the sun was shining, but she was not much cheered by the sight. She stumbled into the kitchen and put the coffee on, hoping she could get a cupful into her interior before she had to be civil to anyone.

When the telephone shrilled she made a dive for it. For the first time in her life she was disappointed to hear Jack's voice. She had hoped it was Norman, full of apologies for his ridiculous behavior the night before.

Jack had a habit of getting the bad news over with right away.

"I can't make it today, Ellen. Another stupid meeting this afternoon."

"I'm sorry."

"What's wrong? You sound terrible."

Ellen forced brightness into her voice.

"I guess I'm sleepy. The Randolphs spent the night—we had a storm—and I didn't get to bed till late."

"What fun," said Jack, who didn't like the Randolphs. "We had a lot of rain too. Is everything all right out there?"

"Oh, yes." Ellen glanced out the kitchen window. "The back yard is sloppy, but the sun is shining; it will dry things off fast. I do wish you were coming. . . ."

"Me, too. What about you and Penny coming in to-morrow?"

Ellen could hear voices in the background. Even on Sunday morning he wasn't free.

"Jack, you're too busy. I know you are."

He spoke to someone, his hand over the mouthpiece, and then addressed her again.

"Look, I'll call you tonight. See what we can arrange."

The telephone had awakened the others. They came yawning downstairs, and Ellen didn't get her pre-breakfast coffee after all. It was noon before the Randolphs left, and she turned, with aching head and drooping eyes, to cope with a stack of egg-stained dishes. Penny had disappeared again. Ordinarily Ellen wouldn't have been surprised; Penny was a normal adolescent, with the tendency of the breed to dematerialize when there was work to be done. In her present mood, Ellen found the girl's absence sinister. There was nothing she could do, except yield to her mounting concern and telephone Norman. She got the housekeeper, who told her Norman was out. Martha was never loquacious; this time she was barely civil. She hung up before Ellen could ask any more questions.

Her head was aching so badly that she took a couple of aspirin and lay down in her darkened room. She did not expect to sleep, but she fell at once into heavy slumber, and dreamed.

It was the old dream of running desperately through a

dark wood toward something she wanted with all her heart and soul to prevent. But this time the feeling of danger was intensified. Danger was all around; it dripped from the trees like blood. She awoke with a cry and a pounding heart—and then realized that the pounding came, as well, from outside. Someone was hammering on the front door.

She knew who it was before she opened the door; Ishtar was crouched on the mat, staring fixedly at the wooden panel. Penny came out of the kitchen as Ellen descended the stairs.

"Take Ishtar," Ellen said shortly. "It must be Norman; she only acts that way with him."

Penny scooped up the cat and Ellen opened the door. It was Norman; but it was a Norman she scarcely recognized. He was wearing the clothes he had worn the night before; they were stiff with mud, torn and stained. He had not shaved. He looked past Ellen at Penny, who held the struggling cat, and he spoke as Ellen had never heard him speak.

"Get rid of that damned cat!"

Without a word, Penny turned and carried Ishtar to the cellar.

"I'm sorry," Norman said to Ellen. He rubbed his eyes with the back of his hand. "I'm sorry. . . . I can't think. Please, Ellen—has Tim been here?"

"No, of course not. Come in. What on earth has happened?"

But she knew, even before she asked—she had known all along. The only thing she didn't know was the precise nature of the act.

"I've been out all night looking. I've looked everywhere, trying to find him . . . before they do."

"Who? What has happened?"

She had to pull at his sleeve to get him inside the house; and then she went straight to the bar for brandy before questioning him further. The brandy helped; he drew a long breath after tossing it down, and rubbed his eyes again.

"I keep forgetting you don't know. You remember last night? My God, it seems a hundred years ago."

"I remember that so-called spirit message, and you rushing out of the house. I knew what you were thinking. . . . Norman, don't tell me it really happened. What did Tim do last night?"

She was aware of Penny standing straight and silent behind her. Penny would be worried too. How worried? How much did she care for the boy? What had she been doing out in the rain last night? All these thoughts, and others, flashed through her mind in a dark kaleidoscope of shapes before Norman finally answered.

"He attacked one of the girls. Beat her badly and would have raped her, maybe killed her, if she hadn't fought him off."

He hid his face in his hands. Ellen sat frozen, staring at the tumbled silver-gilt hair that fell over his fingers. Then Penny spoke.

"Which girl?"

"I don't know. What is her name? Prudence."

"Prudence?" Ellen repeated. "The same one who—"

"Yes." Norman dropped his hands and looked up. His eyes were like pale-blue pebbles, expressionless and dull. "I know what you're thinking, Ellen. But the girl didn't inflict those bruises and cuts herself. I saw them."

"Has she been examined by a doctor?" It was Penny who spoke; her voice was so dry and hard it might have been that of an old woman.

"You don't know this town," Norman said. "Bring in a doctor, to hear of a young girl's shame?"

"There are tests," Penny said. "Tests for attempted rape. How far did he get with her? If he—"

"Penny!" Ellen didn't know why she was shocked; she had always prided herself on discussing such things frankly with Penny and the boys. Perhaps it was the girl's tone—or perhaps it was Norman's expression as he stared at Penny.

"This is beside the point," he said slowly. "If it were any other boy in town, they might give him the benefit of a doubt. But Tim is condemned before he opens his mouth. I tell you, they are out looking for him! I've got to find him before they do!"

How long had she lived here, Ellen wondered? Six weeks? Long enough to accept the terrible truth Norman was hinting at. Six weeks ago she wouldn't have believed it could happen anywhere in a civilized nation. She had been incredibly naive. Mrs. Grapow and the minister . . . the sick, perverse religion that ruled the town . . . old customs, old habits, old ways of doing things. And Prudence's father—

". . . his shotgun," Norman said. "You know Muller, Ellen. He says he'll kill the boy on sight. He's drunker than usual. He might do it."

"I know him," Ellen said. "Oh, God, and I gave him back that shotgun. . . . No, I won't explain now, it doesn't matter. He could always find a gun somewhere. . . ."

"Help me find Tim." Norman spread his hands in a pleading gesture. "I've got to get him out of town. Where is he?"

"Norman, I don't know. We haven't seen him."

Norman wasn't looking at her. He was looking at Penny.

Ellen turned.

Penny was wearing shorts and a sleeveless shirt. Her long bare legs were deeply tanned. Her black hair rippled over her shoulders. She looked delightful.

Her wide, candid eyes moved from one adult face to the other.

"No, we haven't seen him," she said sweetly. "I should think he'd be miles away by this time. He's got money, hasn't he?"

"He hasn't any money," Norman said. "I haven't dared let him have cash."

"You don't know what he's got," Penny said. "He's such a bum, isn't he. . . . Probably he's a thief as well as a vandal and would-be rapist. And you have all those expensive little trinkets just sitting around the house. He could hitchhike to Washington or Richmond and find a pawnshop. If I were you, I'd check my inventory."

Norman's eyes fell. He seemed to be studying his hands, which were tightly clasped on his knees. They were no longer well tended; scratches crisscrossed them and the long fingers bore the colors of the woods—berry stains, and brown smears of sap. Ellen visualized him pushing heedlessly through the tangled woods, in rain and darkness, calling Tim's name. The picture was so like the theme and the landscape of her nightmare that she shivered with sympathy.

"If he does come here, we'll let you know right away," she said gently. "Penny may be right, you know. Go home and check the house. If I were you, I'd call the police. Just report him as missing."

"I can't do that yet," Norman said. "A boy that age— they wouldn't take me seriously unless he were missing for more than one night."

"Tomorrow, then, if he doesn't some home tonight. I'm sure you are worrying unnecessarily, Norman. Muller is a sot, but he isn't really dangerous; give him ten dollars and he'll drink himself into a stupor. The more I think about it, the more I'm inclined to think Penny is right. If Tim started hitchhiking—"

She broke off as Penny darted to the window. Then she heard the sound the girl's keen ears had heard first. It was the sound of a car coming up the driveway.

She joined Penny at the window. The car was one she had not seen before, a battered old Ford that wheezed and stuttered. The driver got out—Mr. Winckler, the minister. He was followed by Mrs. Grapow, and two men.

One of them Ellen knew by sight, though not by name. The other was Muller.

"Don't let them in," Penny gasped.

"I have no intention of doing so."

When she ran out onto the porch, no one was in sight. Evidently the delegation had halted on the path; she could hear a mutter of voices, as if a conference were in progress.

For a moment the whole scene shimmered like a faulty film. It was impossible that she could be experiencing this on her own front porch with its walls of flowering green and its comfortable modern furniture. The yard was sunny and quiet. The sun was far down the western sky; she had slept longer than she realized.

Ellen rubbed her eyes. Surely she was still asleep and dreaming. Maybe she had dreamed the whole summer. Mrs. Grapow was a product of her subconscious, the church and its pastor a fragment of some suppressed childhood terror. . . .

Then they came in sight from behind the rose bushes. Mr. Winckler led the way. His face was set in a sanctimonious frown, but his little eyes shifted uneasily. Mrs. Grapow was behind him. Muller trailed her, at a safe distance. He was not carrying a gun. Ellen assumed the others had prohibited the weapon, not because they wanted to make a pacific impression, but because they didn't trust their ally's aim. Muller was weaving dangerously. Without his prop, he looked uncertain and ill at ease.

Ellen left the porch and closed the screen door behind her. Standing on the stairs, looking down, gave her a psychological advantage, and she meant to keep the intruders as far from the house—and from Penny—as she could.

Ignoring her peremptory gesture, Penny followed and stood behind her on the topmost step. It never occurred to Ellen to call on Norman for help or moral support; but a name entered her mind, and she suppressed a desperate, futile need to call it aloud.

The pastor stopped when he saw her. Ellen didn't give him time to speak.

"What do you want here?" she demanded.

"You know what we want. Where is he?"

"I don't know."

A shadow fell over the clearing. A bank of heavy clouds obscured the eastern sky. From its edge, chunks and lumps of cloud scudded westward. They were dark, rimmed with reflected gold.

Without warning Ellen was gripped by a strange sensation. This had all happened before—a woman, standing at bay on the steps of her home facing a sullen group of attackers. Even the emotional climate seemed familiar— anger mixed with fear and a strong sense of danger. Psychologists called the experience *déjà vu,* and explained it with a variety of rationalizations.

Ellen could have explained it too, but she didn't try. She welcomed the feeling. The strength of that other woman's contempt stiffened her body and allowed her to speak.

"I don't know," she repeated, more strongly. "And I wouldn't tell you if I did. Get off my property, or I'll call the police."

Mrs. Grapow shoved forward.

"Nobody's gonna call the police. We won't have that poor girl's shame made public."

"It seems to me her shame is pretty public already," Ellen said coolly. Her eyes moved to Prue's father, who shied back. "If her father wants to spare her feelings, he had better go home and get rid of his gun."

"He's got a right," said Mrs. Grapow.

"He has no such right! I warn you, and you had better believe me; if Tim is shot, I'll have the police out here so fast it'll make your heads swim. I'll testify that you threatened him—all of you. Accessory before the fact is a serious charge. You could spend a lot of time in prison for that."

"Now you listen to me," Winckler shouted. "This is our business, and we'll handle it ourselves. We don't want outsiders telling us what to do."

Mrs. Grapow nodded approvingly.

"That's right, Pastor. You tell her. Tell her we want to search this place."

"Mother," said Penny, in an agonized whisper.

Ellen raised her voice.

"Penny, go in and call the state police."

"Wait a minute," Winckler began.

"Yes, let's all wait a minute."

It was Norman's voice. Ellen had been so preoccupied she had not heard him approach. He descended the first two steps and stood beside her.

"Hank," he said to the minister, "you're out of line. You shouldn't threaten Mrs. March."

"Well, now, I didn't exactly mean—"

Mrs. Grapow gave the little man a push. He staggered forward a few steps.

"Oh, yes, we did mean," Mrs. Grapow shouted. "Pastor, you get up there and tell 'em, or I will. Norman, you know what that boy is like. None of our girls are safe with him on the loose. Night's coming on, and the good Lord knows what he'll do in the dark."

"I've done everything I can," Norman pleaded. "I think he's gone, Mrs. Grapow. Left town. I tried to find him—"

"You didn't use the dogs. They'd find him quick enough. And spare us the trouble of shooting him."

Penny gasped, and Norman said weakly,

"Now, Mrs. G., you don't really mean—"

"Stop it!"

Ellen shouted. She felt odd. Perhaps it was anger that made her feel so dizzy and disoriented; never in her life had she experienced such outrage and hate. Yes, hate was the right word; she could have exterminated all three of them, including Muller, without a qualm of conscience.

Norman's ineffectual pleading angered her too. A lot of help he was; couldn't he see it was useless talking to these monsters?

She caught hold of the stair rail, and the hard, solid surface under her hand steadied her whirling thoughts. They were all staring at her. Why were they staring like that?

"Stop it," she repeated. "I won't listen to any more of this obscene talk. Get out. Get out! And take that trigger-happy cretin with you!"

She flung her arm out, indicating Muller.

The whole group recoiled; it was as if she had flung a stone. Muller's mouth hung open. A trickle of tobacco-stained spittle slid down his chin. He backed up, step by step, stumbling, but never taking his eyes from Ellen.

Then she knew. They were afraid—even Mrs. Grapow, clutching the spindly arm of the minister. They were vicious and rotten with hate, and they were afraid. Of her.

Something gripped her like a giant hand. It closed over her ribs and sent the breath rushing out of her lungs. The clearing darkened. She heard a voice shouting, hurling words like bullets. The words were unfamiliar, and yet some part of her knew them, knew their meaning and their power.

She came back into her body—there was no other way of expressing it—to see the committee in full retreat. Muller was already out of sight. The minister had abandoned Mrs. Grapow; she thudded after him like an unwieldy brontosaurus.

Norman stood at the foot of the steps, clutching the rail. His eyes were so widely dilated they looked black.

Ellen swayed. Penny caught her by the shoulder.

"Mom, Mom—are you okay?"

"My God," Ellen muttered. "That was me talking! What did I say?"

"I don't know. But it—it sounded sort of like Spanish."

ii

The living room looked very dark with the sun hidden in clouds. It was somehow unfamiliar; the furniture looked wrong.

Ellen shook her head. She still felt queer, but she would not let the feeling conquer her again. It had helped once, but only temporarily. The real danger couldn't be solved by curses.

"Penny." She caught the girl by the arm and turned her around. "Penny, I must talk to you."

"Not now, Mom. We've got to do something!"

"We're doing everything we can. Norman has gone home to check the house, as you suggested; he will make sure the dogs are securely chained. The next step is yours. Answer me, and for the love of heaven, tell me the truth. Do you know where Tim is?"

Their eyes met, on a level. Penny had grown over the summer; they were the same height now. Through all the years of normal naughtiness and misbehavior, Ellen had been certain of one thing: Penny had never lied to her. Faced by a direct question, the girl lowered her eyes.

"Think," Ellen insisted, shaking her gently. "Tim is in danger if he stays around here. We must get him away, Penny."

She was winning. Penny's lips parted. Then she shook her head.

"Honey, please. I want to help Tim. You trust me, don't you? You used to trust me. . . ."

Tears overflowed the girl's eyes. She threw herself into Ellen's arms.

"I do trust you," she mumbled against Ellen's shoulder. "Oh, Mom, if you could only trust me!"

"Honey, darling, I do. I know you have been acting as you thought best, but this is getting out of hand; you can't cope with it alone. Go find him, Penny. I'll call Norman, and—"

She couldn't see Penny's face, but she felt every muscle in the girl's body stiffen. When Penny spoke again, her voice was shrill with strain.

"You don't trust me, you don't believe me. Oh, Mom, let's get away from here. I can't stand this horrible place. Please, please . . ."

"All right," Ellen said. She had dealt with hysterical girls before. The fact that this was her own daughter only increased her efficiency. "All right, Penny, we'll go. I hate the place too. Stop that crying now, and we'll leave right away. Where do you want to go?"

She held the girl away from her. Penny's face was smudged with tears, but she was calmer. Sniffing pathetically, she wiped her cheeks with her hand.

"Washington? We could find a hotel, and call Jack—"

"Sounds great to me," Ellen said, with forced cheer. "Pack your toothbrush and let's go."

They went upstairs and Ellen started packing an overnight bag. Secretly, she was happy to be going. Even the threatening sky did not worry her; if the weather got bad they would stop somewhere along the way. A neat impersonal hotel room would look like heaven, after Chew's Corners.

She felt a slight qualm at the thought of deserting Norman, but comforted herself with the knowledge that she was not abandoning Tim. Penny's suggestion had been a dead giveaway. Tim wasn't in the neighborhood, or Penny wouldn't be willing to leave. Penny's verbal hints, her inexplicable behavior—all pointed to the same conclusion. Perhaps she had arranged to meet Tim in the city. Ellen sensed that it would be unwise to push Penny now; the girl was too frantic. But once they were away, Penny had a lot of explaining to do.

Ellen went downstairs carrying her suitcase. Penny had already gone out to the car. Ellen left her bag by the front door and went to look for Ishtar. Her mind was running along familiar lines—cat food, litter, carrier—when the door opened and Penny came in. The girl's face was ashen under her tan.

"The car doesn't work," she said.

"What do you mean? It started yesterday. Did you leave the lights on, or—"

Penny shook her head. She looked like a mechanical doll.

"The battery is okay. The tires are slashed and someone punctured the gas tank. There isn't a drop left."

The other man, Ellen thought. Four people had gotten out of Winckler's car, but only three of them had spoken with her.

She stared speechlessly at Penny. There was no need to speak; the implications were clear, and far more unpleasant than anything Ellen had anticipated.

"I'll call Norman," Ellen said.

"No!" Angry color rushed into Penny's face. "Is that all you can think of? Call Norman, tell Norman, help poor old Norman. . . . I hate Norman! I'd like to kill him!"

"That's enough," Ellen said. The tone was one she seldom used, and it seldom failed to have an effect. This time it failed.

"I thought it was Jack," Penny went on. "All along I was hoping and praying it would be Jack. Then you come here, and that crazy, sick old— Can't you see what he's like, Mother? I didn't think anybody who loved Jack would be dumb enough to fall for Norman. I thought you had better taste."

"Penny," Ellen whispered. She felt as if she had been struck in the face.

"Mom, I'm sorry. I didn't mean it. If you just knew—"

"I wish I did know. I've been trying to get you to tell me. What has come over you? I'm beginning to think this place is haunted!"

"It is. But not the way you think. The town is okay.

Mom. Some of the people are a little weird, but what town doesn't have its collection of oddballs? It isn't the town. It's one person—one single individual—who is behind all this crazy business."

"Mrs. Grapow."

"No, not Mrs. Grapow!" The girl was frantic; she beat her small hands together and then whirled toward the window. "You don't understand—and you won't, not till it's too late. There isn't time. The time is going, running away—and in the night . . ."

It was only six o'clock, but the sky was as dark as it would have been at that hour on a day in midwinter.

"Maybe we'll have another storm," Ellen said.

"No, it's not going to rain. I wish it would. That might stop them. . . ."

"Penny, what are you afraid of? You don't think we are really in danger, do you?"

"Someone doesn't want us to leave here," Penny said.

"That may have been a precautionary measure to keep us from interfering, or to prevent Tim from escaping in our car. Penny, I can have the state police here in ten minutes!"

Penny laughed.

"Try," she said.

Ellen picked up the telephone. The line was dead.

She had a hard time getting the phone back on its stand, her hands were shaking so badly. Strange, that it should have taken this to convince her; the signs were all there, and Penny had seen them. Still Ellen argued, with her own fear as much as with Penny.

"Another obvious precaution. They don't want us calling the police."

"All right," Penny said, with a certain grim satisfaction. "At least that takes care of calling dear old Norman. Now, Mom, try this one. Suppose we are in danger. The car is out of commission, the phone is dead. What do we do?"

"Why, I suppose we could start walking."

"They would have someone watching. At the road."

Ellen didn't have to ask who "they" were. She was entering into the game, but in a schizophrenic manner; half of her mind "played" in order to calm the girl, but the other half knew it was not a game.

"We could go through the woods."

"They know the woods better than we do."

"Then what do you suggest?" She added, with a feeble attempt at sarcasm, "I suppose you won't let me suggest walking to Norman's."

"No."

"What, then?"

"Set fire to the house," Penny said.

She was in deadly earnest.

"Or maybe the shed," she went on. "The whole town isn't in this. Someone might see the flames and call the fire department."

"My God," Ellen muttered. She said aloud, "All right, honey. I'll get the kerosine and go out to the shed. You—you lock up the house."

I'll run, she thought. Straight through the woods to Norman's. Call Jack—a doctor—rescue squad, there must be one. . . .

"Oh," Penny said. It was a high-pitched squeak of sheer surprise. "Oh, my gosh, you think I'm crazy, don't you? You really think. . . . There's no other way, then. I'll have to tell you the truth."

Ellen dropped into a chair. Her knees would no longer hold her up, and her mind toyed with terrible theories.

Penny turned on the lights. Now that Ellen could see her more distinctly, she felt less alarmed. Penny was pale but calm; her lips were tightly set as she moved purposefully around the room, drawing the drapes and bolting the front door. Then she went to the cellar door and opened it.

"Come on up," she said. "It didn't work. The car—"

"I know, I was listening."

Part of Ellen's mind had suspected the truth, but it was still a shock to hear the deep voice, and see the boy standing there.

He looked different, somehow. The clothes were the same tattered garments he always wore; they were in worse condition than usual, and she deduced that he really had spent at least part of the night in the woods. He had never been heavy, but now he looked gaunt, his cheek- and jawbones standing out sharply from the stretched skin of his face. But none of these changes accounted for the difference in his appearance. . . .

Then she knew. The sullen, shuttered look was gone. He stood tall, his shoulders back. The blue eyes were sunken with fatigue, but they met her eyes squarely.

Penny closed the cellar door and came to stand beside him. She didn't have to do that, Ellen thought dully. They stand together, even when the width of the room separates them.

Ishtar sauntered in and leaned against Tim's dirty ankles. For a while there was no sound in the room except the cat's throaty purr. Tim bent over and picked up Ishtar, who nuzzled at his chin as he cradled her in his arms.

"Ishtar likes me," he said tentatively. He smiled, and Ellen thought, well, no wonder, if he had ever looked at me like that. . . . But he had, the night he brought Ishtar home.

Ellen began to laugh.

"She needs an aspirin or something," Tim said, his smile fading. "Maybe I shouldn't have—"

"No, I don't need anything." Ellen giggled feebly. "I am a little hysterical. I don't know what to say."

"You don't know what to say!" Penny moved forward and Tim followed, as if drawn by a magnet. "I've got to convince you, but quick, that I am right—me, your six-teen-year-old baby—and the whole rest of the world, including my omniscient mother, is wrong. How about that?"

"Wrong about what?" Ellen felt oddly calm. It was the lull before the storm—or the eye of the storm, they had been through considerable uproar already.

"Try this for a starter. That big white house up on the hill—who does it belong to?"

"Not Norman?"

"It belongs to Tim." Penny gestured at the unlikely owner, who looked sheepish. "The house, the car, and about two million dollars. And on his eighteenth birthday, which is next month, he gets the lot."

"Wait a minute," Ellen said. "Nobody gives an eighteen-year-old—"

"Control of a fortune? I know most people don't. You wouldn't. But Tim's mother was different. Didn't you ever wonder where all the money came from? Why that house has been redone and redecorated so recently? Tim's mother was a Peabody—one of the meat-packing Peabodys. When she was eighteen she ran away from home and married Tim's dad. It was one of those crazy marriages everybody says won't work, but it did. She hated the social bit. She just wanted to live in the woods with a lot of animals around. She said she had sense enough at eighteen to choose her own life, and she figured her son would, too."

"How do you know this?" Ellen demanded incredulously.

"I was ten when she died," Tim said, in the slow, deep voice that was so attractive without its bitter undertone. "We used to talk a lot. She didn't talk down to kids. My dad was a pretty swell guy, too. Then, like overnight—" He made a helpless and very eloquent gesture; and Ishtar, whose bottom had been left dangling, bit him. He put the cat down and went on. "The lawyers said Norman was going to be my guardian. I never liked him much, before. He was, like, you know, kind of dumb with kids. Like ho ho ho, if you know what I mean. Kept looking like he wanted to pat me on the head, but he was afraid he'd get his hands dirty. I didn't mind so much. I didn't care about anything just then. And he wasn't bad, you know? Just stupid."

"All right," Penny said briskly. "Keep in mind, Mom, that I can prove everything I'm going to say. Will you accept my first point, for the moment?"

"Yes," Ellen said weakly. Penny's manner brought back evenings in front of the fire in the old house in Bethesda—evenings of laughter and furious debate, with Penny taking on all three boys, and Jack supporting first one side and then the other, as the spirit moved him.

"Okay. Next point—and I can prove this, too. Tim hasn't seen a doctor, neurologist, psychiatrist, or counselor. He has never been a patient of Dr. Abrahamson's."

"But Norman said—" The expressions on the two young faces stopped her. "How do you know?"

"I guess you won't take Tim's word," Penny conceded. "How about Dr. Bishop's?"

"Penny, you didn't. . . . How did you do it?"

"I told him a lot of lies," Penny said coolly. "About you. He likes you a lot, Mom. He fought me quite a bit, but he finally agreed to check. Tim has never been a patient of any psychiatrist Dr. Bishop knows in D.C. He was definite about Abrahamson."

Ellen was shaken. The information about Tim's inheritance was relatively unimportant. Norman had always given her the impression that the money was his; but vanity was a minor vice. On this point, however, Norman had lied, deliberately and unequivocally, and she could not think of any innocuous reason for the lie.

While she sat silent, thinking it over, Penny did something that shook her even more. The girl dropped on her knees in front of Ellen and took both her mother's hands.

"This is the clincher," she said. "This is what you won't believe. But it's true, Mom. It's true and you've got to believe it. Tim never hurt an animal in his life. He had a dog when his parents died. Two weeks afterward he found it on his bed. It was dead. Poisoned. On his bed, Mom!"

Ellen shook her head dumbly. She ached for Penny; the girl's eyes were dark with horror. Penny believed the story. But she had gotten it from Tim, and Tim. . . . Ellen looked at the boy. He returned her gaze with a somber stare. Penny clutched her hands tighter and went on, the words pouring out.

"Norman got him a puppy. He didn't want one. You don't, Mom, not right away. You know. But he got it anyway and Tim loved it. Norman got the big dogs at the same time. They were pups too, but big and strong even then. They killed Tim's puppy. It got shut in with them by mistake, *he* said, and he hadn't fed them that day, because he was training them to be watchdogs."

Ellen was half convinced by the sheer horror of the story. Surely no boy of ten—or even of seventeen—could invent an idea so coldly diabolical.

"This is Tim's version," she said.

"I know how it sounds," Tim said.

"I'm not through yet," Penny announced. "I'm only beginning. Mom, would you like a drink or something? You look kind of funny. And this is going to get worse."

"I think maybe I would," Ellen said. "Penny, Tim—I'm trying very hard. It isn't easy for me, but I'll try."

"Thanks," Tim said.

It was not an eloquent speech, but his look added another pebble to the slowly mounting weight in Ellen's mind.

She accepted a glass of sherry from Penny, and took a sip.

"Go on," she said.

"When Norman offered to get him a kitten, Tim said no," Penny took up the tale. "Norman got it anyhow. Tim tried to lose it, in the woods, but it came back; it was so little. The dogs—"

"Please," Ellen said. "That's enough. I get the picture."

It was a literal picture, a visual image so distinct it sickened her.

"It happened twice more," Penny said. Her voice shook. "Tim finally ended it the only way he could. He pretended he didn't care. When he found the—the dead animals, he would just laugh and shrug. Then he'd run out in the woods and throw up."

"I said, I get the picture. It's horrible, Penny, but you're forgetting one incident. I actually saw Tim—"

"I was killing it," Tim said. "My God, I had to kill it quick. You heard it screaming, but you didn't see how bad it was hurt."

"It's too coincidental," Ellen argued, only fleetingly aware of the incongruity of debating such a crime with its perpetrator. "That I happened to come along at that precise moment—"

"It was no coincidence. Look, Mrs. March, he arranged that appointment with you, right? He knew when you'd be coming. To get me on the spot, all he had to do was tell me there was an injured squirrel on the path. I'd have gone to help it anyway, but knowing you were coming, I ran out there as soon as he told me. I didn't want you to see anything ugly."

"It was a pretty farfetched scheme. What if his timing had been off? If you had been late, or I had been early. . . ."

"It was worth taking the chance," Tim said. "What's a squirrel? No big deal to *him*."

Ellen would never get used to the way his voice changed on the pronoun.

"All right," she said. "It's possible. I'll go that far. What next?"

"I haven't finished about the animals yet," said Penny. "Tim is crazy about them, like his mother. They spent a lot of time in the woods together, before she died. Tim knows the woods and the wildlife like a naturalist. He watches animals, but he never dares tame them or bring them home. Right now there's a poor old stray cat he feeds; but he can't get too friendly with it for fear it would follow him home."

"It's a white cat," said Tim. He gave Ellen a shy smile. "I guess maybe you've seen it."

"I guess I have. Well, it's a relief to know I didn't imagine the cat. A small relief, in the middle of this madness. . . . But with Norman so afraid of cats, how could he bear to have kittens around when you were small?"

"They didn't stay around long," said Tim, in a voice that made Ellen wince. "He isn't too scared to kill them."

"I thought you might say the phobia was a pretense."

"No, why should he put on about a thing like that? I could have used it," Tim said. "You know—toss cats on his bed and like that. But it would have been kind of hard on the cats. . . . It's a funny phobia, you know? What really bugs him is the idea of touching a cat, or having it touch him. He can carry them in baskets and boxes. That's how he got Ishtar that day."

"Are you trying to tell me he took Ishtar out of the shed?"

"He has a trap he uses," Tim said, with horrible calm. "He baits it with fish or liver or something. I saw him bring Ishtar home that day. He couldn't give her to the dogs while they were chained up, in the daytime. You wouldn't believe she was that dumb, to walk right up to them. I guess he was going to wait till dark and then let them loose. I sneaked her away before he could do it. But he let the dogs loose anyhow."

"Wait a minute," Ellen said, pressing her hands to her head. "You're making him sound like a monster. I don't see—or do I? I suppose you have checked Norman's financial status?"

She spoke sarcastically, and was taken aback when Penny nodded.

"Jack did."

"But Penny, you could get Jack in serious trouble that way! He has no business telling you—or using his sources for personal reasons—"

"He'd do anything for you," Penny said. "You've got a lot of admirers, Mom. Course I had to lie to him a little bit too—"

"I suppose you told him Norman wanted to marry me for my money?" Ellen was amused, exasperated, and oddly pleased.

"Jack is down on anybody who wants to marry you for any reason whatsoever. Gol, Mom, you really are dim."

"It's gotten pretty dark," Tim said quietly. "There's a wind rising."

It wailed around the house like a lost soul. Ellen glanced uneasily at the windows.

"Norman's finances," she reminded Penny.

"They are a mess," Penny said. "Jack thinks he's been embezzling Tim's estate."

"Jack said that?"

"Oh, well, not exactly. He said he'd had some funny hints from people, and for me to keep you from doing anything silly till he could look around some more. He knows a lot more about what's been going on than you think," Penny said coolly. "And he said he didn't like it one damn bit."

"I don't either." Ellen shivered. "Listen to that wind."

"It isn't the wind now." Tim went to the window. "It's the dogs."

"They're loose!" Ellen started to get up.

Penny gripped her hands more tightly.

"They were bound to be," she said obscurely. "Mom, listen. We don't have much time, and you're not convinced yet. I can see you aren't. I'm not through with my case yet."

"There's more?"

"You've only heard half of it. Do you think this witchcraft business has been coincidence too?"

"What are you trying to say?"

Penny glanced over her shoulder. Tim, at the window, nodded.

"I'll make it fast," she said, turning back to her mother. "This town has a weird, sick religion, and Mrs. Grapow doesn't like you much. Start with that. Then remember the day you talked about a coming storm—and the storm came. Now that *was* a coincidence. It would have been laughed at and forgotten, if somebody hadn't made a point of it, all over town. Then you were dumb enough—I'm sorry, Mom, you couldn't possibly anticipate what would happen—you got carried away and told the kids' fortunes. That was when the fun began. Those fulfilled predictions weren't coincidence. They were too accurate. Take them one by one."

Penny glanced again at Tim. He did not speak, but she seemed alarmed by what she saw; her words tumbled out.

"You made your predictions vague, naturally. That left the joker—let's call him Norman, shall we, instead of X? —plenty of latitude. When you warned Klaus about a car, you meant he should drive more carefully. But when he was almost hit by a car, that could fit the prophecy too. Anybody can rent a car. And Norman was out of town that day."

Ellen started to speak, but Penny hurried on.

"It would be impossible to trace the necklace Sue Ann got. It was expensive, but not unique; there must be a dozen jewelry stores in nearby towns that carry those things, and the buyer would be smart enough to pay cash. But somebody sent that necklace, to fit in with your promise of 'presents.' It didn't come from the spirit world.

"Joyce and Steve was a good guess. *He* didn't have to do anything about that—except harp on it. The cruelest thing he did was send that letter to Chuck, the one that was supposed to be from Harvard. I saw that letter. It had a regular printed letterhead. But a person can order something from a printer as easily as he can rent a car.

Norman probably had that done in Washington, so it would be hard to trace. But we could try."

Ellen was dazed, not only by the intelligence and persistence with which the girl had acquired her data, but by its cumulative effect. The prophecies had always bothered her; it would be comforting to believe they had been engineered by a material agent.

"But that trick would certainly be discovered," she objected. "If Chuck doesn't hear something more soon, he'll write Harvard and find out—"

"By then," Penny said, "it won't matter. It will be too late."

"Nobody would trace it to *him,* anyhow," Tim put in. "The kids would just think somebody played a mean joke."

"What do you mean, it will be too late?" Ellen demanded.

"Don't you see the point of the whole thing? Norman has been planning this for years, Mom. I think at first he just tormented Tim out of spite. Remember that night when you told me you thought he was in love with Tim's mother? I think his feelings were a lot more complicated than that. When he had her son under his thumb. . . . Anyhow, it wasn't long before he realized he could end up with a tidy fortune. He loves money. All those expensive ornaments, and that ostentatious car. . . . There was no hurry because he was both guardian and administrator. He could nibble away at Tim's estate and nobody would ask questions till Tim came of age. So Norman worked up a little scheme. Somebody would ask questions if Tim died under suspicious circumstances, with all that money involved. Norman decided he would get someone else to do his dirty work. And I bet he enjoyed every minute of it. Slowly, year by year, he has made Tim look like a monster. Oh, Tim is no angel. . . ."

She gave Tim a look that belied her words. Tim blushed.

"I did beat up a lot of guys," he admitted. "I was a mean kid for a few years."

"But the rest of it—the really dirty things—Norman did," Penny went on. "He and Tim look a lot alike. In Tim's old clothes, in the dark—"

"My God," Ellen interrupted in horror. "Are you telling me it was Norman last night—with Prudence—"

"Just look at the probabilities, Mom. Look at Tim! Do you think that flabby female would have escaped with a few cuts and bruises if Tim had really wanted—"

She glanced at Tim, who was beet-red, and took pity on him.

"He has better taste," she concluded. "And, believe me, Mom—he wasn't that hard up."

Ellen decided not to pursue the suggestion.

"But Norman—"

"He sent her a note, supposedly from Tim," Penny said. "She's got a thing about Tim."

"Of course," Ellen whispered. "How could I be so stupid?"

The look on Prue's face, the day Tim came to the store. . . . the fair-haired dream prince at the wedding . . . "I've got to go to the dance. I've got to go with. . . ."

"A lot of the girls think he's sexy," Penny continued. "I told you, that blond Heathcliffe sulk is very effective."

She grinned at Tim, who grinned back. For a moment the two young faces were so alight, Ellen's eyes were dazzled.

"But when did he . . . Oh, Lord. I suppose he ran right out of here last night—"

"After writing that corny message," Penny said. "If the lightning and wind hadn't given him his chance, he'd have had a fit or pretended to hear noise, or something, to create a disturbance and scatter the papers around. He played the whole crowd of us like a violin, Mom. I didn't realize what was going on till it was too late to stop it. And I was dumb; I figured I would let him go ahead, see what he was up to. Mom!" She stared at Ellen. "You believe me. You believe me, now."

"It fits together too well," Ellen said unwillingly. "He wanted me out of here—out of town. He tried to frighten me—the dogs, hints about Tim. . . . The townspeople think badly of Tim and they don't like interference. If anything happened to Tim, they wouldn't make a fuss. But I would. He knew I would."

"You're such a sweet, gentle little busybody," Penny said. "You look harmless, but everything you did confirmed Norman's assessment of you as a potential danger. Stalking out of church, talking back to Mrs. Grapow, hassling him about getting Tim to a psychiatrist. . . . Gosh, Mom, you have to admit you asked for it."

"I guess I did. I babbled a lot about the police, too."

"That's why Jack was worried. He said you were such a nosy little devil, if there was trouble brewing you were bound to be in the thick of it."

"I wish he were here," Ellen murmured. Then she started up. This time Penny made no attempt to hold her back.

"Look here, you two. I may or may not be convinced of the truth of this admittedly wild story. It's too much to take in all at once. But I'm willing to go along with you, to the extent of taking precautions. I can't afford not to. What are we going to do?"

"We can't stay here," Penny said.

"Where else can we go? Is there anyone in town, Tim, who would shelter you?"

Tim shook his head.

"Wait a minute," Ellen exclaimed. "What about Ed Salling? I'll bet my last dollar he's all right."

"He lives on the other side of town," Penny said. "We'd never make it."

"Then why go anywhere? The house is sound, well built; Norman wouldn't dare try overt violence. . . ."
Ellen shook her head; no, she couldn't believe it, she

couldn't see Norman as a killer, stalking them with a gun or knife. But she had promised to believe. . . . Doggedly she went on.

"We'll sit up all night and keep watch. As soon as it's light, I'll walk out of here and go straight to the highway. Norman wouldn't attack me. . . ."

Her voice died away as they turned to her with the now familiar look of pitying contempt.

"Mom," Penny said gently, "you still don't get the picture. Norman isn't going to attack anybody. He doesn't have to. The town will do it for him."

Ellen sat stunned, her hands clenched in her lap. Naive was not the word for her. Criminally stupid, that's what she was.

She had to admit it was an ingenious method of murder. The tinder was there, at hand; but without Norman to light the match and fan the flame, it would have smoldered harmlessly for a few more years before dying of itself. Norman's plan was almost foolproof. The town was not uniquely evil. In any group there were a few—sometimes more than a few—who could be aroused and sent out like hounds on a trail. They enjoyed the hunt and the panic of the prey. Five thousand years of civilization had not eliminated the breed; probably nothing ever would. They were so easily inflamed—by passionate words, by liquor, by the queer quirk in the brain that allows some people to kill for pleasure.

And once the pack was howling down the trail, the job was as good as done. If some drunken Neanderthal in the mob didn't fire the actual shot, Norman could do it himself, with relative impunity. In the cold light of dawn, when the blood lust had been assuaged and the corn whisky had worn off, the mob would slink home, silent with a shared guilt. No one would ask questions. No one would answer questions. Tim's death would be written off as a sad but inevitable accident, and Norman would go home to his lovely white house on the hill and put a black armband around his sleeve. Norman knew what was proper.

"He'll have to kill all of us," she said aloud.

"No," Tim said quickly. "He wouldn't dare do that. That would raise a stink."

"Jack would tear this town apart brick by brick if anything happened to you," Penny added. "Norman knows it. But that won't help Tim. It would be our word, not just against Norman's, but against that of the whole town. We couldn't prove Norman had done anything criminal."

"Then Tim is the one in danger," Ellen said. "Can we hide him?"

"Where? If they want to come in," Penny said grimly, "we can't keep them out."

"Then he must get away."

"Never mind," Tim said softly. "It's too late. Here they come."

Ellen heard it then; fifty centuries of atavistic terror recognized the sound her own ears had never heard. Once heard, it could never be forgotten—the sullen roar of an aroused mob.

Twelve

Ellen went to the window. Tim held the draperies back so she could see.

They came by car and on foot, along the driveway and out of the woods. Some carried torches. There were flashlights too, and electric lanterns. Someone turned on a car's headlights. The front lawn was as bright as morning.

They gathered in a huddled group on the grass a safe distance from the house. At first glance they had seemed to number in the hundreds, but Ellen realized there were only twenty or thirty people. Most were men, but there were a few women. Among the latter, of course, was Mrs. Grapow. She stood in the front ranks, with the pastor beside her. Her allies were not all human. She had Norman's dogs. One hamlike fist held both leashes without visible effort, though the dogs were straining forward.

Now that the moment had come, Ellen was conscious

of relief. The menace was real, and there was a peculiar comfort in knowing that her imagination was healthy.

"I'll talk to them," she said.

"Don't go out." Tim caught her arm. "Talk through the window, it's not so exposed."

"Yes, right. Can you get out the kitchen door while I keep them occupied?"

Penny was one step ahead of her. She came running back through the hall, her hair flying.

"There are more of them out in back. They're all around the house, Mom."

"If worst comes to worst, Tim will have to try," Ellen said. Then, despite her fancied calm, she shied back as a high-pitched shout echoed through the night.

"Miz March! We know he's in there. Send him out and we won't hurt you or your girl."

"And just how do you suppose they found out he's here?" Penny muttered.

Mrs. Grapow had stepped forward a few paces. So, Ellen thought, she's the spokeswoman for the group. It was appropriate. In her long dark dress, flanked by the two great dogs, she looked like one of the more unsavory pagan goddesses—Hecate, perhaps, or the hippopotamus deity of the ancient Egyptians.

"Send him out," she bellowed. "Or else we'll come in and get him."

"He isn't here," Ellen yelled back. "Get out of here, all of you."

"We know he's there! You better watch out, or we'll tend to you too! There's some here that thinks you're worse than him."

Mrs. Grapow's grammar was deteriorating, Ellen thought with grim amusement. The amusement soared, suddenly, into an upsurge of exhilaration. In a way the feeling resembled the earlier seizure, when she had hurled unintelligible curses at the intruders; but this time she was fully conscious of what she said. It was as if something had learned, from the first experiment, that it had gone too far. Now it was gentler and more skilled. Ellen felt mildly, pleasurably drunk.

"Get your fat carcass off my lawn," she shouted, enjoying the epithets. "And take that horde of morons with you! By God, I'll sue you for every penny you've got, you dirty-minded, foul-mouthed, paranoidal old—"

"Mom—hey, Mom!"

Penny's voice was shaking. Ellen glanced at the girl over her shoulder and saw that she was laughing. A chip off the old block, that's what Penny was. The boys would be proud of her. They hadn't raised her to be a sissy. . . .

Mrs. Grapow had fallen back a pace. The threat to her moneybags hurt, Ellen thought triumphantly. It wasn't enough, though. Mrs. Grapow couldn't back down now without losing prestige, and power meant more to her than money. Not that the woman was thinking that clearly. She was beside herself with rage.

"All right, boys," she screamed. "Let's go—"

"Wait, wait!" The pastor pushed forward, waving wildly at the surging crowd. "Mrs. March—don't be a fool! We aren't going to hurt you, not unless you make us. Give the boy up. Let's not have trouble now. We don't want—"

"You're the ones who are making the trouble," Ellen yelled. "You come any closer and I'll have you put in jail." She deliberated for a moment and then went on, forming every word distinctly, "You're a lecher and a crook and a psychotic petty tyrant and a nasty little wizened meager skinny—"

"All right," the pastor shouted. "All right! I tried. It's your own fault."

"Mom, Mom." Penny shook her. "I admire your derangement of epitaphs, but you're just making them mad. Stall for time!"

The leaders of the mob had gone into conference. The torches flared in the wind. The two dogs sat staring balefully at the house. They worried Ellen more than the humans did; in her present mood she felt she could outface, and outfight, any two men in the crowd. But the dogs were something else.

Mrs. Grapow turned back, her fat face shining like an orange moon in the torchlight. Before she could move or speak, Ellen shouted,

"One more step and I'll put the curse on you. May you get so fat you can't walk. May your store burn to the ground. May your tongue turn black and wither and drop off. I pronounce this in the name of Satan and all the devils in hell, and furthermore—"

"Stop that!" It was the pastor who shouted; Mrs. Grapow stood stock-still, staring. "Now look here, Mrs. March, that sort of thing isn't going to help—"

"Take it off me!" Mrs. Grapow spoke to Winckler, but her yelp was loud enough to be heard in the house. "Take it off, Pastor, don't let my tongue—"

"I will, I will. Don't worry, Elvira, the power of the Lord is with me—"

Ellen interrupted this pledge with a remark that surprised her. She was familiar with the phrase, but had never expected she would have occasion to use it.

The minister darted forward.

"You're just making things worse for yourself, Mrs. March. I'm going to give you ten minutes. I can't restrain these righteous citizens any longer. You send that young devil out here and we'll leave you alone. Think it over."

He turned to reassure Mrs. Grapow. He looked ridiculous, standing on tiptoe to pat the big woman's heaving shoulders.

"Well," Ellen said. She cleared her throat; it was dry from all that yelling. Turning from the window, she saw that Penny and Tim were standing side by side staring at her. Their hands were clasped and their eyes were wide.

"I never heard you talk like that," Penny said.

"I'm just getting started. We have ten minutes and we

had better make use of them. This is your chance, Tim. It isn't much of a chance, but it's better than staying here."

"Right," Tim said. He tried to free his hand, but Penny refused to let go.

"Mom, he'll never make it. There are men all around the house. They've got lights and—and guns."

"I'll have a look."

It did not take Ellen long to realize that Penny was right. Every exit was covered. She returned to the living room.

"Okay," she said briskly. "Then we'll make a stand. Let's get everything we can piled up against the doors. Collect any object that can be used as a missile. We'll retreat to the cellar if they break down the doors, Luckily the cellar door opens inward. Tim, can you quickly rig some kind of bar on the inside? There are tools and some scraps of wood downstairs."

Tim's jaw was hanging.

"You are a real crazy lady," he said seriously.

"Go, on, get moving. I'll stay here and keep an eye on things."

Tim was back in a few minutes.

"There are old bolts already on the doorframe," he reported. "I found a piece of wood that fits."

"Good. Help Penny shove that sofa against the door."

Tim obeyed. He came back to the window, and Ellen saw him stiffen as he looked out.

"Get a load of who just arrived."

The car was the old station wagon Norman used for rough work and bad weather. Trust him not to risk the Rolls, Ellen thought—and then felt a faint stir of hope. Maybe the kids were wrong about Norman. Maybe he could disperse the mob.

He looked frantic enough as he got out of the car and ran toward the waiting group. Ellen strained her ears, but at first she could hear only a murmur as he spoke with Mrs. Grapow. Then Norman's voice rose.

"I told you you couldn't take the dogs. What the hell do you mean by stealing my—"

"Public need," said Mrs. Grapow. "You can't stand in the way of the people, Norman."

"You're all crazy," Norman shouted. "Crazy, insane. . . . Hank, Mrs. G.—stop this and go home. I promise you, I'll deal with Tim."

"You go home," Mrs. Grapow said. "This is no place for you, Norman, and you ain't the man to stop us."

Norman turned toward the house.

"Ellen," he called, making a megaphone of his hands. "Don't worry, Ellen. I'll go for help . . . the police . . ."

Mrs. Grapow raised a huge fist. Ellen watched in horrified fascination; she didn't have time to call out a warning even if she had been inclined to do so. The fist fell, and Norman collapsed onto the ground, where he lay still.

"Five more minutes," Mrs. Grapow shouted.

She gestured; two of the men came forward and dragged Norman's limp body to the rear.

"You don't suppose . . ." Ellen began.

"That puts him in the clear," Penny said tightly. "Mom, don't start wondering. That was all an act."

Ellen stood watching through the window as the young pair went back to barricading the doors.

"Three minutes," the minister shouted.

There was a cry from Penny, and the sound of a scuffle, Ellen whirled around.

The big sofa, which had been moved with such labor to block the front door, was pushed out far enough to allow someone to pass. Tim had one hand on the door-knob. His other hand and arm were hindered by Penny, who clung like a furious puppy in spite of his efforts to dislodge her. She couldn't have held him if he had not been reluctant to hurt her.

Ellen ran to them and added her strength to her daughter's. Tim resisted for a moment; the muscles in his arm felt like ropes. Then he relaxed and put his arm around Penny. She clung to him, clutching his shirt front. Tears of fright were streaming down her face.

"No, you don't," Ellen said, panting. "What's the matter with you?"

"You've got to let me go! They'll leave you alone then. If you don't . . ." He ducked his head toward Penny, whose face was hidden against his dirty shirt.

"We have a hang-up," Ellen said slowly, "about throwing people to the wolves. If you went out there, Penny would be right behind you. I couldn't stop her. Because I'd be right behind her."

He believed her. That he could do so, after seven years with Norman, was a magnificent tribute to the man and woman who had been his parents. I wonder if I could do as well, Ellen thought humbly. Maybe I shouldn't have been so emotional. He's going to cry.

Tim had learned discipline the hard way. After some struggle, he got face and voice under control.

"Okay," he said gruffly. "Hey, Penny, cut it out. You're getting mud all over your face."

Ellen went back to the window and left them to talk. The incident had removed her last lingering doubts about Tim, and if she was being illogical, then logic be damned. He cared enough about Penny to walk out in cold blood to face that pack of human wolves.

Ellen knew she would have to watch him. If he could get out of the house without their following, he would try again.

Another car came up the driveway. Its headlights flared, sending long, queer shadows fleeing across the lawn. The car was unfamiliar but the man who got out of it was not. She gave a little cry, and Penny and Tim came to join her.

"I don't believe it," Penny gasped.

"Who is it?" Tim asked.

"Jack," Ellen whispered.

"It's my uncle," Penny said. "Oh, wow—of all the people I'd like to see right now . . ."

His tie was askew and he was bareheaded; the torchlight reflected redly from his high forehead. He didn't look at the house, but went quickly across the grass toward the mob. Mrs. Grapow went to meet him. They talked for several minutes, while the three inside the house watched in an agony of fear and hope.

"It won't work," Ellen muttered. "What in God's name is he doing here? He can't—"

Jack's comments seemed to be having some effect. The mob's amorphous outlines wavered. Winckler was no longer in evidence; Ellen finally located him, safely concealed behind a couple of stalwart and very intoxicated farmers.

But Mrs. Grapow was not so easily cowed. She had been bossing men all her life, and a single man, without a gun, did not intimidate her. She thrust her face into Jack's, arguing and baring her teeth. He said something that seemed to annoy her, for she began to shout.

"Get going, mister. Let's see you run. If you like 'em so much, you can just join 'em. Come on, run—get moving, or I'll set the dogs on you."

She slackened her hold on the leash. The two great black beasts lunged; only Jack's quick backward leap saved his legs. He glanced at the house, and then at his car. Ellen read the thoughts that raced through his mind; she knew what his decision would have been, if he had been allowed to make it. The car was not only a means of reaching for help, it was a weapon, and Jack would not scruple to use it as such.

Mrs. Grapow knew what he was thinking, too. She moved to intercept him. She let the lunging dogs drag her forward, and Jack had to retreat. She was bellowing with laughter. When Jack turned to run, with the gaping jaws snapping at his heels, her laughter rose to a howl.

Ellen, Tim and Penny reached the door in a jumble. Tim heaved the couch back; the women worked at the bolts and the lock. Ellen flung the door open as Jack came bounding up the stairs. Without a word of greeting he turned and helped Tim push the couch back into place. Then he went to the window.

"Give us five minutes," he shouted. "I'll talk to them— I'll convince them."

Then he turned and grinned at Ellen.

"You surpass yourself," he said. "Only six weeks, starting from scratch, and look what you worked up!"

A few days earlier Ellen would have burst into tears and fallen into his arms. Now she grinned back.

"I guess we do need a diplomat. Why didn't you ask for fifteen minutes while you were at it?"

"I'm not sure what to do with even five minutes. This is rather confusing. . . ." His eyes finally left her face. "This, I presume is Tim?"

"Sir!" said Tim, staring.

"Hi, Penny. Your face is dirty. . . . All right, troops. How do we get out of here?"

"The house is surrounded," Ellen said. "We were going to make a stand."

"I'll bet you were. No dice, Ellen. Half that crowd is roaring drunk and the other half is hypnotized by Madame Lefarge and her dogs. They'll set fire to the house if they can't get in any other way. I'd rather take my chances out there than be roasted alive. That blocked-up door in the cellar. Where does it lead to?"

"The witch's tunnel," Ellen said slowly.

"So you said in one of your letters. Where does it end up?"

"I don't know. I don't even know if it's passable."

"Then let's find out. Get a flashlight. Penny, keep an eye on the window, but don't get too close. They're about ready to start throwing things."

A rock crashing through the glass lent emphasis to his words. Jack didn't even look back.

Ellen and Tim followed him downstairs. He picked up an ax as they passed through the room where Ellen kept her tools. When they had descended the slimy stone stairs, Ellen silently indicated the door; Jack swung the ax and brought it down with a crash. Rotted wood splintered and fell.

Tim glanced at Ellen. His eyes were shining with admiration, and she thought wryly, he's found himself a hero. He ran up the stairs and returned with a hatchet.

"We need something heavier," Jack said, glancing at Tim. "There's a sledgehammer under the workbench upstairs."

Tim took off as if someone had lit a fuse under him. Jack leaned debonairly on the ax and smiled at Ellen. His face shone with sweat, but that was the only sign of concern she could see.

"Lucky for us you let the boys dump all their junk here."

"You wanted them to put it in storage," Ellen reminded him.

"I am sometimes wrong. Rarely. But you can't blame me for failing to anticipate this particular problem. . . . Ah, Tim; got it? Okay, see what you can do with it. Ellen, hold the light steady."

Cleared of its overlayers of wood, the doorway looked even less accessible. It had been bricked up as well as boarded over. A solid wall of green-lichened brick confronted them. Before Ellen could voice her dismay, Tim swung the sledge. Ellen ducked back from a shower of sharp fragments. A breath of something foul and dank-smelling reached her nostrils; when she dropped the arm with which she had shielded her face, she saw that the wall was not so formidable after all. A jagged black hole gaped where Tim had struck. The surrounding bricks were buckling.

"Mortar's no good," Jack said calmly. "Must have been a hurry-up job. Have at it again, Tim. Watch your eyes."

Tim's cheek was bleeding where a splinter had struck him, but he grinned as he turned to comply.

Suddenly Ellen remembered.

"Ishtar! I can't leave her here."

"Not the witch's familiar," Jack agreed with a smile. "Tim, I think that does it; we just need a hole big enough to crawl through. Ellen, give Ishtar a couple of those tranquilizer pills you use when she travels. Hurry up, I want her out cold when I carry her."

Ellen dashed up the stairs.

Penny was standing against an inner wall. There were several rocks on the floor now; and as Ellen passed the living room, a gun went off. It sounded unpleasantly close, but nothing came through the window.

"Get downstairs," Ellen yelled, as she passed.

Ishtar was under the bed. She was too smart to stay in a place where people were yelling and throwing things. Ellen captured her and rammed the pills down her throat. When she returned to the subcellar, Jack and Tim were dragging boxes into a jumbled pile in front of the door.

"They'll find it eventually," Jack said, balancing a carton on top of the heap, "but we needn't make it any more obvious than we can help. Careful when you squeeze in, girls; try not to upset our camouflage."

He turned the flashlight into the tunnel, and Ellen saw what lay ahead of them.

The walls and floor were of beaten earth, shored up with rotting timbers. The walls shone greasily in the dim light. The whole structure appeared to be on the verge of collapse.

"In," Jack said concisely.

Ellen hung back.

"I can't. It's a horrible place. . . ."

"Upstairs is more horrible," said Jack, as a fusillade of shots rattled the windows. "They're just letting off steam now, but it won't be long before those bullets will be coming through the windows, soon to be followed by people. After you, Ellen."

So she went in, with his hand steadying her and the languid body of the cat clutched in her arms.

When they were all inside, Jack reached back through the aperture to pull some of the piled-up boxes against the door.

"Okay," he said. "Let's get moving. Tim, can you see what's ahead?"

"No, sir."

"Take the flashlight. You can have the dubious honor of leading the procession. Ellen, give me the cat. Ouch. She isn't out yet, I see."

"I gave her a triple dose," Ellen said anxiously. "I hope I didn't overdo it."

"We'll take her to a vet and pump her out once we get clear, just in case," Jack promised. As always, he had time for her minor worries even in the midst of catastrophe.

The tunnel was so low the men had to stoop and so narrow they had to walk single file. The miasma was sickening. The floor was slippery with something that shimmered like mold. Ellen's head began to swim.

"How much farther?" she groaned.

"The farther the better," said Jack from behind, where he was bringing up the rear.

Ellen knew what he meant. The farther they got from the house, the better their chance of avoiding the mob. If they could get out—if the tunnel wasn't blocked . . . if the foul air didn't overpower them . . . if the mob didn't find the door too soon. . . .

Her courage seemed to have deserted her; she would

have welcomed the support of the crazy mood that had
held her earlier in the evening. The only thing that kept
her moving was necessity—and the knowledge of Jack's
presence. Ellen realized she had not even asked him how
he happened to arrive so fortuitously. There had not been
time. Nor was there time now; they had other things to
worry about.

The air grew thicker as they proceeded. Ellen felt as if
she had been walking for hours. Once they were held up
by a giant tangle of roots that crisscrossed the tunnel like
a spider web. They were brittle and dead, however, and
Tim crashed through them with one thrust of his
shoulders, ignoring Ellen's cry of warning.

"You could bring the roof down!"

"We don't have time to fool around," Jack answered
her, as Tim proceeded. "Air's bad. Hurry up, Tim."

Ellen was finding it difficult to breathe by the time they
stopped. The tunnel ended abruptly, in a rough wall of
dirt.

She looked around, baffled and afraid. Was the wall a
cave-in? It must be; there was no visible exit. They would
never dig through.

Tim knelt on the floor.

"There was a ladder here once," he reported, holding
up a scrap of rotted wood. "Must be a trapdoor above."

"I'll stand on your shoulders," Jack said promptly.
"I'm heavier, but you're younger."

"Yes, sir."

Already they worked like a team. Tim knelt and
cupped his hands; Jack climbed on his shoulders, supporting himself against the wall. Then Ellen realized that
the low ceiling was gone, and that a shaft opened up
above them.

"This is going to be interesting." Jack's voice echoed
gruesomely from the air above her head. "There is a
trapdoor. It's half decayed, but I'll bet there are three feet
of rocks and dirt on top of it." His voice went hard with

strain. "Make that four feet. It won't budge. Your turn, Tim."

They changed places.

"I'm gonna put my back against it," Tim called down. "Can you stand up then?"

"I'll try. . . ."

Jack's face darkened with effort.

"No," he gasped, falling back to his knees. "Damn it—"

"Something gave," Tim said. "I felt it. Once more . . ."

Ellen watched with alarm as the veins on Jack's forehead bulged. She was about to expostulate when there was a muffled shout and a creaking crash and a sudden rush of air. Jack fell flat and Tim's legs dangled absurdly. They twitched upward and disappeared.

Jack sat up.

"I think I slipped a disk," he said, groaning. "I'm too old for this sort of thing."

Tim's voice floated down to them.

"Lift Penny up to me, sir."

"Stop calling me 'sir,' " Jack said in a muffled bellow.

He lifted Penny so that Tim could catch her hands. Ellen went next. She saw Jack button the now limp body of the cat under his shirt as Tim heaved her out; then she held Tim by one leg, with Penny holding the other, while he leaned down to give Jack a hand up.

"The flashlight is still down there," Jack grunted as he rose to his feet. "I turned it off."

"Better not to use it now anyhow," Tim said.

Instinctively they had lowered their voices. The wind made rushing noises in the treetops high above their heads, but the place where they stood was very still. It was also very dark. There was no moon, and the leafed branches overhead cut off even the faint diffused light of the night sky.

"Where are we?" Ellen whispered.

"Good question," said Jack. "It's up to you now, Tim."

"I know where we are," Tim said. "Wow, we came a long way. We're half a mile from the house."

"You must have eyes like a cat's," Jack said.

"I'm used to the dark. Only—where are we going?"

"Another good question."

They were all silent for a minute. The night noises were soft but distinct; an owl hooted, and a wakeful bird answered quaveringly. Ellen fancied she could hear a distant murmur of voices. Then she heard another sound and caught blindly at Jack's arm.

"The dogs!"

"We'd better get moving," Jack agreed. "Head for your house, Tim. They won't think of looking for us there. All I need is five minutes at a functional telephone."

"Martha and Will—" Ellen began.

"Didn't you see them?" Tim's voice was flat. "They're at your place. Come on, this way. We'd better hold hands."

"What about the trapdoor?" Penny spoke for the first time. Ellen could see her dimly now, a dark shape next to the dark shape that was Tim.

"Leave it open. Maybe someone will fall into it," Jack said.

Their progress seemed to Ellen maddeningly slow. She had no idea where they were. She had surely walked in this part of the woods, but there were no landmarks in the dark. Then she began to see more clearly. She thought at first her eyes were adjusting to the darkness, but as the light strengthened she realized what it was, and groaned aloud.

"The moon's out. Darn it!"

"The light is the least of our worries," said Jack. "Listen."

They stopped walking. The baying was continuous now, and closer.

"That's the danger," Jack said. "Tim—"

"Yeah," Tim said. "This way."

The light was strong enough for Ellen to see the stream. Tim led them straight into it. The water felt pleasantly cool on Ellen feet; she didn't even mind her soaked shoes. Very little seemed of consequence with the dogs following their trail.

"Takes us out of our way," Tim said, reaching out a hand to steady Penny as she slipped on a stone. "But I think we better do it."

The moonlight came and went. Tim set a rapid pace. He was the only surefooted one; Ellen could hear Jack slipping and swearing behind her, but his hand was quick at her elbow whenever she slipped. The intervals of moonlight grew longer. They were making good time, she thought. It couldn't be far to the house on the hill, even if they were going a little out of the way. The howling of the dogs faded.

Yet as they stumbled on, with the water lapping at feet and ankles, Ellen was aware of a mounting tension. Danger. Danger. The word was so clear in her mind, it might have been written in fiery letters against the trees.

Of course there was danger. They weren't out of the woods yet, literally or otherwise. But the prospect had certainly improved since she had stood at the window, with Mrs. Grapow giving her five more minutes. There was no sign of pursuit; even the barking had stopped. The woods were silent and peaceful, with moonlight sifting through the leaves to dapple the forest floor and waken pale sparks from the bubbling water. Then why did she feel as if an imminent peril were walking close behind?

Tim led them out of the stream. He seemed more confident; he smiled at Penny as he turned to help her over the bank. Then he extended a hand to Ellen. Jack gave her a useful if inelegant boost from behind. He followed her up, and then stood still, raising his hand.

"Listen!"

At first Ellen couldn't identify the sound—a high, shrill keening that rose and fell. Fantastic theories raced through her mind before the strangely elusive knowledge clicked into place.

"Sirens," she exclaimed. "The police or the fire department."

"I don't believe it," Tim muttered.

"Do you suppose they did set fire to the house?"

"We'd see the flames if they were high enough to alert a neighbor." Jack turned to look in the direction from which they had come. "Maybe you've got a few friends left, Ellen."

"We can go back, then," Penny said eagerly.

"No!" Ellen's voice was sharp. She shook her head dazedly. "I don't know why I said that. What's the matter with me? I feel funny. . . ."

"No wonder." Jack's hand closed over her arm. "It's been a wild night. I think you're right to be cautious, Ellen; I'll reconnoiter, before we go rushing back. Here, take the cat."

He handed the limp furry bundle to Ellen. Ishtar was snoring horribly.

"Excuse me, sir." Ellen had a wild desire to laugh; Tim's formal manners were so unlike his former behavior. "You don't know the way. Better let me—"

"Oh, no." Penny clutched at him. "It's you they want."

A debate ensued. Finally they agreed to stick together. Tim would lead them to the path that connected the two houses, and they would see if there were any signs of activity.

Ellen couldn't think of any reasonable objection to the plan, but as they went on, the sense of mounting danger grew stronger. The sound of the sirens had reassured her momentarily, but now it was as if something else guided her brain—something that didn't recognize the sound of official protection, something that cried aloud with every step, "Watch out! Watch out!"

After a while she recognized a landmark. They were not far from the path. In another moment Tim stepped

out into a small glade—the same one where Ellen had
found Tim with the injured squirrel. Not a propitious
spot; was that why she felt . . .

Jack was behind her and Penny and Tim, side by side,
were just ahead. Ellen felt the way she felt when she had
flu. Her head was swollen and her stomach was queasy. A
strangled cry burst from her lips, and a man stepped out
into the clearing from the shelter of the fallen oak.

"I thought you'd end up along this path eventually," he
said.

His voice was under better control than his face. It was
a mask of distorted features. His mouth twitched uncon-
trollably.

"Ah," Jack said. "Norman, I presume."

"And you must be John Campbell. I don't know how
you got here, but you are under a misapprehension. Get
the women out of the way, Campbell, while I take this
unfortunate lad to the authorities."

Ellen took the single step forward that brought her to
Tim's side. Penny was wound around him like a vine.

"Ellen, get away." Norman lifted the shotgun. "He's
dangerous. You of all people ought to know that."

"So dangerous you need a gun to escort him to the police?" Ellen said. "Isn't it odd that it's the same kind of
gun the local hunters carry?"

"Just a moment," Jack said. He had not seemed to
move, but Ellen realized he was standing beside her.
"Let's talk. Mr.—do you mind if I just call you Norman?
I feel I know you so well."

"See here, Campbell, I don't know what these two silly
females have told you—"

"Oh, you know how women are," Jack said soothingly.
"Put that gun away, Norman. Then we can talk sen-
sibly. . . ."

"I'm the boy's uncle," Norman said. "You don't think
I'd hurt him? I just want to get him to the police."

"Then the police have arrived?"

"Someone called them." Norman's features twisted alarmingly. "I'd have called myself, but they held me prisoner. You saw that, Ellen? You saw Mrs. G. hit me?"

"I saw," Ellen said. She was afraid to say more; the man was so unstable, the slightest word might set him off.

The light was strong in the clearing; it was almost as bright as day. Norman stood under the shelter of the trees. The moonlight flickered across his face as the boughs moved. He smiled.

"You see, Campbell, the boy is dangerous. I hate to admit it. But after last night—he attacked one of the town girls. How you can trust your niece with him. . . . But maybe you weren't told about that incident?"

"No," Jack said. "That's terrible."

"You know Ellen." Norman's voice was horribly confidential. "You know how she is. Mind you, I think she's very nice, very sweet. But she doesn't understand this boy. If I didn't have a gun, he'd escape. With Penny, maybe, as a hostage. I can't take that chance."

"I see what you're driving at," Jack said.

Penny gave her uncle a look of horror and disbelief. Tim didn't turn his head; but Ellen, whose shoulder was touching his arm, felt the sudden telltale slackening of muscle. She knew what was going through the boy's mind. After running headlong into walls of hate and mistrust all his life, he had finally found two adults who seemed to trust him. Now they were acting like all the others. They were ready to give him up. Ellen wouldn't have been surprised if he had snatched at Penny and tried to run. She wanted to reassure him and Penny. Jack didn't believe a word of the specious excuses, he was only trying to get Norman off guard. But she couldn't speak without warning Norman.

"Oh, hell," Tim said, in the old familiar growl. "This is a waste of time. Get lost Penny. I'll go with old Normie if that will shut him up."

He took a step forward. Ellen grabbed at him. Penny

was hanging onto his other arm and yelling. Ellen heard Jack utter a wordless explosive sound. He moved. Then the gun went off.

Ellen was blind and deaf for a few seconds. When her stinging eyes cleared, she saw that Jack was on the ground.

He sat up before her heart had missed more than two beats.

"Damn it!" he said distinctly. "Thanks a lot, you guys."

Norman had retreated behind the fallen trunk. It formed a barricade that made it impossible for anyone to tackle him.

"It was an accident," he mumbled. "I'm not used to this thing. Don't make me do anything stupid, Campbell. It will be your fault if anyone gets hurt. Tim's fault, too. I don't want to hurt anybody. . . ."

Jack got to his feet. He was squarely in front of Tim now; when the boy realized this, he tried to push forward. Jack elbowed him back.

"You came dangerously close to the death house there, pal," he said to Norman. "I'm through playing games with you. Hand over that gun."

For a moment Ellen thought the forceful tone would do the trick. But Norman had gone too far to give up.

"No," he said. "No, you don't. You're all crazy; but I'll save you in spite of yourselves. Get over here, Tim, or I'll shoot. I'm going to count five, and then I'll shoot, and I don't care who else is in the way."

Then Ellen saw it, on a branch over his head. The moonlight must have touched it with a vagrant ray, for its white fur seemed to shine. It was only there for a moment, but in that moment she made out every detail, thanks to the queer, luminous light that shone around it. It was small and fat and long-haired; the whiskered face had a delicate pink nose, and eyes that glowed like two miniature red taillights.

The cat dropped straight down onto Norman's bare head.

Norman screamed. Ellen had never heard such a sound from a human throat. The gun fell. Norman stumbled backward clawing at his face, which was hideously trans-formed—covered with agitated white fur, like a monster out of H. G. Wells.

She stood frozen with horror, clutching the limp body of Ishtar. Jack dived forward and got to his feet holding the shotgun. He handed it to Tim and then turned back. There were sounds from the darkness under the trees, but they did not continue for long.

Thirteen

Ellen was standing by the kitchen window when Jack came downstairs. It was a beautiful day. The sun was shining and the roses were blooming and the mocking birds were at their favorite game of teasing Ishtar. She crouched on the steps rumbling like a volcano as the graceful gray shapes swooped at her with squawks that sounded like whoops of avian laughter. The pleasure of the sport was always one-sided, and Ishtar's mood that morning was worse than usual. She was sulking about the indignities she had suffered the previous night.

Ellen turned as Jack came in. His chin was covered with a hideous salt-and-pepper stubble, and his clothes—the same he had worn the night before—had not been improved by their noctural adventures. But he greeted her with his broadest smile as he took the cup of coffee she handed him.

"This is like old times," he said.

"Are the kids still asleep?"

"Uh-huh. Tim reminds me of Phil, the way he sleeps —all over the bed, sheets wound around him like the snake and Laocoön." Jack's smile faded. "You realize this is the first time in seven years that kid has gone to bed without dreading the next morning?"

"He must have doubted his own sanity at times—wondered if he really had done the things he was accused of doing. I can't see how Norman managed it."

"Only too easily. Tim was man-size when he was fourteen, not unlike his uncle in appearance. Before that time it was even easier. Norman would take advantage of every accidental disaster; he probably arranged a few himself. Whenever anything happened, he'd rush to the victim's house waving his checkbook and babbling apologies. And don't think of Tim as Sir Galahad, lifting his pure pale face heavenward. All normal kids are hellers. . . ."

A reminiscent gleam warmed Jack's eyes. Ellen laughed.

"Yes, I've heard of some of your exploits. Men! You all stick together. . . . Jack what are we going to do about Tim?"

"I'm glad you have accepted it."

"What?"

"That Tim is going to be part of the family."

"Now just a minute, I didn't mean that! Penny is only sixteen, I'm not having her involved with. . . . I like Tim and I feel sorry for him, but—"

"That's a very unworldly attitude. Most mothers would snap at two million, even if it came with Jack the Ripper. Don't you think we had better grab him before he gets out into the world and sees what else is available?"

"If you think I'd sell Penny for *twenty* million . . ."

She saw the twinkle in Jack's eye and stopped in amused confusion.

"You ought to be ashamed of yourself, leading me on."

"I am, as always, in complete agreement with you,"

Jack said. "But dammit, Ellen, that relationship is a little staggering. I've never seen anything quite like it. The way she went to bat for him, wholeheartedly, with shrewd, adult intelligence—"

"Because the minute she saw him she knew he couldn't do anything wrong," Ellen murmured.

"Well, there were other reasons. If you start from the premise that prophecy is uncommon these days, there had to be some explanation for your astounding success as a fortune-teller. It stretched coincidence to the breaking point. The factor I find most inexplicable is your failure to see that yourself. If you had, you would have seen a lot of things. Were you so bemused by—"

He stopped suddenly, and Ellen, who had joined him at the kitchen table, looked at him in surprise.

"No," she exclaimed, as his meaning struck her. "No, not by Norman. I never was—I didn't ever. . . . It wasn't Norman. It was something else."

Jack started to speak, but for once Ellen was too concerned with her own needs to notice his. This was something she had to say; only by speaking of it could she exorcise it.

"I didn't dare admit it before," she went on. "I can now, because Penny has explained the other things that frightened me. The things I saw are equally susceptible to a rational explanation. But there were so many of them, they sort of piled up."

She told Jack about the shadow. He listened with the faint frown that indicated concentration; when she had finished, he nodded thoughtfully.

"Suggestion."

"You don't know how real it was. It . . . she . . . the figure was *hanging*, Jack."

"Uh-huh." He followed her thoughts as readily as if they had been his own. "Did you ever find out which room Mary died in?"

"Of course I did. According to Ed, it was her room. Her bedroom. You see the implications—"

"Sure, I know about bedrooms." Jack's smile was half-hearted. "It can fit the other part of the legend you heard from Tim. The theme is common, Ellen—the sanctimonious Puritan, and the beautiful, amoral woman. A novelist could handle it in several different ways. She lured him into her bed and destroyed his self-respect—so he destroyed her. Or she lured him on and then rejected him, so. . . . He strung up the body so that the rope would cover the marks his hands had left on her throat. . . . Maybe we ought to collaborate on a book. Horror stories sell well these days."

"Oh, Jack, you always say the right thing. But you can see how it affected me. I swear, there were times when I did feel possessed. The more trouble I had with the town, the more I identified with her."

"Understandable. Ellen, would you like to ask a priest to come out here? Father Kelly would do it. Not for exorcism, only to say a few prayers."

He was quite serious, and Ellen considered the question as seriously.

"No," she said, after a moment. "I don't think so. I don't think it's necessary. It sounds odd, Jack, but I was never afraid of *her.* Anyhow," she added, smiling, "we might be mistaken about Mary's religion. If she wasn't Catholic, Father Kelly might irritate her."

"Then you don't intend to give up the house?"

"Heavens, no, not after all I've been through. I mean, the worst is over. I don't think I'll have any more trouble with the townspeople."

"No. Your friend Ed told them off, but good. Too bad he's as isolationist; he'd be great at the U.N."

They both fell silent, remembering what had happened after they returned to the house with a moaning villain in tow. The state police had the situation well in hand; the mob had been dispersed and the ringleaders arrested. Their cronies were only too eager to testify against them. Mrs. Grapow was the only one to resist. She was howling out Scriptural admonitions when Ellen's party arrived, but her outrage didn't last long after Jack began his story. His accusations against Norman included attempt to commit murder and aggravated assault. The trooper's first reaction was one of incredulity; but Jack's identification papers were impressive, and Norman made no attempt to deny the charges. He did not speak, or take his hands from his face, not even when he was led off to the waiting police car.

The memory that warmed Ellen's heart, however, was the action taken by some of her neighbors. Ed Salling had not called the police; that would have been against his principles. He had just come to the rescue, driving hell for leather in his old truck, with as many responsible citizens as he could collect in a hurry. He had not realized the seriousness of the situation until a delegation of the town's teen-agers descended on him demanding help. All the young people, including Bob Muller, had taken part. Joyce had called the police. Then they had piled into Klaus's jalopy and come to join the fracas. They were preparing to organize search parties when Ellen arrived.

No. She did not think she would have any more trouble with the town.

Jack cleared his throat.

"Ellen. . . . I don't suppose you—that is, would you—"

Ellen didn't hear Penny and Tim before they entered the room. Penny always floated, and after his years of woods-wandering Tim moved like Natty Bumppo. Jack stopped speaking. Ellen noticed that he looked annoyed, but she had other things on her mind. Feeding Tim kept her fully occupied for some time. As she dispensed eggs and ham and pancakes, she remembered that sleeping wasn't the only normal activity Tim had been unable to enjoy. He must have choked three times a day on Martha's cooking, mixed as it was with sanctimonious verbal bullying and vicious commentary on his mother. Ellen fried two more eggs on the strength of that, and reminded herself to ask Tim if she could be present when he fired Martha.

No one said much while the two young people were eating. Jack was unusually silent. When the edge had been taken off Tim's appetite, he addressed the older man.

"Sir . . .?"

"Don't call me 'sir,' " said Jack, scowling at a half-eaten piece of toast.

"What should I call you?"

"My lord?" suggested Ellen, removing the toast, which Jack was crumbling into an unsightly mess. "Your holiness? Most excellent, worshipful—"

The corners of Jack's mouth turned up.

"I answer to my first name," he said.

"Could I?"

"You might as well." Jack pushed his chair back and considered Tim, who stared at him like a devoted dog. "You must be feeling slightly disoriented this morning. But I suppose it isn't too soon to consider the future."

"I know what I want to do."

"What?"

"Be a vet. Could I?"

Jack smiled reluctantly.

"You don't have to be anything. You'll be a wealthy man, even after my employer takes his share of the loot."

"But I want to be a vet." Tim dismissed two million dollars with a shrug of his broad shoulders. "The thing is, could I? I mean, I was pretty rotten at school. I've done a lot of reading, but I never studied. I would have flunked if the teachers hadn't passed me to get rid of me."

"Veterinary medicine." Jack thought about it, pulling

at his lip. "It's a rough course. No harm in trying. Give yourself a year with a tutor, or at some stiff prep school before you try for college."

"Saint Edmund's is a very good prep school," said Penny looking innocent.

"Uh-huh," said Jack drily. "It's also about a mile from Rosecroft, isn't it? What I had in mind was a year abroad. I haven't had a chance to tell you, Ellen, but Phil says he doesn't want to go to college this fall. Wants to bum around for a year. I've agreed on condition that he spend the year with me and report for periodic tutoring. No reason why Tim couldn't join us."

Tim's eyes were as big as saucers. Ellen let out a small, inaudible breath of relief. Poor Penny; she looked like a child who has not found the expected stocking on Christmas morning. At that moment Tim had forgotten her very existence. Which was just as it should be. There was good, sound stuff in Tim; few adults could have survived Norman's seven-year campaign as well. In a few years. . . . Ellen allowed conventional maternal plans to occupy her mind.

Then she looked at Jack, and was glad he was staring fixedly at his plate while he gave Tim time to react to his suggestion. Her face would have betrayed her feelings. How could she help loving him? He lectured her about involvement, but he was the first to hold out a helping hand to anyone who needed it.

An altercation outside interrupted the flow of silent sentiment. Hissing, howling screaming—the sounds were suggestive of a small war.

Tim was on his feet.

"Cat fight," he said cheerfully. "Hey, do you think—"

"Ishtar!" Ellen ran to the door.

Ishtar was crouched by a lilac bush. She was swollen to half again her normal size, and her body shook with throaty Siamese growls. The other cat was invisible. Presumably it had retreated under the bush.

From his greater height Tim saw more than Ellen did.

"It's my cat," he said, his face alight. "The white one. That's weird, that it should come around right now, like it knew. . . . Could I bring it in? Please?"

Ellen thought of fleas and worms and ear mites and enteritis.

"Sure," she said, without a second's hesitation. "If you can catch it."

Tim went out. Ishtar didn't budge, but she made a rude remark to Tim over her shoulder.

"I'll get Ishtar," Penny said, and followed Tim. "Thanks, Mom."

"It's the least I can do. I'll have to adopt that cat, whether Ishtar likes it or not. After all, it—"

The door shut in her face and she turned to Jack, now her sole audience.

"After all, it did save our lives."

"It did what?"

"Saved our lives." Tim, Penny, and cats had disappeared. Ellen heard Penny laugh, and a scream of rage from Ishtar. She went on, "If that cat hadn't jumped on Norman last night, somebody would have been hurt."

Jack's face was a study in perplexity.

"What are you talking about, Ellen?"

"But you must have seen it. On the branch, above Norman. It jumped, or dropped, or—" Her throat closed up as she saw Jack's expression. "You didn't see it?"

"I guess it could have been an animal. . . . I didn't see anything in the tree, but then my complete attention was concentrated on Norman."

"Didn't you see anything?"

"I saw something that looked like moonlight. As if the leaves had shifted and let the light through onto his hair. He yelled and tripped, or something. . . . dropped the gun. . . ."

"There was a cat," Ellen said. "A white cat. Jack, his face. It must have been scratched—clawed—"

"There wasn't a mark on him, Ellen."

They stared at one another.

"Jack," Ellen said. "I've been meaning to ask you. I didn't have a chance last night. Why did you come? How did you happen to arrive at the last minute, like the *deus ex machina* in the play?"

"You won't believe me."

"Try me."

"I was sitting in my hotel room," Jack said slowly. "It was late afternoon. The sun was still shining. I was working on some papers. All of a sudden—it's hard to put into words, but—I heard you. Your voice, calling me by name. Something took hold of me, like a hand pulling strings in my mind. My thought processes weren't affected; I knew perfectly well what I was doing. I tried to telephone you. No answer. The operator told me there was something wrong with the line. I called the desk, then, and ordered a car. Wasn't till I was halfway here that the thing relaxed, whatever it was. I couldn't turn back, though. I didn't try. I drove the way I've always forbidden the boys to drive."

"I see."

"You do believe me!"

"Yes."

"Did you call me, Ellen?"

"Not out loud." Ellen was remembering the first confrontation with Mrs. Grapow and the minister. It must have been at about the same time. . . .

"Well," she said calmly "Mary was a busy little ghost about five P.M. She had me in her clutches for a while, too. You should have heard me curse."

"I have heard you. You don't need any help from ghosts."

"But you did. And what made you think of the tunnel? I'd forgotten it myself."

"That's a point against your possession theory. If your witch wanted to remind us of an escape route, why drag

me into it? You claim to be possessable—or whatever
you want to call it—"

"She could only convey emotions to me," Ellen said.
Her eyes were fixed on the sunny window, but her
thoughts were elsewhere. "She needed a—a vehicle, a living person who was receptive and responsive. The first
day I came here, that burst of savage triumph. . . . Ed's
aunt didn't feel anything all the years she lived here. But I
was too receptive—too much like her. When she tried to
reach me, she blew the fuses, like an overloaded circuit."

"Ellen, a few minutes ago you were ready and willing
to rid yourself of ghosts. What's come over you?"

"You," Ellen said simply. "People can't evaluate
themselves; maybe I am superstitious and suggestible, capable of hallucinating shadows and cats and curses. But
you are not. I know you. It would take something genuinely out of this world to make you behave in such an extraordinary fashion."

"Well, it wasn't a damned ghost," said Jack furiously.

"Then what was it?"

The cat fight had retreated to a distant part of the yard.
Jack looked at the door with a trapped expression.

"Those damned kids keep coming in," he said unfairly.
"They don't give me a chance. . . . I'll tell you what I
think it was. I've never doubted the possibility of extrasensory perception, particularly at moments of extreme
emotional stress. When two people are very close, maybe
one can transmit emotion to the other, if the need is
strong enough. I felt your need. You were in danger, and
—you couldn't be in danger without my knowing it,
Ellen. Ellen—could you—I mean, is there a chance
that—"

The kitchen door opened. Jack groaned and banged
his fist on the table.

Penny came in, carrying Ishtar, who squirmed in her
hold like a demoniacally animated fur muff. For a moment
the light caught her eyes and they glowed crimson.

Penny rushed Ishtar to the cellar as Tim entered carrying another cat. It was a long, lean, mangy-looking animal with a hunted expression, but it lay quietly in Tim's arms. He'll make a good vet, Ellen thought. We're going to be overrun. Snakes, mice, birds. . . . I'll let him have an elephant if it will make him look like that.

She opened a can of cat food and the animal began wolfing it in loud, unseem gulps. Tim sat on the floor, legs crossed, stroking the bony back.

"It knows me," he said proudly. "Most of them growl if you touch them while they're eating."

Penny came back. She joined Tim on the floor and looked up at her uncle.

"What's the matter? You look mad."

"Did either of you see a cat last night?" Jack asked. "Ishtar?"

"A white cat. In the tree, over Norman's head."

Tim shook his head.

"I closed my eyes," Penny admitted. "When he started counting, I just closed them and prayed."

"It had blue eyes," Ellen said. She wasn't arguing; she was simply stating a fact. "Only blue eyes shine like that in the dark, like red beacons. I saw them as clearly as I see you."

"No," Penny repeated. "Is that the wrong answer? You still look mad, Uncle Jack."

"That's not why I'm mad," said Jack, in a growl reminiscent of Ishtar's.

"Oh?" Penny's eyes moved from Jack to her mother. She grinned. "Haven't you gotten around to it yet? I thought we were settling the future this morning."

"If you wouldn't keep interrupting me—"

"What are you talking about?" Ellen asked curiously.

"He wants to ask you to marry him," Penny said, and then shifted hastily on her bottom till she was behind Tim and his cat. Her uncle had risen purposefully, his eyes fixed on her. "Well, I was just trying to help," she said plaintively. "You're so slow. Why don't you get it over with?"

"Hmph." Jack scratched his chin. "Maybe you're right. I can't stand the suspense. Ellen, would you?"

"Certainly not." Ellen's cheeks were flaming. "You'll go to any length to save me from my own incompetence, won't you? I told you I'm not afraid."

"But I am." Jack seemed to have forgotten about their audience. "I'm afraid of being without you. I didn't miss the kids, Ellen; I missed you. I've never spent a more miserable six weeks. Now, wait, let me spell out all the inducements before you turn me down. You won't have to give up your house—or your ghost. We'll leave a saucer of milk out for it every night, the way they do in Ireland for the fairies. Another year of this rat race and I'm retiring. I want to sit and watch the roses grow. Maybe I'll write that book I keep talking about. Can I come here? Please?"

"You're just asking me because you feel sorry for me." Ellen had forgotten the audience too.

"Words fail me," said Jack.

He took one long stride, over cat, dish, and fascinated listeners, and put his arms around her.

After an interval he lifted his head.

"Am I asking you because I feel sorry for you?"

"No," Ellen said.

Still holding her, Jack turned his head.

"Get out of here, you guys."

Ellen didn't hear them go. A good while later she was aware of something twining around her ankles. She started convulsively and Jack let her go.

"I guess there will always be a cat between us," he said, frowning at the white mongrel. It was purring hoarsely. The food dish was empty.

"It wants more to eat," Ellen said. "Did you really mean that, about keeping our ghost?"

"I was kidding about the milk."

Ellen bent over and picked up Tim's cat. It continued to purr, lifting its scrubby head as her experienced fingers found the sensitive spot under the chin. Its eyes were half closed with pleasure, but there was no mistaking their color. They were a pale yellow-green.

Ellen put the cat down.

"We'll put out the milk," she said.